THE GREATEST HITS OF WANDA JAYNES

THE GREATEST HITS OF WANDA JAYNES

BRIDGET CANNING

BREAKWATER

P.O. Box 2188, St. John's, NL, Canada, A1C 6E6

WWW.BREAKWATERBOOKS.COM

A CIP catalogue record for this book is available from Library and Archives Canada.

Copyright © 2017 Bridget Canning

ISBN 978-1-55081-670-9

We acknowledge the support of the Canada Council for the Arts, which last year invested $153 million to bring the arts to Canadians throughout the country. We acknowledge the financial support of the Government of Canada and the Government of Newfoundland and Labrador through the Department of Business, Tourism, Culture and Rural Development for our publishing activities.

PRINTED AND BOUND IN CANADA.

 Canada Council   Conseil des Arts
for the Arts   du Canada   Canada Newfoundland
Labrador

Breakwater Books is committed to choosing papers and materials for our books that help to protect our environment. To this end, this book is printed on a recycled paper that is certified by the Forest Stewardship Council.

FOR JON WEIR

1

THERE are not enough people in the hallway. When Wanda Jaynes leaves class, she tends to slap on her excuse-me-I'm-a-very-busy-instructor face as she manoeuvres past students on the way to her office. But right now, it is an unencumbered path.

Silhouettes of hunched shoulders line the exit by the employee parking lot. Lots of faculty out for a smoke when it isn't break time, and no one's laughing or carrying on. She passes students staring into their phones, muttering to each other. Whatever's happened has the stink of fresh injustice and old exasperation.

In her office, she locks the door and refreshes her computer screen. One new email with that tiny, terrifying red flag. Subject: *New Budgetary Changes for the Newfoundland Institute of Learning*. Here we go.

Wanda sits and reads. And even as the bile within her alters the barometric pressure of her core, it's hard not to be impressed with the political wording. Pretty slick. Just last week, she taught a lesson for English 3102, "Jargon and Clarity." Something like that. The students had to paraphrase technical terminology into everyday speech. And this section of the email is prime for translation: *Due to the provincial government's budgetary shortfall, the service delivery model for Adult Basic Education will become the responsibility of our partner colleges in the private sector.*

"So, class, one way we reword this is," Wanda says, "due to mismanaging tax dollars, we're getting out of paying instructors money to teach poor people, like you. Privatization, bitches."

And more words: *The current ABE program will continue until the semester's end with no renewal for the fall.* The term and her contract end in less than six weeks. They'll finish up and gut the place. Her office is closet-sized, they'll use it for storage. She'll be packed up with the GED guidebooks and grade-twelve curriculum guides, all forced to drop out together.

She spins her chair away from the monitor. On the wall before her, the shape of her head reflects in the glass frame of her Bachelor of Education. When she received her first contract at the institute, displaying her credentials seemed like a good idea. A professional idea. Look, see how qualified Wanda is. In the glass, her bangs have separated in the middle, the way they do when she gets frazzled. Her head now resembles one of those toy Lego people she played with as a child, with the snap-on plastic hair, the kind she could pry off and replace with a hat or helmet. Look, see how interchangeable Wanda is.

Not that anyone gave a shit about her credentials. Andrea once admired the wooden placard hanging by her teaching certificate: *Teacher, You May Not See The Fruit Of Today's Work, But You Have Seeded A Lifetime Of Knowledge.* A convocation gift from somebody, maybe Ivan's sister. She remembers a twinge of annoyance on how all the first letters are unnecessarily capitalized. But it was nice to think someone could consider her effective. A potential, successful educator.

Wanda closes her eyes. She will not cry. She will not exit this building in front of students and colleagues looking like a sad, soon-to-be-sacked, sack. Because people don't look at trees and wonder who planted them. And has she really *Seeded Knowledge*? Assisting grown men as they compose argumentative essays on which ATV is the best. Twenty-two zero grades distributed so far for plagiarized papers, many where the students didn't even bother to change the font, straight cut and paste from Wikipedia. Ignoring the twitch of hands as they text under desktops. She flinches at the thought. So much easier to say nothing, keep on going, pretend she doesn't notice.

She fishes out her cellphone to text Ivan. One missed call from Mom. Nope, not returning this call today. When Mom hears the news, it will be a full-on fret through the Could List: *Maybe you could do a Special Education degree. Maybe you could get a job at Stella Maris and move back home to Trepassey. Maybe Ivan could get something more reliable. If you got pregnant now, you could just go on maternity leave.*

And then the phone will pass to Dad to deliver warnings: *Make sure you keep up your work until the end. Don't burn any bridges— one program shuts down, they start another. You want to stay in their good books. You're over thirty now, you need to focus on stability.* Ivan says it's because she's an only child. "If I didn't have a sister to share the brunt of my mother's insanity," he says, "I'd be a hermit on a hill."

The computer dings. A second email: *Meeting Request*, from Trevor Dowden, Department Head. Subject: *Upcoming changes and their impact*. The *impact* means laying off contract employees everywhere, so permanent ABE staff can take over positions in programs not being privatized. Andrea has permanent status and already teaches in degree programs. An image of Andrea hugging a rock-climbing wall pops into her head: teeth bared, fingers dug deep into handholds. Seeds of knowledge or not, it really doesn't matter how good or bad a job anyone does. Seniority first.

The meeting is scheduled for Monday. Maybe it's policy to give bad news on Fridays, so everyone goes home, drowns their sorrows all weekend and are too strung out by Monday to make a nuisance. She clicks "yes" to the invitation, then texts Ivan.

> Bad news at work.
> President just emailed
> everyone. Cutback City.

> I just saw. It's all over Twitter.
> I'm so sorry.

> Thanks. Ugh.

> Come home outta it. Don't worry about anything, I'll take care of supper & rally the troops.

> Thank you. xo

> xo

> You know what? I wanna read this email. What do bureaucrats say when they tell people their livelihoods are meaningless? Greedy fucks.

> We're going to be okay. I love you.

They will be okay. And poor. Her fingers drum the desk to the rhythm of their bills: mortgage, house insurance, student loans, car payment, car insurance, health insurance, phone bill, power bill, oil bill, credit-card bill, security-system bill, food, parking, house repairs. Her parents' anniversary at the end of the summer. Ivan's niece's birthday. Summer in general with invitations for patio beers, barbeques, festivals, concerts, trips. Ivan gets private renovation projects with carpentry and repairs, plus gigs with the band. Those bring in about half the bills. Groceries here and there. This autumn will bring EI and insecurity. She hugs her belly. It clenches and releases like a sweaty fist.

Come home outta it indeed. Why not. It's Friday, no one can expect her to stay and do teaching prep in the wake of this shit storm. She'll print the email and leave. When Trish and Leo are over later, it will be easier if they read it for themselves. She won't have to explain her situation over and over, like it's an anecdote to be perfected. And Ivan will be angry enough for everyone. He's good at that.

A knock on her door. Andrea. Here we go. Wanda takes a deep breath and opens up. Andrea leans into the office. Her arms make a tee stance bracing the door frame. In the small office, Andrea is an Amazon who doesn't mind blocking an exit.

Andrea tilts her head in sympathy. "Did you read the email?"

"Oh yes."

"Hard old stuff."

"Yep."

"Everyone's already getting out the seniority list to check their status." Andrea shakes her head. Her earrings make little tingling sounds. They are cats with tiny bells on their tails "Human Resources are coming next week. This kind of thing freaks people out. Bad for morale."

"Well, they should come," Wanda says. "That's their job."

"What will you do?" Her head towers over Wanda. Andrea's hair is cropped short with frosted tips, creating a mesh of stripes through her dark-blond hair, like tabby-cat markings. Maybe she has a cat fixation. Maybe she wears whiskers and a clip-on tail around the house. An image from *The Jungle Book* flashes in Wanda's head: Bagheera the jaguar, high on a tree branch, watching Mowgli below. But Bagheera was a mentor and Wanda should stop telling herself she has Mowgli hair.

"There's not much I can do if they don't have a spot for me," Wanda says.

"But you've been here, what, three years?"

"Four."

"You'll have recall rights. I imagine there's a bunch who would rather retire or take sick leave than start over in a different program."

"Yes, that's a good idea," Wanda says. Recall rights still go to permanent staff first. Andrea knows this. Wanda clasps her purse and jacket. Time to go home, have a drink, and process all this noise. "Sorry, but I have to run. And I've got something out on the printer."

"Yes, get your résumé done, my dear," Andrea says. "No one can say how you spend your time now." She leans back and fills Wanda's office with her trademark gut-laugh: *ha-ha-ha-Ha!* A laugh that could come with its own slogan: *When Andrea's amused, everyone knows it.*

Wanda shuffles out, maintaining her neutral expression. Easy for Andrea to empathize when she knows her job is safe. Andrea likes to brag about how her practical science and math background is always in demand. "I don't have to worry about being replaced by spell-check," she said last year. And then poked her thorny elbow into Wanda's arm and let loose big guffaws, *ha-ha-ha-Ha!* She glares at the Wet Floor sign by the copy-room door. It's been there for as long as she can remember. Andrea will keep her job, Wanda will lose hers, and still, none of the leaks around the building will get repaired.

In the copy room, Mona crouches by the photocopier, clearing a paper jam. Her white hair is swept back in a braid, but stray wisps give her a frizz halo.

"This stupid thing," Mona says. "If you don't turn every knob, it doesn't co-operate." She yanks a crimped sheet from the copier's bowels. "It wanted to make paper dolls with this one."

"I guess they won't be replacing it anytime soon," Wanda says.

"Have you heard anything?" Mona says.

"I'm not holding out hope. You?"

"Oh yes. I'm gone. My position will be made redundant at the end of the school year," Mona says. She tries to shut the front panel, but it jars.

This is a surprise. Mona has been a technology instructor with ABE for twelve years. Every day, her warbling voice echoes in the classroom next to Wanda's, like fingertips chirping on fresh-washed dishes.

"Is there anything you can do?" Wanda says.

"I'm writing a letter. There are too many things I don't understand about this decision. They say the program isn't successful. But how do they gage success?" Mona opens a side panel and tugs out a crumpled piece of paper. "I didn't realize teaching computer skills to high-school dropouts and single mothers was for profit."

"It's disgusting." And Wanda feels it, a hot grain of disgust, like the pea in the princess's bed. Unavoidable, but too far buried to reach.

"It's just…God. You get so fucking angry." Mona flicks up the side panel so it clicks into place. The copier hums in response. Her cloud of white hair seems to crackle in the air.

Wanda nods and keeps her face even. *Mona said fuck.* Mona sticks with darns and hecks. But there it is, *fucking*, all wrapped up in Mona's warble. She should respond with something kind. Something with equal passion. "It makes you wonder how politicians come up with these decisions," she says. "I mean, to sit in a room and vote on this kind of thing...you have to think people get bullied into it on some level."

"All politicians are bullies," Mona says. "They make horrible decisions, all the time, with no regard for anyone."

"It's terrible."

Mona looks up. Her eyes are dark and even. "Every time I drive by the Confederation Building, I think about Haliday's farm. You know where that is?"

"I think so? I think I used to know."

"It's way in back," Mona says. "Sam and I used to take the kids there." She presses a square on the touch screen. The copier's insides purr. "Sometimes, I think about that farm and its distance from the Confederation Building. I bet there are certain points where you'd have a clear shot at the top two floors. It wouldn't take much." Her finger hovers over the touch screen. "I wonder if I should pause this."

Wanda swallows. How to respond? Laugh? No, she should say something to match Mona's intensity. Ivan would know what to say, like last weekend, during one of his antigovernment rants. "Ever hate someone so much," Ivan said, "you know that if you murdered them, you'd spend the rest of your life masturbating about it?" Trish did a spit-take and they all laughed. Then again, they were super high at the time.

"They probably already have bulletproof windows," Wanda says.

"Yes. Probably first thing passed in the budget."

They both chuckle. Ho-ho, indeed. Neat sheets of paper start to pile out the side of the copier. "I'm making copies of the seniority list for a few people," Mona says. "It's long. But everyone wants to take it home for the weekend."

"Understandable."

"How about you?" Mona says. "Forming a plan?"

"Just do up my résumé, I guess." She shrugs. "I'm sorry, Mona."

"It's all you can do," Mona says. "I'm writing letters though. The union needs to step in. And students are angry. There will be protests."

"Well, let me know what you do," Wanda says. Then suddenly, "I'd be interested in writing letters." Really? A neat, organized, expressive letter to those in charge? She can do it—she teaches people how to do it in Business English. But now, with the idea voiced and airborne, it's clearly fruitless. A student uprising? Most are on income support with subsidized tuition. They'll wander over to a private college, fill out a form. Any letter she writes will receive a polite response. They'll suggest she find work at a private college. Maybe she'll make half her salary there.

"Will do. Thanks, Wanda," Mona says. She picks up the stacks of paper: "Oh, they're nice and warm." She hugs them to her chest and exits, her shoulders high with forced pride. Her collapsing white braid flaps against her back just enough to break Wanda's heart a little.

Wanda makes it out of the building without interceptions from students or coworkers. The parking lot is nearly barren. Everyone is gettin' gone. She drives out of the lot and onto the highway. The sky is polished blue with wisps of clouds, like scuff marks. The sky doesn't care she's losing her job. Smug-ass sky.

Half a tank of gas left. Gas—another expense to be trimmed. But if she's not commuting to a regular job, they won't burn much gas. Unless she returns to subbing. Fucking hell. Early mornings in starchy dress pants, wondering what kind of fire she'll be thrown into today. If she gets a job teaching high school, there's the expectation to volunteer after work: *We need a teacher guide for the prom committee. We need someone to help with Student Council.* And she'll have to deal with parents again. She can still hear Cody Grant's mom's cigarette tongue over the phone, the call home to discuss his expletive-laden tantrum when his iPhone smashed on the grade-nine classroom floor: "It's no wonder he don't behave right," Mrs. Grant growled. "All he eats is junk."

And all these things, they were par for the course when she first became a teacher, when it seemed the easiest way to do something good. "On your way to battle the massive, naked onslaught of stupidity," Ivan likes to say. But he just enjoys quoting Werner Herzog. Maybe she should get out of it. Be part of the teacher statistics, the fifty percent who quit after five years. But it's been seven years and she's reached *comfortable*, that rhythm they told her about in university, when lessons are developed and time management is a friend. Sure, the ABE students are all over the place: addicts required to prove they're enrolled to keep their welfare, young men who live in their parents' basements, single mothers fighting exhaustion and defeat. But Wanda showed up every day and gave them things to do and it felt like enough. Then again, maybe it's the Generation X in her: Find the easiest, least shitty job. Do it with minimal effort. Pat self on back.

Home. Ivan's jean jacket hanging in the front porch is instant solace. The house smells like chili—he's warmed up the batch she made earlier in the week. He comes out to greet her.

"There's beer in the fridge and wine on the table," he says. "I'm glad you're home." She lets her face rest in his neck. His skin exhales outside air and kitchen heat. She runs her hands down his side and along his belt, under his navel.

"Hi, Wanda!" Trish waves from the doorway of the living room.

"Oh. Hey," Wanda says.

Ivan presses her to him. "You should see the ideas Trish has for the album cover. It's going to be beautiful," he says. He kisses her neck and releases her. "But later. Let's get you sorted."

Trish scurries over for a hug. Her arms are light on Wanda's shoulders. "Oh honey," she says. "I'm so sorry. It sucks so hard."

Wanda's hand lands on the warm flesh of Trish's lower back, a spot where her blouse has shifted up. She moves her hand away. Did she jerk her hand away? Trish doesn't seem to notice.

"Where's Leo?" Wanda says.

"He's coming soon," Trish says. "He's jamming with Ray."

"Are you supposed to do that too?" Wanda says to Ivan.

"Not when you just got bad news," he says.

Trish regards Wanda at arm's length. She shakes her head. "Let's get you a drink."

In the dining room, Trish's laptop is set up on the table beside two empty beer bottles. Ivan has put out wine, glasses, and an ashtray. A landscape photo is displayed on the screen, rocks, sky, and water. "Will that be it?" Wanda says.

Trish pours Wanda a glass of wine. "No, we decided that one's too dark. Too much like the EP."

Guilt jabs Wanda's core. She still hasn't given the new recordings a full listen. Not that she hasn't heard the songs performed buckets of times.

"So, what is happening, exactly?" Trish says. "All I see are people flippin' out on Facebook."

"Hold on," Wanda says. "I'll get the letter."

She goes to the porch to get the printed email from her purse. Ivan's voice reverberates in the dining room. Trish giggles. What did he say? Something short and snappy. She brings the paper to the table, lays it in the middle with flair. "Voila. The centerpiece."

Ivan lights up a cigarette as Trish reads. Why can't he wait to do that? Or go outside? She hasn't eaten yet. Now the dining room will stink. But he likes a smoke when he's annoyed.

Trish sighs. "Education's always the first to be slashed and burned. So nasty."

"No it isn't," Ivan says. "Not everywhere. Look at the success of school systems in Scandinavian countries. Look at the influence of Confucian thought in East Asia. We treat education as a frill because we are a culture in de-fuckin'-cline." He stabs the air with his lit cigarette, his exclamation point. "Western society is breaking down. Everything is hyper polarized." He holds his hands out, like he's about to pick up something: a box, a baby. "Look at the way information is presented. How people argue. We must be right-wing or left-wing. Scientific or religious. Masculine or feminine. No grey areas allowed, no mixture. And here's Wanda, a well-rounded, dedicated educator, who chooses to teach the lost ten percent, the ones who don't make it through high school for a plethora of reasons. And what do we do? Put a price tag on it. Declare its value with a dollar sign. It's capitalistic and unrealistic and shameful."

"Hear, hear," Trish says.

Wanda sips her wine. The intellectual segregation of society, for reals. It would be nice to just rest her head on the table. On her forearms, like kindergarten naptime. Perhaps the two of them had more to drink than those two empties. She pushes the ashtray a few inches towards Ivan. He taps his cigarette in an empty beer bottle. Ashes dust the side. "Ivan's just mad 'cause the government's ruined our summer," she says.

"How so?"

"What, you mean the road trip?" Ivan says.

"We wanted to drive down to see my friend Sharon in New Jersey in August," Wanda says. "But if I don't know about employment in September, maybe we should save our money." She glances at Ivan. They haven't discussed this yet. Maybe she's jumping the gun.

"Yeah, well, not going to the States doesn't break my heart," Ivan says. "That place is a disaster. Back in a sec." He bounces off to the kitchen for refills.

With Ivan absent, the only sound is Trish's fingernail scratching at the beer label. Her eyes downcast. Pick, pick, pick. Nothing to say to Wanda, but all kinds of things to say to Ivan. This is a new thing. Wanda has noticed how lately, when Ivan's around, Trish's laugh increases in pitch and volume, spills out at tripping speeds. Like last week, that perfect spit-take. *Pfft. Omigod. Yer so funny, Ivan.*

What would Trish say if Wanda asked her about it, right now? Looked her in the eye and tweaked her head towards Ivan's back: *What's all this about, Trish?* Now that would be unreasonable. Wanda would look like a psycho bitch. Trish and Leo are their best couple friends and regular drinking buddies since she and Ivan started going out. Leo and Ivan have been in at least three bands together. Maybe Trish has a little crush? It can happen in long-term relationships, right? Trish and Leo have been on the go for close to ten years now.

"So fidgety," Trish says. "I'm dyin' for a cigarette."

"Tell Ivan not to smoke in front of you. He knows better."

"Oh no, it's fine."

"Well, even if he's a weekend smoker, he shouldn't be doing it in the house." Wanda gestures to the walls. "He'll have the whole place painted in tar."

"It's such a luxury to smoke inside these days, who am I to stop anybody?"

"I guess." And pause. "So how's the album art going?"

"Okay, I think. I mean, it should connect with what we designed for the EP. But this album's so much lighter, you know? It should be a really positive image."

Wanda nods. She's well aware of the theme, thank you. The EP was "dark" because they were exclusively Ivan's songs about his childhood and losing his father, about their lack of money and opportunities. Stuff he'd worked on for years. Trish may have known Ivan longer, but Wanda's part of the family. This she knows.

Trish's eyes dart up as Ivan saunters back. He passes her another beer and straddles the chair beside her. Wanda considers the two of them, side by side. Like a pair of salt and pepper shakers. Here's Ivan, caramel-coloured from installing gutters all week. Hasn't shaved since Wednesday because two days gets him the optimal sexy scruff. His hair hangs in black ringlets, glossy and effortless.

And here's Trish, pale skin, white-blond hair sliced and diced haphazardly to frame her pixie face, her kittenish blue eyes. She and Ivan are candy from the same shelf in the confectionary, both decked out in cool, aloof shirts. Ivan in his faded Nick Cave and the Bad Seeds t-shirt, Trish in some flouncy blouse she found at the Sally Ann, lavender with a bow in the front. Check Trish out, she can even rock frumpy.

Wanda gazes down at her own outfit. Horizontal black-and-white-striped top paired with Friday casual jeans. Her brown Mowgli hair dangles to her collarbone, no-nonsense bookends for her face. Everything about her is parallel lines. Once, back when she was subbing, she had a few days in a grade-eight class. One student, obviously not doing his work, had emptied out all the leads from his mechanical pencil and arranged them into a figure of a woman. "I'm making a picture of you, Miss," he said. She told him to put it away. That night, she stared in the bathroom mirror and examined the unremarkableness of her face. Wanda Jaynes, you could draw her with dotted lines and get the gist.

In the early days of her and Ivan, they'd go drinking with her cousin Brian and his boyfriend, Max. There was a house party, some themed event where everyone wore glitter and extravagant hats. Ivan smeared streaks of shiny blue face paint on his cheeks, like football eye black. They created a dramatic contrast against his dark skin and glorious cheekbones. "Fucking ridiculous how hot your sexy Portuguese boyfriend is," Brian said. "I don't know how you do it. I can handle Max 'cause he's my hot equal. If he looked like Ivan, I'd feel like crap all the time." And then he backtracked: "Not that you're not gorgeous yourself. You're so pretty."

The front door opens with a jangle of brown bottles. Leo lays the beer case on the table. He kisses Trish and gives Wanda's shoulder a squeeze. He points to the letter on the table. Wanda nods and he holds it with both hands to read it, like it's an ancient scroll in danger of crumbling.

"The needs of the budgetary shortfall?" he says. "Who came up with that? Someone's gotta hard-on for jargon."

"Good name for a band," Ivan says. "Leo McLean and the Budgetary Shortfall."

"Ivan Medeiros and the Shortfall Needs," Trish says.

"I'm sorry, Jaynes," Leo says. "This fucking sucks." He pulls a small bag of weed out of his shirt pocket. Wanda's shoulders relax. Leo's presence brings equilibrium. Leo, the good listener, the insightful commentator. Next to Trish, he could be her sibling with their delicate features, Leo's eyes round and soulful, full lips that buckle together in thought.

"Smells like you guys are making chili," Leo says.

"Yeah, you want some?" Wanda says. He nods. She goes to the kitchen and ladles chili into two bowls. What else. Maybe some cheese. Maybe some sour cream. Maybe a couple of minutes to herself.

She opens the fridge and stares at the shelves. How shitty of her to feel this way. She knows it's partly because her closest friends have left. Sharon's job at Montclair is working out well. She might never leave New Jersey. And Nikki, in Montreal, how she complained about it at first: "Everyone is obsessed with how you dress up here, it's so shallow." Sharon and Wanda rolled their eyes. Nikki, who makes a point of counting all the ball caps on male heads in a bar, who tweets about the depressing state of men's fashion.

Besides them, everyone on Facebook has a baby and no spare

time. Or freshly divorced and on the prowl. Brian and Max broke up last year. Now he has a new fleet of single drinking buddies.

Perhaps loneliness is a feeling unrealized until considered. She's always around people. Weekends with Ivan and their friends, in their echo chamber of shared opinions. All week in class, answering questions, making sure to be *on*. Maybe this busy little life keeps her from dwelling on the possibility of loneliness. And suddenly, here it is, and it's been gathering quietly, like dust bunnies and mold. Waiting for action. She closes her eyes. The refrigerator air prickles her skin.

Ivan's arm encircles her waist. "Look at this," he says. He holds out his smartphone. The title of a recipe: Green Thai Curry.

"Leo says it's deadly," he says. He kisses the back of her ear. "I want to make it for you tomorrow night."

"Yeah?"

His hand presses against her stomach, the edge of this thumb against her breast. "Do we have all that stuff?" His thumb makes a slow circle. It's hard to read the list on his phone.

"We need coconut milk," she says. "But I can get some tomorrow after the gym."

"You're going to the gym?"

"Have to," she says. "I haven't done anything in two days." The gym membership—another possible cutback. She should sit down with a sharpie and a clean piece of paper. Write out the track listing for The Budgetary Shortfalls.

"So dedicated," Ivan says. "Tomorrow night. I'll cook, you relax." She cranes her neck so he can kiss it.

Back in the dining room, she stares at the paper, the email, in the middle of the table. The sweat from their drinks have left damp spots on its edges. She crumples the page and tosses it underhand to the wastepaper basket in the corner. It lands over a foot away.

"Fail!" Ivan, Trish, and Leo sing in unison. A flush of petulant defensiveness runs through her. *Little brats.* Maybe it's some residual feeling from childhood: striking out at the pitch, missing the shot. She never had good aim. The act of squinting and lining up the projection—softball, darts, pool—and always off. She ignores their jeers, picks up the paper ball and drops it in the bin.

2

THERE are too many damned people in the grocery store. Wanda figured if she arrived early enough, it wouldn't be this maggoty. But no. Saturday morning and the vast store hums with humanity. With her gym right next door, she's in it with the rest of them, fresh from her workout, pink-faced and ravenous. And a good chance she will bump into Someone She Knows. Someone She Knows never manifests when she's dressed up, having a good hair day. But grocery shopping in her yoga pants? Guaranteed.

She checks the time on her phone: 10:07am. As she was leaving, Ivan reminded her the chimney inspector will be by the house at 11:00 and he won't be home. So, groceries, get out, get home, deal with Chimney Dude, and finally, finally eat. What's that word Leo uses for feeling irritated due to hunger? Hangry. They joked about it as a band name: The Hangry Fits. Ivan Medeiros and his Hangry Feelings. Low Blood Sugar Hangry Magic.

She taps the Our Groceries app on her phone. The items are arranged in order of the actual grocery aisles, so she doesn't backtrack, no returning to the dairy section from produce. What does she need? Two-percent milk. A birthday card for Fiona. Ivan should get his niece the friggin' birthday card himself, but whatever. He also wants to make that green curry, so coconut milk and fresh ginger. There's an abandoned cart in the middle of the entrance. She grabs it and heads to the card section.

Children's Birthday Cards are divided into Cards for Boys and Cards for Girls. A boy card with a picture of Yoda: *Clever and strong you are. One of my Jedis you will be.* A girl card which comes with shiny nail stickers, a picture of a cartoon cat in high heels: *You sparkle and shine. You're cute. Happy Day!* Is the juxtaposition on purpose? Boys, you're smart, stay cool. Girls, put some shiny crap on your nails and smile. Toys, too—were they this gender specific when she was little? What did she play with as a child? Legos. Barbie had adventures with her teddy bears. Sharon said she used to play with He-Man figures. Nikki had a train set. Ivan is right, things are extra polarized. Blue for boys. Pink for girls. Pink for breast cancer, the girl cancer.

Wanda finds a card with a puppy and a kitten on the front, blank inside. Ivan will just have to write something nice to Fiona. One of the back wheels on the cart jars and refuses to co-operate. No wonder it was left there. Good judgment, Wanda.

She shoves the cart hard to turn into the meat/poultry section. An elderly woman in an itchy-looking purple coat, the shade of artificial grape food colouring, has planted her cart in the middle of the thoroughfare. The woman bends over the display, examining a package of chicken thighs with a tiny magnifying glass. She gives the package a whiff and lays it down. She picks up another and scrutinizes the surface, sniffing and peering. A warm, damp spot forms on the back of Wanda's neck. She shoves the cart hard to get around the purple coat lady. She grunts a little. Purple Coat Lady doesn't notice. *Go ahead, missus, keep breathing over all the raw chicken.* Beneath the purple coat, she wears brand-new white sneakers and blue jeans. How Seinfeldesque. *Hey lady, why don't you scrutinize how you're monopolizing that space? Or some shoes from the new millennium?* Wanda hisses "fuck" under her breath as she angles her cart past her. No acknowledgement. She officially hates Purple Coat Lady.

Wanda reaches the World Foods section and scans the shelves. Jars of curry sauce, ramen noodles, basmati rice, canned lychees— no coconut milk. Which means it could be in three other sections: Baking, Health/Organic, or with the pop, lined up with bottles of bar mix and grenadine, for the piña-colada shoppers. It would be nice to ask someone. She glances around; no staff in sight. The coconut-milk search now means backtracking into the Bad Aisles, with the Doritos and Pepsi. How is she supposed to stick to the outside perimeter of grocery stores, like all the healthy shopping tips suggest, if they don't put the goddamn products in logical places? She could just walk out. Leave the cart right here. Let the two-percent milk sour. Let some wage-monkey teenager on staff restock it.

The Baking Supplies aisle is one back. No staff here either. She goes slowly. White sugar, brown sugar, white flour, whole wheat flour, shredded coconut. No coconut milk. Her eyes dart over the bags of chocolate chips. She could rip the corner off a package, make a spout, fill her mouth with perfect chocolate nibs, turn them into shrapnel between her molars. A blond woman with a baby in a carrier looks up from the packs of artificial colouring and regards her oddly. Have to get out of this aisle.

Here's a guy in a Dominion apron. Shaved head, neck tattoo. Wanda practically shoves the cart in front of him to get his attention: "Excuse me?" He stops. A flicker of impatience shadows his face.

"Do you know where I can find coconut milk?"

"Milk?" He blinks at her. The neck tattoo reads "*infinity*" in what appears to be the Aristocrat font.

"No, coconut milk."

"Ummm…"

"You know, cans of coconut milk. For making curry? Sometimes it's with the Thai food, but I couldn't find it in the imported section."

"I don't know. I work in the deli."

"Do you know anyone who would know?" Her tongue feels eel-like, forked at the tip. She is the most sarcastic snake in the world.

"Yeah, yeah, hold on now. Ummm…," *infinity*'s hand touches the outline of a smartphone in his apron pocket. "I don't see anyone around right now. Does it come in a carton?"

"No, it comes in a can."

"Maybe with the canned vegetables?"

"I think they're fruit."

"Maybe with canned peaches and stuff. Aisle three," *infinity* points and disappears in a puff of apathy before she can object.

Wanda pushes the cart towards the beverage aisle, the back wheel twisting out as it turns, like a palsy. There they are. Cans of coconut milk next to the pineapple juice, each with a picture of the brown husk sliced in half to expose their fresh white inners. Wanda takes a can. $1.99. She has definitely spent $1.99 of her time trying to locate this product. The little bastard would fit nicely in her purse. When she was in high school, she shoplifted a few times, gum, cheap perfume, make-up. An appealing act right now. Is anyone looking? Are there cameras? Plain-clothes security? She looks down the aisle. Purple Coat Lady pushes her cart out the end, turns right, and disappears. She's alone. She eyes her purse. It's oversized and puffs out a little, an extra shirt for the gym is inside. It would dull any clinking sounds, like keys on metal. It would disguise the can's shape. She looks down the aisle again.

A loud cracking sound booms through the store. She jumps. If she didn't know better, she'd say it was a gunshot. Maybe someone dropped something heavy, from a height, the top of a shelf. Maybe something fell from the ceiling.

But that would mean a scream of surprise and then quiet. Not screams and screams and more screams.

And the woman, Purple Coat Lady, appears in Wanda's view of the end of the aisle. She runs across the entrance. The horrible boom comes again and her purple shape falls and Wanda can just see her legs and her shoes at the end, her white sneakers on her blue denim legs, twisted in mid-run. There's blood.

"He has a gun! He has a gun!"

Another huge cracking sound. It *is* a gunshot. Someone is shooting. Someone is shooting people in the store.

People run and scream, there are echoes of screams. Someone flies past her. "Run!" Wanda moves towards the start of the aisle, by the main entrance. The doors are clogged. People everywhere, piles of them, shoving, falling down. Wanda's knees buckle and she leans on a shelf. Which way to go. Have to get out. Where is her phone? She runs back to the cart. She grabs her purse with her left hand, still holding the coconut milk in her right. There is yelling. Another shot. Screams. How many of them are there? There is nowhere to go. Fire exit. Wanda starts up the aisle towards the back of the store, towards the deli. She can get into the back, there must be a way out.

At the end of the aisle, she looks both ways, like she's about to cross the street. People scramble behind the meat counter. She looks to the right, towards Produce. There is a fire exit in the corner. She can just run, run as fast as she can. No signs of danger to the right.

She looks left and there he is. She knows it's him before she sees the gun. He's the only calm person in the store. He takes deliberate steps, holding the handgun in his left hand, scanning the area. Short hair, pale face, black jacket, the sporty-looking winter kind, faded jeans. A fine spray of acne scars on his cheek. A backpack. He has supplies. He is prepared.

She stands inside the aisle. She cannot run, she cannot move. His eyes meet hers. They are dead and black and leaking tears, old batteries she found in the basement once, wet and poisonous. His gaze lands on her and he starts to turn, his hand with the gun sways towards her, like a crane with a load, it's coming, please, fuck, no. But his battery-eyes flicker and he hesitates and she sees his decision. He has spotted someone else, someone beside her in the next aisle. He raises his arm to point at the something, the someone to her right. First this one, then the next one. She hears a sob and a thud to her right, someone behind her in the next aisle. There is begging and sobbing in some other language. She does not understand the words, but their urgency gauges her insides. She sees his blank need, so obvious in the fluorescent light. He takes aim and she just wants to stop the aim, just wants to stop, and when her elbow jerks back, there is a thunk, a bottle knocked off the shelf, some kind of heavy liquid, and there it is, the back of her hand, straight out from her face, her fingers flared open, and there is the can of coconut milk on a rotation through space as it strikes, right there, his forehead, thwack, and he crumples and lies scattered on the tiles like a condemned building.

3

THE people in the bedroom speak with top-notch enunciation: "*A nightmare came to life in one of St. John's largest grocery stores today...*"

"Ivan." Her voice has a crust. Bed sheets tucked up to her chin. The air is stuffy and contains flickering lights. Those people need to stop flashing lights at her.

"*Can you please tell us what happened today?*"

Wanda looks around the bedroom. She is alone, but voices blare around her. The clock radio on Ivan's side reads 10:02pm. The door is open to the computer glow from Ivan's office across the hall.

"*I was in the produce section when I heard the shot.*"

"Ivan!"

"I'm here."

"Turn down the volume."

"Oh Jesus, sorry." The volume drops, but just a smidge. That man is half deaf. She tears the blankets down, pulls the sheet over her head. Air fans in. She closes her eyes. No matter. The witnesses might as well be reporting from the foot of the bed.

"*Everyone was running for the doors...people dropped everything and took off...food all over the floor, everybody runnin', slippin' in it.*"

The sound stops and starts. Ivan is hunting and seeking, clicking on different news sites, CTV, CBC.

"The second shot happened, I wanted out, but the doors were blocked with people. I ran, hid behind the counter in the bakery. There were others ducked down with me, we were all just frozen there. I prayed and prayed, Lord Jesus, save us."

"When I saw his gun pointed at me, I just thought, 'get down.' And I dove for the floor. The bullet hit a cereal box. Rice Krispies rained down on me. And he went on, he must have thought I was dead. When I think about it, I believe God told me to get down. Get down and don't move."

Wanda opens her eyes. The light from the doorway makes the bed sheets resemble snowdrifts at night. She and Ivan arrived home shortly after eight. There was a note on the front door, something written in a frustrated scrawl—the chimney inspector was by. She staggered to the bedroom, stripped off, and got into bed.

The police station took hours. The same questions asked over and over—gently, but with thorough deliberation. She watched her own hands tremble as she drank tea out of a small Styrofoam cup. Over and over, she told the story. The man, the gun, the can, his head, he fell. There was a main cop, her name slipped out of Wanda's mind instantly, but she took care of her and the other witnesses. She had kind and serious eyes and was good at her job. There was another cop, a young guy, talking to Ivan in hushed tones. Ivan was handed a card, a pamphlet of some kind. *That's for when I go crazy*, she thought and marvelled at that idea. Do the police know it will happen? Maybe they're just being proactive.

She exhales and the sheet parachutes out slightly. Coming in for a landing. Her legs ache in a weary, empty way, like they were squeezed and wrung out. How fast did she run? When he fell, she turned and ran, straight down the aisle. The automatic doors were open and there was a clear exit. Her feet hit something wet and she skidded but kept going.

Wanda jams her knuckle in her mouth and bites. The purple coat woman and her silver hair and the red streak on the floor. She ran until she was outside and caught up in the police officer's arms, a wall of blue uniforms and she heard a high-pitched wheezing sound, like the slow release of air from a balloon and she realized it was her.

"I saw him. He was...his face was...dead, no expression and he just...he was like a robot. Robot eyes. Nothin' in them."

Wanda flings the sheet off and sits up. "Ivan! Turn it down!" Silence. Ivan appears in the doorway.

"I'm sorry, I'm so sorry. You okay?"

She rubs her face. "I need to sleep."

"I'll come to bed. Do you need anything?"

"Water, please."

"Be right back." He closes the door. She lies back down and chews her lip. A glass of water would be fantastic. And a long, solid cry. She closes her eyes. The backs of her eyelids are tinged with a muddy glow. Maybe all those fluorescent lights have stained them, like a sunburn. She's looking at the residue of some kind of radiation. The red smear on the floor tiles. She flinches. Shake that image off.

The swish of the door: Ivan with a tall glass of water and an outstretched palm. He holds out a little blue pill.

"Remember when we came back from BC and I complained to Mom about jetlag? She left half a bottle of Valium here."

"God love her pill-poppin' socks," Wanda says.

Ivan laughs sudden and sharp. She takes the pill and a sip of cool, cool water. "What's on the news?"

"Shock. And theories," he says. "Some think he's a crazed anti-consumer activist. Some think it's like a Montreal Massacre thing. Some say he's ISIS."

"He's a white guy."

"Yes. So the retort is that he's a Christian fundamentalist. And the retort to that is that he could be a convert to Islam and then ISIS again. And so on." Ivan brushes her hair from the side of her face. He was pale when he showed up at the police station and a hint of it remains, like a thin coat of primer.

"How are you?" she says.

"Don't worry about me."

"How are you?"

"Relieved. Never been so relieved in my life."

"Me too. I think. I'm so tired."

"Who do you...who do you think he was?"

"Dunno. He just looked like some guy to me." She reaches and he passes her the water. It's rare to be parched enough to actually sense liquid enter the bloodstream. Her veins can feel how cold the water is. "He looked…consumed."

"Consumed by what?"

"I don't know. He looked sad."

"Oh, baby. I'm sorry this happened to you." His eyes shine down on her. "And I'm sorry the news was so loud. I can't turn my brain off."

"Take a Valium sure." It's already starting to work. Or maybe that's a placebo effect. There's a warm thickening in her empty legs.

"I might."

Her blinking slows. Ivan strokes wisps of hair from her forehead. "I'm so amazed by you," he says. "You are amazing." His breath escapes in a snagging sigh that quivers his bottom lip.

"Mazing," Wanda says. The muddy-eyelid glow fades to black.

She is immersed in a thick, stuffy shroud. The comforter bunches around her head like a wreath. When she shifts, the synthetic fibers scrunch inside it. She thinks of the times she played hide and seek with her cousins—when was that? The summer before grade five. Once, she hid in the unfinished extension they were building on the house and she climbed behind a roll of pink insulation. All that summer, she'd been curious to touch the insulation, thinking it would feel fluffy and soft. Instead, it was starchy and dry and made her skin feel powdered with some kind of crystallized, chemical dust.

Hide and seek. Run and hide.

An exclamation muffles through the pulp. It is Mom's voice. Wanda pushes back the comforter. The day peeks through the cracks in the blinds. Mom's voice is downstairs now, was downstairs all along. She can hear Ivan too, speaking in appreciative and polite tones. Then Dad, offering something light and jovial. Ivan laughs. Mom and Dad, up early for the two-hour drive into town from Trepassey. The clink of silverware on plates. They came in because of the shooting. Ivan was on the phone yesterday, calling to let people know.

Did Ivan put the pot away? Yes. He would do that, he's not stunned. Mom and Dad fear "all those downtown drugs." Like no one in Trepassey has a draw. Like she and Ivan aren't in their thirties.

But they both know if there was pot evidence around the house, Mom and Dad would inflate with disappointed silence. And then, some slow intro into a "concerned discussion." Which could probe Ivan into impassioned statements on legalization and her mother's response climbing to its limit of shrill. So shag that. When parents visit, it means scour the place for green crumbs and roaches. And in Ivan's mother's case, no evidence of cigarettes either, even though they are just weekend smokers, really. Because Mrs. Medeiros does not debate her feelings. Last spring, she spotted a couple of butts on the ground. Wanda said they were left by friends. "Ivan's father was a gasping rake at the end," Mrs. Medeiros said. "Don't even let your friends smoke. They think it's a choice, but they're pawns to those bastard cigarette companies."

No, if Ivan called Mom and Dad, he would straighten up the place. And now they are here, doing what they do in a tragedy: arriving armed with worried eyes and more food than necessary. Casserole dishes filled with meatloaf, scalloped potatoes, and condolences.

Actually, scalloped potatoes sound deadly right now. She slides herself to the edge of the bed and stands. A sour briny taste has formed in the back of her throat. Her legs are rubbery and newborn. Valium is an effective drug, yessir. She shrugs on her robe and wipes the tightness from her eyes. The pressure of yesterday tweaks in her hips, but she needs to go downstairs. Show that she is okay, put something clean in her mouth.

Ivan and her parents mill around the dining room, laying plates on the table, opening Tupperware containers. They pause when she enters. Mom comes over first for a hug. She's all soft-cotton shirt and bread-baking smells.

"Oh lovey," Mom says. "What a thing to happen. What a terrible thing." Her voice vibrates with exhausted concern. If Mom slept, it was brief, jerked into consciousness by fretful thoughts, finally getting up to putter and bake until they took to the road. "We're so happy you're okay," Mom says. Her fingertips sink into the terrycloth on Wanda's back.

"Of course she's okay," Dad says. When he hugs her, he holds her so tight she can feel his words reverberating on her ribs. The lines from his corduroy shirt press into her cheek. "More than okay," he says. "She's a hero."

Ivan told them. Obviously, they should know. Dad hasn't shaven; a few strands of her hair stick to his cheek like Velcro.

"Let her eat," Mom says. "She must be starved." The table is laden with easy-to-grab items: buttered toast, green grapes in a bowl. Long slices of cantaloupe like orange smiles lie on a wooden cutting board. Wanda takes one and on the first bite the sweet juice floods out the bitterness in her mouth and throat. She almost groans with the relief. She eats it without pausing and takes another. She could do this all day, fill the cracks and crevices of her insides with cure-all cantaloupe juice.

"Jane, do you want me to put these on?" Ivan gestures to a Tupperware container of small pink bundles. Scallops, wrapped in bacon.

"If Wanda wants them."

Wanda nods while she chews.

"Did you sleep well?"

Nods.

"I just can't believe it," Mom says. "You see this kind of horror show down in the States, but you don't imagine it happening here."

"People lose their minds all the time," Ivan says.

"Is that what it was?" Dad says. "Are they sure he didn't have some kind of agenda?"

"I think we would know by now. Other shooters had notes. YouTube manifestos, like that creep in California who blamed all women for his virginity."

"So, this guy had nothing?" Mom says. "What makes someone go off like that?" She lays wrapped scallops in rows on a baking sheet, making a platoon of pink snails.

"What makes people do all the awful things they do?" Ivan says. He glances at Wanda. "I'm going to put more coffee on."

Wanda selects another slice of cantaloupe and sinks her teeth in. So good. Her eyelids flutter involuntarily. From now on, she'll use her nose for breathing and mouth for fruit only.

"Have you talked to Sharon or Nikki?" Mom says.

"No, Mom, I just woke up."

"I just want to make sure you have supports, dear. Your friends should know."

"So, what happened?" Dad says. He drops a tea bag into his mug. Earl Grey, with the string and little tab. "You knocked the guy out?"

"Yes."

"You hit him in the face?"

"No. Well, maybe. His forehead, I think."

"With something from the shelves?"

"A can of coconut milk."

"Let her eat," Mom says. "You should eat too."

"And it knocked him out," Dad says. He exhales with a whistle, jigging the string of the tea bag vigorously. "Wow. That close to him. You must have really whipped it."

"Why do you have to fixate on that?" Mom says. "Let her collect herself."

"If she doesn't want to discuss it, she'll tell me," he says. "And when my daughter does something brave, I want to know about it." He pulls out the tea bag and dumps it on the edge of his plate. "She saved the people in that store yesterday. It's natural to have questions."

"Honestly, I don't remember throwing it," Wanda says. "I remember being terrified. Then he fell down. And I ran."

"Good for you. Smart, smart girl," Dad says.

She grins in spite of herself. A memory pops up, some incident in junior high. She got detention for smacking some boy. Who was that? Sheldon White. He called her a whore and she hit him, open-palmed across his jaw, just as the teacher walked in. Dad picking her up late from school, asking what happened: *He called you what? Next time, make sure no one is around when you clock the little bastard.*

Mom bites into a slice of cantaloupe and frowns. "There's a taste of onion on this. Is that knife clean?"

"It should be."

"Probably from the cutting board," she says. "Wooden cutting boards, they hold flavours, even when they're clean. You know what your Aunt Sheila does? She has different coloured cutting boards for different items: green for vegetables, red for meat. Cuts down on germs."

Ivan's eyes meet Wanda's over Mom's shoulder and he nods too enthusiastically. *Yes, let's go out and get a rainbow selection of cutting boards.* Wanda bites into another slice. It's there, faintly, the taint of onions. Maybe garlic too. She forces herself to swallow.

"I'll just stick to grapes," Dad says, plucking one from the bowl. "Who said *peel me a grape*? Marilyn Monroe?" His moustache ripples as he chews, like a flexing caterpillar, mouse-brown with specks of grey. That's how she used to think of his moustache, some furry creature trained to hide his facial expressions. What does he look like without it? It dates him now. 80s dad. She remembers being stuck at a neighbour's house during a winter storm—Carly Bennett—she went over after school to watch Much Music. The weather got bad and Carly's parents didn't want her to walk home alone. She wanted to stay, have a slumber party. But Dad came to get her in the blizzard, bustling into the Bennett's porch chased by a flourish of snowflakes, grinning at them all, crusts of frozen snot dangling from his moustache. The next day, Carly pointing to a picture of cave stalactites in their science textbook: *Your dad's moustache boogers.*

"Have you talked to your mother?" Dad says to Ivan.

"Yes, she's in Florida. Coming back in a couple of days."

"And your sister and her family?" Dad says.

"They're in Corner Brook visiting my brother-in-law's folks. I talked to Sylvie last night, they'll be in next week."

"How's that adorable niece of yours?" Dad says. "Fiona, right?"

"She's great. A character. Her ninth birthday is coming up."

"They're so great at that age." Dad smiles down at his hands. Yes, let's bring up Fiona. *And speaking of kids…* Wanda receives direct questions about the possibility of children, but they spare Ivan that kind of scrutiny. Maybe because they know Ivan will not perform Wanda's dance around the subject and he will flatly state he has no interest in children.

"How's the music going?" Dad says.

"Oh, good," Ivan says. "Getting the finishing touches on the album."

"What's the name now? Rogue something?"

"The Rogue Skaters is the one I'm in with Leo. But I also play bass with Ray Wakeham's band, Ray and the Autumn People."

"Oh yes," Dad says. "Clever name. Sounds like good fun."

Good fun indeed. A sudden weariness descends over her. She wants to be clean, a shower, a lie-down in a cool place. She wants to be away from Mom and Dad and their tug-of-war nurturing.

"I need to get a wash," she says. "And I should put on clothes."

Mom's voice from the kitchen goes up an octave: "Don't feel like you have to get done up on our account."

"Yes, you do whatever you need to do," Dad says. "Relax." A tiny drop of tea hangs from his moustache. Maybe his facial hair isn't brown at all, but stained with years of tea and toast and an assortment of safe, brown foods. She is suddenly irritated; why is she explaining to her parents that she needs a shower? It's not like they're invited guests. Mom shutting the cupboard doors too loudly, already frustrated how this kitchen is not laid out in the same format as hers. Dad and his cup of Earl Grey. So proud when she hit Sheldon White, but didn't say anything to the teacher who gave her detention.

"I need a shower, really," Wanda says. "I didn't get one last night." She hops up, tightening the belt on her robe. She should tell them what else she needs. Who knows who they've spoken to already.

"You do what you need to do."

"Also," she says, "I don't want anyone to know what I did. To the shooter."

"The knockout?"

"Yes. I went through it all with the police. I really don't want to be asked a pile of questions about it from everyone I know."

"Well. It's an understandable reaction," Dad says. "Especially now. You're tired."

"Yes, lovey," Mom says. "We won't say anything until you do."

"I'm not going to say anything."

"Of course. Not right now."

"No, not now, not ever. I don't want this to be a thing."

"But, um, it will be a thing," Ivan says. "I mean, the cops said you'd have to give a report in court."

"And I will. Later. Court won't happen for months."

"You know, sweetie," Mom says, "it's a horrible thing what's happened. But you don't need to act like this is *bad* news. This is different."

"How so, Mom?"

"Well, Wanda, whenever you get bad news, you avoid discussing it. I know it's why you didn't call back Friday to talk about what's happening with your job."

"I don't like talking about shitty, negative things," Wanda senses Dad's moustache grimace-prickling. Whatever, Dad, it's a shitty little swear word.

"But this isn't a negative thing."

"Mass shootings are pretty negative, Mom."

"Honey. You stopped it," Dad says. "What your mother is trying to say is this is something good."

"I don't even remember doing it."

"You still did it though," he says. "And we're all thankful."

"Well, I don't know how anyone can be thankful about any of this," she says. "I mean, I get it, it happened. It's on the security footage. And when that man goes to court, I'll have to tell the story over again, in front of him and everyone else. And I have nothing to say other than it happened so fast I don't really remember it. So, until then, please keep it to yourselves."

Dad's mouth opens to speak, but she turns on her heel and bounds upstairs to the bathroom. She locks the door and sits on the edge of the tub. Exhales. The peace of a secure door. How is it these people can maintain such a weak understanding of her? A bit of space. A bit of empathy. Not that hard, people.

She turns on the hot water and adds small suggestions of cold. She pulls the lever on the faucet and watches the water rain out of the shower head. The mist rising, the patter on the tile. The mirror fogs up and the room becomes a blur of steam before she removes her robe and stands under the nozzle. The impact of the water both causes and soothes goose bumps on her flesh.

All this will pass. It will be okay. It's early May. Time cures and all that. Soon it will be summer. Sharon and Nikki will be here for concerts and cabin times. A cabin party, somewhere far away, near water, that would be nice. Sharon's parents have a great spot out in Salmon Cove.

She met Ivan at that cabin. It was supposed to be a small get-together, but Nikki kept inviting people: her roommates, her cousin, a bunch of guys in a band. Ivan striding across the lawn carrying an orange cooler, a quick "hi" on introductions and his eyes bouncing over to Nikki. Little Nikki, training for the Tely Ten, tiny, tan and tight all over, a little package of herself in blue shorts. Ray Wakeham unveiling the bag of shrooms after supper, the earthy taste in the back of her throat. Later, Ivan pointing to a plastic grocery bag, Foodland, snagged in the branches of a tree: "Look at that. Way out here and there's still litter." And Wanda was too euphoric to go there. "How special is that?" she said. "There's isn't a Foodland for twenty miles. It made it all the way here. That's a bag of dedication."

And Ivan's peel of laughter from a deep warm pocket in his belly, genuine with a note of surprise. And then he ended up next to her when they all walked the quad trail around the barrens and the dusk light in her dilated pupils made everything look like TV static and when she said this, he held his hands in front of his face: "Everything has thickened."

Later, in the kitchen, Nikki referred to doing hot knives as hash tags and Wanda and Ivan made sure no one let her forget it. And the next day, when they were leaving, he said to her, "You should come see us play. We're at The Levee on Thursday." He found her eyes and waved from the side window of the car as they drove away.

This summer, they can go back there. Reconnections. Making new fun. The shower sloughs off what feels like a thousand layers of grime and sweat. When her fingertips are puckered, she gets out. She returns to bed. Cool air tender on clean flesh.

Her parents are gone when she wakes up. 3:52 in the afternoon. Jesus, the time. Ivan sits in the living room with the TV low and crackling. The bowl of fruit remains on the table along with today's *Telegram*. Wanda chews a grape and examines the front page. A colour photo of the Dominion-store parking lot, yellow tape, people huddled together, hands over their mouths.

Grocery Store Massacre Shocks City

In a year when international news of mass shootings has reached an all-time high, it seems the city of St. John's is not immune. Citizens express shock and grief over yesterday's incident which resulted in three fatalities.

The shootings occurred in one of the city's largest Dominion stores on Saturday morning. According to police and witness reports, the shooter, Edward Rumstead, 42, entered the store shortly before 10:30am. He produced a handgun from inside his jacket and began shooting. He moved throughout the store, shooting four times, killing one staff member and two customers. He shot at and missed Mrs. Geraldine Harvey. Mrs. Harvey stated that she lay on the floor and pretended to be dead after Rumstead shot and missed.

The names of the victims have been released. Michael Snow, 22, a third-year university student and part-time cashier at the Dominion branch. D'arcy Fadden, 37, a chemical engineer and father of four-year-old twins. Dr. Ella Collier, 59, a professor of economics at Memorial University.

According to police reports, Rumstead was knocked unconscious by a customer in the store. The customer then exited the store and alerted police that Rumstead had been struck on the head and fell down. Police surrounded the area and entered the store, where they found Rumstead lying unconscious.

Rumstead carried a backpack which contained a second loaded handgun and boxes of ammunition. No other details have been released on the identity of the customer or the nature of how Rumstead was incapacitated. Currently, Rumstead is in police custody and undergoing psychiatric evaluation.

No motives have been revealed as to why Rumstead decided to open fire in the Dominion store. Sources state he lived at home with his widowed mother in the West End of St. John's. For several years, he worked as a custodian in industrial warehouses, but he had been unemployed since 2011. Neighbours describe him as a quiet man without much to say.

Neighbour Clifford Pomeroy: "You'd see him outside, working in the yard or cleaning his mother's car. He might nod or wave at you. Honestly, I'm completely shocked, but it goes to show, you never really knows anybody."

Oliver Loblaw, CEO of the Loblaw/Dominion chain, has released a public statement expressing condolences: "It is with deep sadness that we at Loblaw/Dominion received the news of the tragic shootings in St. John's, Newfoundland. Our Newfoundland and Labrador customers are dear to our hearts. We offer them our sympathy and support during this difficult time."

Outpourings of sympathy for the victims and their families are already appearing at the scene of the crime: people have left flowers, notes, and gifts along the north edge of the Dominion parking lot. A candlelight vigil for the three victims will be held there tonight at 7:00pm. The store remains closed to the public at this time.

In the living room, Ivan flicks between the weather channel and the news. Rain, drizzle, and fog all day and for the next three days. There are enough bright lights on screens and in minds right now. RDF solidarity.

The news spins panic circles. This here happened, this happened here! Everyone has an angle and a point: *Soon security guards at school, metal detectors at the mall, criminal profilers, neighbourhood watch. Well, that's unnecessary—overall, St. John's has the lowest rate of murder in North America. This is knee-jerk paranoia. No it isn't, and if there was security with guns, there would have been only two shots fired, him shooting and him being shot. If there were more guns, this would happen more often. #grocerystoryshootingNL #EdwardRumstead #NLmassshooting #RNC #thoughtsandprayers.*

Wanda imagines their radius of neighbours. Who knows what the people around you are like, really? Like Pascale next door, with her glum face and steely hair, her furtive glances and quick nods. Last winter, Pascale left a note tucked under their windshield wiper: *I didn't spend hours in the snow, shovelling out a spot in front of MY house for YOUR car.* Ivan ranted about how ridiculous it was for a neighbour to leave a note and not just ask them to move the car. "It's all street parking, what does it matter?" They call her Pascale Aggressive behind her back. And what kind of person is Pascale, really? Maybe she's hoarding weapons. Maybe she cooks meth. Maybe there are missing girls tied up in her basement, concealed by soundproof walls.

Leo calls. He tells Ivan how spooky it is downtown. Bars and restaurants empty, no one walking. People want to cluster in well-lit homes with their curtains drawn. Friends and family have called all day, sent emails and text messages. All day, Ivan has answered the phone, texted one-handed, repeated the same combinations of words: *Wanda was there, but she's fine. Just shocked and exhausted. We're dealing.*

On the couch, he rubs her knee under her robe. "That candle-light vigil tonight. You want to go?"

"When is it?"

"Seven o'clock."

Wanda takes the remote and changes the channel. There must be an episode of *The Simpsons* on somewhere. Why do they even have cable? Something else to cut back.

"If you want, we can all go," he says. "You, me, Trish, Leo. Up to you."

Some commercial, an elderly woman on the ground. She can't get up, her face in anguish. The announcer is saying something. Wanda's mouth dries. The woman in the purple coat, how did that feel, those seconds she ran before he shot. Did she feel her purple coat get heavy on her back, blood pooling out. She swallows, a scrape in her throat.

The ad is for some medic-alert product. A remote control with a large button. Seniors can wear it like a necklace.

"Look at that thing," Ivan says. "Does it come in different colours and patterns? Panic button fashion."

"I'll go," Wanda says. "We can all go. I'm okay with that."

"Alright," he says. "I'll text them."

4

SHE and Ivan bundle into the back of Leo's Tercel. Trish smiles at them from the passenger seat. She hasn't been able to hug Wanda yet, but she reaches back and pats her knee. Both she and Leo are mellow, but wide-eyed. They make blithe comments and offer her things— gum, a cigarette, a bottle of water.

The perimeter around the store is fenced off with yellow tape and traffic is backed up. Cops direct vehicles to parking spaces. Cops everywhere. Are there reasons to be afraid? What about copycat stuff? Maybe public gatherings are not such a good idea. Maybe this is how people develop a fear of crowds. Get your agoraphobia on the go.

Leo parks by the furniture store across the street. Streams of people descend on the vigil area, some carry bouquets of flowers and gift bags. Trish wanders ahead with her camera, tuning it for the low light. They follow her through crowds and around parked cars, the length of her back clad in a smart-looking raincoat, tomato red. Ivan walks with Wanda, his fingers interlocked with hers.

The crowd has gathered by the back of the parking lot. A long awning is set up over a portable wall sheltering three large portrait photos, hung high enough to be visible over the crowd. Wanda stops when she's close enough to focus. The first photo is a dark-haired man, mid-thirties, holding a fishing rod. His hand is propped on his hip in a jokey pose. The father, D'arcy. Next, a smiling young man with cropped reddish hair, the cashier, Michael Snow. His arm dangles casually on the shoulders of a petite blond girl. Probably his Facebook profile picture, probably his girlfriend. A youngster, like he just turned old enough to drink. The third photo is Purple Coat Lady, the professor, Dr. Collier. Her hair sways over her forehead in a polished wave. She wears black with a simple silver necklace. Dr. Collier gazes into the camera with accomplished wisdom, probably a photo from her professional profile, her biography of achievements. Wanda swallows back the swell in her chest.

Short wooden steps have been constructed underneath the pictures to hold offerings. They are staggered with bouquets, homemade signs, wreathes of flowers, teddy bears. A Boston Bruins hockey jersey is propped up under the photo of D'arcy Fadden. Someone has strung white Christmas lights along the top of the awning. The display radiates through the murk and sadness. People stand hunched over, many hold candles—special ones in jars to stay lit in the damp. Two women with university logos on their backs stand near the photo of Dr. Collier, they wipe their eyes and shudder. The parking-lot grey mixes with the mist, smudging everything but the candlelight and the myriad of jewel-toned Gortex jackets.

"Were you there?"

An elderly woman stands at Wanda's shoulder. Her eyes are swollen and tight. She wears a navy-blue raincoat with long yellow buttons, like Paddington Bear's jacket. A red canvas bucket hat is clamped down over her head. She holds a Mason jar containing a glowing white candle.

"Yes, I was there." Wanda is aware of her hands in her pockets. She should have a candle too, out of respect. Where does she get one? Was she supposed to bring one from home?

"I can tell," the woman says. "The ones who were there are the ones not crying. You all look like you had the juice shaken out of you."

"Well…we did," Wanda says. "I'm pretty dehydrated." Nice one. Fuck sakes.

"I would feel the same," the woman says. "I'd also be drunk. Or at the edge of temptation, anyway." She rolls her small wet eyes to the sky. "Had to give that up a long time ago. I'm Dallas Cleal, by the way."

"Wanda Jaynes." She offers Dallas her hand. Dallas takes it, but holds it still instead of shaking it. Her hand feels brittle, but warm and soft. She looks into Wanda's face with quivering lips.

"I should be sad, but I'm so angry," Dallas says. Her voice is flat and cracked, the tenor of old cement. "Ella. Poor Ella."

"You knew her?" Wanda says. Purple Coat Lady. "Dr. Collier, right?"

"Oh yes. For years. We taught together at the university. Philosophy for me, economics for her. But we did cross-discipline courses with the Women's Studies department." She sighs. "Ella did so much good. She did research. She wanted to find ways to get away from financial dependence on oil. Wind, recycling. Manure even. She found a guy down near Codroy, a dairy farmer. He knows how to make energy from cowshit. 'We could feed it back into the grid' she said."

Dallas drops Wanda's hand. She retrieves a pack of Benson and Hedges Menthol out her pocket and hands her the candle. Wanda roots in her pocket for a light, but Dallas pops a smoke in her mouth and lights it off the candle flame.

"And now she's gone. She went to the store and she's gone." Dallas sucks hard on her cigarette.

"I'm sorry." Maybe she should tell her she saw Ella in the store. No, she might make Dallas upset. Or become overwhelmed herself— who knows what she might disclose then.

"Look at this bunch," Dallas gestures to a group of about a dozen people in royal-blue raincoats. They stand to the side of the awning with clasped hands and bowed heads. A woman with long red hair cradles a stack of pamphlets like a baby.

"Who are they?"

"They call themselves The Workers for Modern Christianity." Dallas's raisin eyes glint with malevolence. "They show up everywhere: funerals, protests. They say they're giving support to the masses. Load of bull. They only want to enlarge their membership base."

"Like, missionaries?"

"They're bible literalists in the way they believe everything is the will of God, as in he is sovereign. 'The lot is cast into the lap, but every decision is from the Lord,' kind of thing. Which you know, fine for them, you want to say. Until you check their website and see the links to gay reprogramming camps. And when it comes to women and men, they have all our assigned places mapped out."

"Really? Shit."

"I just can't trust anyone who hands out propaganda at something like this. Who sees people in this state of mind and thinks *membership drive*?" Dallas gestures to the three figures by D'arcy Fadden's photo, a woman, two kids. Maybe his twins.

"Yes, it's pretty gross."

Dallas takes a harsh mentholated drag. "What did you say your name was again?"

"Wanda Jaynes."

"Wanda Jaynes, you take care of yourself. You tell your beautiful people you love them. Do it before they're gone. But you know that, Wanda Jaynes. You know that now, anyway."

Dallas moves her smoke over the Mason jar for a moment, like it's an ashtray. Then she remembers and flicks the ash to the side. She shuffles towards the awning and stops beside a cluster of people. Her mouth moves. Heads turn. They don't know her either.

Wanda watches the red-haired woman with the pamphlets make her way down the line. She stops in front of the photo of Michael Snow and proffers a brochure to an elderly couple. The woman looks up, her face pink and streaming. She waves a hand to dismiss her. What are you doing, Red-Haired Lady? That woman could be his mother. How to Get a Smack in the Face.

Wanda shakes her head. A familiar, residual relief expands through her, the one she first experienced at twenty when she realized she believed in nothing. Shelly Knowling, her roommate at the time, had discovered spirituality in the form of karma and the power of personal energy. *Everything happens for a reason* was Shelley's response to both positive and inconvenient events: finding money on the street, missing the bus, contracting ringworm. Wanda was in the library, doing research for a sociology course on African children and HIV. After hours of literature on desperate statistics and Western apathy, she broke down in tears in the stacks. No, there is no reason for this, no check and balance. There is no God keeping score, no source, no magic energy. Things happen all the time, for no reason at all. The sudden acceptance was a tonic. Years of Anglicanism and shrugging agnosticism and, finally, something felt right. She went home and told Shelly, who promptly burst into tears.

Leo arrives beside her. "Hey, Jaynes." He slips a small silver flask into her hand. "I'm driving, but you help yourself."

"Thank you, sir." She takes a sip. The shock of Scotch glows warm against the cold grey. "Where's Ivan?"

"Right there."

Ivan stands about twenty feet away, shaking hands with someone. It's the cop from yesterday, the young looking one. What's his name? The cop notices her and nods. He is all soft round mouth and gaze. Gawd, he looks about twelve. Wee baby cop. She goes over.

"Ms. Jaynes. How are you doing?" Baby Cop says.

"I'm okay. Processing I guess." What's his name? He got her water and held her hand. What a forgetful arsehole she is.

He leans into her ear: "I know they don't know you personally, but this town is grateful for you." She glances at his profile. His lashes are Minnie Mouse long. "All you need to do is look over there to know it."

She follows his gaze. On the ground to the side of Dr. Collier's picture is a separate cluster of gifts and flowers. No photograph, but a number of Bristol-board signs and notes are tacked to the wall. She reads a yellow cardboard sign, words in a child's handwriting. *Thank you, Hero. We love you.* There are masses of similar pictures and signs. *Thank God for the hero. Thank you for saving my father. Thank you for saving my sister.*

"People need to say thanks, even when they don't have a face or a name," Baby Cop says.

She swallows and tastes bile. Everything inside her is full to the brim.

"I know you're in shock," he says. "Your boyfriend says you don't want people to know what happened. And as an officer, I don't feel I should ever encourage a citizen to take matters into their own hands. But that said, I want to say thank you myself. After seeing the contents of that backpack and witnessing his state of mind... well, things could have been much worse."

"Thanks," she says. The urge to stroke his cheek is strong. Her hand even floats up, but she tucks her hair behind her ear instead. "That's nice to hear."

His brow wrinkles slightly. Adorable, like an intense kitten. "I'm wondering about something. No pressure. But there is someone who wants to meet you."

He nods towards the end of the parking lot. A man and woman, both Asian, sit on a bench. The woman bends forward, swaying back and forth. The man next to her keeps one arm around her shoulders. He mutters into her ear.

"The security footage shows her in the aisle next to you, when you confront the shooter."

She remembers the sounds next to her, the pleading. "I remember her voice," Wanda says. "I didn't understand the language."

"Yes. Her name is Liang-Yi. Her family came here from Taiwan when she was a teen. She said it looked like she was about to be next when you threw that can. Would you like to say hello?"

The woman, Liang-Yi, presses her hands to her face, like otherwise it will slide off.

"I don't want to disturb her," Wanda says.

"I don't think she'll mind." He sniffs and his delicate nostrils flare. What do people do when he writes them up for speeding? Pass him their license and a cookie?

Wanda nods. Baby Cop walks in front of her. The Asian woman's long dark hair drapes forward. Like in that Japanese horror movie, *The Grudge*. Jesus, Wanda, don't compare her to *The Grudge*.

"Excuse me, Ms. Chen?" Baby Cop says. Her face emerges from the hair sheath, heart-shaped and dainty. Her mouth is parted in mid sob or gasp.

"Do you remember me from yesterday?" he says. He extends his hand to her. "Constable Lance." Yes, that is his name! Remember it. Lance, rhymes with trance.

"Wanda, this is Liang-Yi Chen. Ms. Chen, this is Wanda Jaynes. Wanda was the one who threw the can." Threw the can. The can thrower. Wanda don't want to work, she just want to throw the can all day.

Liang-Yi sits up. The man beside her asks something and she

rattles back at him in Mandarin. They both erupt: "Thank you, thank you."

Wanda's hands have no purpose. Putting them in her pockets feels rude, yet they can't seem to dangle right. Liang-Yi stands and takes both Wanda's hands in hers. "I told my brother that I thought my life was over. All I could think was he had chosen me to die. And then he fell." Her hands tighten on Wanda's. "Thank you."

"You're welcome." What a stupid thing to say. Like she held the door for her.

"I have so much I want to say. But my English is not good when I'm upset."

"Your English sounds great to me." Maybe she could teach ESL when ABE ends? How hard would it be?

Liang-Yi peers at her. Her eyes are ridged with wet light. "How did you do it?"

"I don't know," Wanda says. The laughter spurts from some unconscious well. She clamps a hand over her mouth. Liang-Yi peers at her. Wanda shakes her head. "I don't know. I don't know. I remember being terrified. Then he was on the ground."

"You are like a baseball player," the man next to Liang-Yi says.

Liang-Yi ignores him. "I wish I was like you," she says. "I remember everything."

"Baseball player. Monster slayer," the man says.

"I'm neither of those," Wanda says. What is there to say besides all she remembers is fear? That her stomach may always feel like a jar of mustard pickles at the thought of yesterday? She glances towards Ivan. He cranes his neck, looking around for her. "I should go," she says. "My boyfriend is looking for me." She retracts her hand and steps back.

"I don't know how to thank you," Liang-Yi says.

"You don't need to. You don't need to feel that way."

Liang-Yi coils her empty arms around herself and nods. "I understand. But thank you, anyway. Thank you, Wanda Jaynes."

5

THE flickering red lights tease through Wanda's eyelids. What is wrong with Ivan he can't close the bedroom door? She peeks around the room. 1:17am.

It isn't the door. The lights are outside. They flash through the cracks in the venetian blinds. She approaches the window and peels down one of the slots. Whenever Nikki would look through blinds like this, she'd say, "80s detective show."

The flashing lights belong to a police car. A uniformed cop stands on the sidewalk. Headlights make silhouettes of bodies milling about. Cameras flash, people hold their phones straight-armed from their bodies. Wanda recognizes a few of her neighbours and a local reporter.

"Ho-lee fuck!" Ivan's voice downstairs.

"What's going on?"

The doorbell rings. Ivan's footsteps hammer across the floor. The front door opens. She cannot make out what Ivan says, but he's using his Mature Voice, the one he uses for employers and senior citizens. "No, I'm afraid this is all a surprise. We'll keep that in mind."

The door shuts. Ivan moving around, his feet on the stairs. He enters with his laptop.

"Okay. So, this is happening." He sets his laptop on the comforter. The YouTube page is open to a video entitled ST. JOHN'S GROCERY STORE SHOOTER TAKEDOWN.

"The security footage?"

"No. Someone filmed it."

She blinks at the screen. The paused video shows three grocery aisles and the edge of the produce section, shot from above. "Someone took a video?" she says.

"Yeah. Apparently, someone was hiding in the upstairs security office. There's a window that looks out over the store. They hid on the floor and propped their phone against the glass."

"Fuck."

"It's messed up. People are fucked. Everyone is filming everything all the time."

"This can't be legal. They can't just put that up."

"It was just on the news. Less than an hour online. 40,000 hits already."

She hugs her knees. "I might ralph."

"Do you want to see it?" He looks from the laptop to her: "It's up to you."

Get it over with. She nods. He clicks Play.

The video shows the end of the two aisles, side by side. Wanda stands in one and, in the other, the Asian woman—what was her name? Liang-Yi. Her long dark hair hangs along her shoulders and she wears jeans and a blazer. She and Liang-Yi are separated by the aisle shelves. The man, the shooter, Edward Rumstead, faces them, his back to the camera. Wanda cringes as she sees herself. She resembles one of those pop-out paper dolls, the kind which came in books with perforated lines, outfits with little tabs to fold over their limbs. She slicked back her hair in a ponytail for the gym and it makes her head look extra round and ball shaped. A hairstyle to avoid, really. She wears her sky-blue coat from work, the one they gave out free to all employees with the institute's emblem, although in the video, the acronym looks like a smudge on the left side of her chest. Black pants, grey sneakers, big puffy green purse, like a dangling watermelon in her left hand. As Edward Rumstead turns with the gun, Liang-Yi falls to her knees in a begging stance.

"Stop." She buries her head in her knees. "I can't watch this."

He snaps the laptop closed. "I'm sorry." His body around hers, warm hands on her back.

"What the fuck is going on outside?"

"There are a few reporters. I don't know from where. And… people, people who want to know who you are. And people who know you." He pulls out his phone. "I turned the volume down hours ago, but my voicemail is full and I have several hundred million text messages. Yours will be the same."

"What a mess."

"I told the reporters you need rest. But I imagine they'll be out there for a while."

"How long is a while?" Her brain is a ball of lint, stuffy and purposeless. She lies down on her side and curls up. "Everybody knows. I can't believe everybody knows."

"Yes, they do." His hand smooths down her spine. "But you know, they were going to find out anyway, when the trial started."

"Not necessarily. I might have figured out a way to avoid it by then. I could have made a plan."

"Maybe it's better that it's happening now."

"How?"

"It beats the stress of waiting?" He shrugs.

Her hands cover her face. "Can't deal with this now." She snatches the edge of the sheet and tugs, trying to get it out from underneath her.

"Of course, sweetie. I'm going to turn off all the lights. That'll give them a big hint."

"Can I have one of your mom's Valium? And can you cover the window? Their light is getting in."

"Whatever you need." He kisses her cheek and leaves the room. She puts her face in her pillow. More than 40,000 views. More than the population of Trepassey. More people than she's ever known, all watching the worst moment of her life. Sitting at their screens. Probably eating chips. Touching their keyboards with their sticky fingers, typing some semi-literate observation. Clicking the mouse to share it with the followers of their egos. Look at this now. Something else, isn't it.

She shifts her hips and her muscles whine. She ran straight down that aisle. What if he hadn't been knocked out? He could have shot her in the back. Imagine *that* video. The addition of a second or a centimetre would make it a snuff film. Or, angle the camera slightly, it could have caught the distant shape of Ella Collier's corpse at the end of the aisle.

Ivan returns to the bedroom with a bath towel and a glass of water. He produces the small blue pill. She accepts it open-palmed. She downs most of the water while he drapes the towel over the blinds. A few cracks of light escape around the edges, but the room feels cloaked. He gets into bed and lies behind her, the big spoon. She fits herself into the cleft of his chest and becomes small and encapsulated. He presses his lips to her neck, sighing into her. Soon his breathing is rhythmic and lulling.

The pill settles in. With her body finally still, the leftover ringing of the gunshots, the pitch of panic, feet scrambling, all those things continue to circulate, but they thin out. She leans her back into Ivan and squeezes her eyes closed against the images. She matches it until the pill thickens her awareness, making it too marbled and solid to permeate.

The next morning, she opens the window just enough to flick out her cigarette ashes. No one below seems to notice. Two shiny, official vans are parked in front of the house. A bearded guy stands with a TV camera. A young man with slightly spiky dark hair holds a microphone into the face of a short, apple-shaped woman, her hair a familiar mop of greying brown waves. Pascale Aggressive. Maybe it's not about the shooting. Maybe the media have a separate reason to talk to Pascale. *Here's Pascale Fleming, owner of the largest My Little Pony collection in Eastern Canada. Pascale Fleming, no one expected her to be the madam of a highly successful brothel.*

Wanda pads down to the living room. Ivan is nowhere to be seen, but he has closed up the house: windows darkened, doors bolted. The TV is on, but muted. *St. John's Woman, Hero* tickers along the bottom of the screen. Her picture flashes on the screen, her sitting on the rocks at Cape Spear. Where did they get that? Her LinkedIn profile. Ugh, that hasn't been updated in a long time.

A news anchor mouths words. She perches on the edge of the couch and presses the volume button on the remote.

"Now, watch this amazing video, captured on the cellphone of a

worker from the Dominion store. Here we see the take-down of Rumstead by Ms. Jaynes. This clip was posted to YouTube last night and has already received close to eight hundred thousand hits."

Eight hundred thousand motherfucking views. Her guts gnaw at her. Not even twenty-four hours and it's happened for almost a million people. It will be a million people today.

The anchor continues: *"The video shows Rumstead turning towards Wanda Jaynes when he notices Liang-Yi Chen in the next aisle. Just as Rumstead points the gun at Ms. Chen, Ms. Jaynes hurls a can at Rumstead...."* She scrambles for the remote. Change the channel, now. She leaves the TV on an infomercial. A woman gushes over the power of her food processor.

"Good morning."

Wanda jumps. Ivan stands behind her. He's rosy cheeked—he was outside.

"Where have you been?"

"Up on the roof." He flops onto the couch. "Just to see how many people are out there." Ivan reaches for the remote. "They interviewed Pascale Aggressive."

"What do you think she said about us?"

"Oh, she'll be kind." He flips through the channels. He stops at an image of the store, a headline. "I think it was CTV who interviewed her. We can check later."

"I need coffee." And some food. And a private helicopter to a secret island.

"I'll get it." He bounds up to the kitchen. She moves to the window and peers out. The spiky-haired reporter glances her way. Can he see her eye in the crack in the curtain? Peek-a-boo, Wanda Jaynes! There are logos on the vans and microphones: CBC, CTV. Three people who look like reporters stand about, smoking, sipping from coffee cups. A man walks by, his dog on a leash in one hand, cellphone aimed at the house in the other. People know where she and Ivan live. Google the address, get the street view, takes about five seconds. He—Edward Rumstead—is in police custody. What does that mean? In jail? A mental institution? How many friends does he have? She swabs a hand across the back of her neck. So many people outside and here she is, clammy and hidden, snooping out like a nervous child at the annual middle-school pageant.

A noise, an exclamation and the coffee-drinking reporters perk up. They scramble into a cluster. From behind the hunched blob of reporters bounces the top of a grey salt-and-pepper cap. Oh shit. The crowd parts and there's Dad, speaking into a microphone. His face holds the same controlled expression as when he had to talk to Wanda's teachers or a member of the clergy. Through the swaying bodies, she glimpses Mom, her mouth sealed in a prim line, her arms clutch a large brown paper bag. Again, with the food. What better way to recover than stress eating? Maybe Wanda can gain ten pounds this week.

Dad nudges his way through, his hand clamped on Mom's sleeve. Spiky-haired reporter leans in with a question and Wanda sees her father mouth his name: Arnold Jaynes. The reporter does the same with Mom. Wanda's mother, *Jane Jaynes*. Spiky Hair gives a wide polite smile to swallow the chuckle. Sure thing, Jane Jaynes. What a winning argument for why women should keep their maiden names.

Her parents detach themselves and make their way up the walk. They hesitate at the bottom of the step. Mom's eyes get big and she mouths excited words. Wanda stands on her tiptoes to peer down. The front steps are riddled with envelopes, bouquets of flowers, stuffed toys. How did those get there? Mom says something to Dad and pushes the paper bag into his arms. She bends at the waist and starts gathering up envelopes and gift bags, fully presenting her backside to the media bundle.

"Here you are, miss." Ivan holds a tray with a coffee mug, a neat boiled egg in a cup.

"Ivan. My folks are outside. Get them in here. My mother's arse will be all over the front page of *The Telegram*."

Ivan places the tray on the coffee table and unlatches the door. "Come in, come in," he says. Calls arise from the street. "Ivan, can you answer a question? Mr. Medeiros, how is Wanda today?"

"Oh my. Oh my goodness." Mom shuffles in, her arms full of envelopes and gift bags. "I thought these should come in. It's calling for rain."

"Mom, don't worry about that."

Mom removes her coat and stands, shaking her head. She wears a forest-green sweatshirt with a picture of a Canada goose on it. "Well, I guess the cat is out of the bag now," she says.

"What did the reporters say to you?" Ivan says.

"Oh, they asked our names," Mom says. "Asked about Wanda." She sits on the sofa, smoothing her slacks with both hands. "Strange job, to stand outside someone's house all day."

"Well, she's the big story now," Dad says. His voice is tight. He's sooky about something.

"Will you speak to any of them?" Mom says. She leans forward with a secretive air. "You want to make sure you talk to the good ones. Ones who won't do the story…you know," her hands wave in a flourish, "everything with sound effects and neon letters under your face, that kind of sensational news. Like American TV."

Dad enters, brushing his hands on his khakis. "Stick with the CBC," he says. "They don't go in for as many theatrics."

Wanda perches on the armrest of the sofa. Mom looks her up and down. "You look tired," she says. "But better than yesterday."

"I guess."

Dad settles on the couch, eyes down, picking his hands. What's his problem? Oh, she wouldn't let him tell and now everyone knows and he has no one to tell. Fuck sakes.

"Well, Ivan and your father can bring the rest of those gifts in. You relax. I'll make lunch and supper. Whatever you need."

"Oh, Mom, you know, we're fine." What if her parents don't leave? She fills with a panicky claustrophobia. "I'm fine, I just need to rest. Still feeling out of it."

"I'll prepare a few meals to tide you over," Mom says. "You won't have to worry about anything."

"Ivan and I both cook. Really, this isn't necessary." Mom will cook way too much for the two of them. The Jiggs-dinner, cured-meat cure-all.

"It's no bother. Let's see what you have in the freezer." Mom pops off the couch and strides to the kitchen.

"Just let her do it," Dad says. "She's nervous. All this, all over the news…she needs to help." He settles on the couch. "Pass over some of that stuff." He gestures to Ivan.

Ivan passes Dad a handful of envelopes and he starts opening them, prying a nail under each flap. Ivan takes a few as well. Like two old men, whittling on a porch. Men who speak only when necessary. In some grunting man-code they believe is sacred.

"Gift certificate in this one," Ivan says.

Pots clink against each other as Mom moves about in the kitchen. Everyone has something to do. What should she do? She could go upstairs, haul on her track pants and sneakers, and run wordlessly out the door. If she charges, the media will clear out of the way. Photos of her back, disappearing down the stretch of sidewalk. Catch all of ye later.

"Nice note," Dad says. He stands a card on the coffee table: white cardboard with a picture of yellow roses on the front, *Thank You* in gold letters.

"Another gift certificate, a yoga place."

"People are so generous."

Wanda's eyes turn to the gift bags. Sharp peaks of tissue paper. A white teddy bear holds a red satin heart. "How did they all get here?"

"They were dropped off this morning."

"By who? Can random people figure out where we live?"

"No, honey," Ivan says. "Most are from the vigil. One of the organizers dropped them off, a minister."

"How does he know where we live?"

"Pascale goes to his church. She called him." Ivan's voice even. Okay then.

"These guys say you are entitled to free pizza forever," Dad says.

"Really?" Ivan takes the note from Dad, a blue flyer bearing the words Eddie's Pizza.

"Their mom was in the store," Dad says. "They say they will feed you forever."

"She...she made it right?" Dr. Collier. Purple coat, red smear.

"Yes, honey, she made it," Ivan says. "It's their way of thanking you." He lays the paper on top of the yoga certificate.

In the kitchen, Mom has begun chopping. The house is open from the living room to the small dining area into the kitchen, but she pitches her voice for everyone to hear. "It's something to think all those people know where you live." The fridge door opens with a light smack. "We saw a video the other day of how easy it is to break into a house. Do you two have insurance for that kind of thing?"

Dad peers into a gift bag. "Some soaps and things in here. Fancy bath stuff."

"Did I tell you two about Delphine's daughter?" Mom calls. The faint sound of scraping, a carrot peeler. "She got married last summer. Put a notice in the paper about the time and place of the wedding. Then she posted on Facebook that people could drop off wedding gifts at her house. Puts up the address and everything. So, during the ceremony, someone broke into the house and stole all the gifts. Cause they knew no one would be there." Furious scraping. "They should have got someone to stay in the house with the gifts. I mean, you're paying for the wedding anyway, just hire a babysitter for the gifts."

"A gift-sitter," Dad says. He unfolds a piece of paper stuck in a card and ponders it. "Someone wrote you a poem."

"A gift-sitter as a kind of insurance," Mom calls. The freezer door opens with a smack. "You too should really think about getting theft insurance if you don't have it. Especially as time goes by. Making a life together and everything." Dull thuds of frozen objects being moved around. "Nothing in here is labelled."

"Really, not a bad poem at all," Ivan says.

"I'm going to lie down," Wanda says.

"If you want." Dad continues to tear open envelopes. If he could sit around in his underwear and do a repetitive activity all day, he'd be content.

Upstairs then. Wanda closes the bedroom door, turning the knob slowly, with the softest click. She picks up her phone and presses On. Notifications light up like a Christmas tree. She goes through her email accounts. Trevor Dowden, her supervisor, has written an email. *"We're all thinking of you. Take as much time off as you need. I can get a substitute in for you, no problem."* A substitute. Probably someone on a part-time contract, looking to gobble up as many hours as possible. Her thoughts take Dad's voice: *these instructor positions are so cutthroat. Even when there are layoffs, they start new programs all the time and recall people. Every drop of seniority matters.*

She checks other notifications: thirty-seven text messages. Does she even have that many contacts?

Trish: OMG! Honey, I hope your OK! Xoxoxoxoxox

Leo: Everything OK? Saw the news, saw the video.

Sharon: Holy fuck, you're fucking internet famous or some fucking shit. I am in awe of you and want to shake you and want to kill that guy. Call me please. Call collect even if you want, if that's even still a thing.

Nikki: Oh, Wonderful Wanda. I love you. I'm thinking of you. xo

Missed calls: her parents, Ivan's mother, Ivan's sister, numbers from work—probably Trevor Dowden, more likely Andrea. Several unknown numbers. She stares at the phone. It would be nice to hear Sharon's voice, but their phone calls always take at least an hour. Sharon and her tales of working at Montclair, her research position with the Institute for Advancement of Philosophy for Children, her animated impressions of New Jersey accents. Sharon's balance of gentle questions and ferocious loyalty.

Or Nikki in Montreal, the way she sinks in when she listens. "I want to hear the whole story," she'd say. "Hold on." And the fizz of a beer opening and the shift of her body settling in the chair. Nikki, always serious about giving you her attention, even though she's definitely been up to something cool, a client at the spa, a night out with friends. Sometimes Wanda thinks about how they all met through their Education degree and all ended up in different places. Nikki doesn't give a shit about teaching now and Sharon still loves picking it apart. She presses reply to Sharon's text.

Hey Shar.

OMFG. WTF.

SMH.

Jesus woman. How are you doing?

Well, there's media outside, ½ million people know who I am, I almost got shot 2 days ago and my mom is downstairs making jiggs dinner.

Jiggs dinner? My condolences.

Ha ha.

You're everywhere. You have hashtags.

Oh hell.

Nikki called and said, Wanda's hashtags are trending. And I said, they're called hot knives, stupid.

Yes!

So, what are they? I'm afraid.

#WandaJayneshero, #grocerystoreshootinghero and #NLheroWandaJaynes. The last one is from an ongoing Twitter row.

Really?

Yeah, some guy posted that your heroism is due to being a Newfoundlander. We're friendly and fearless, see.

Obvs.

It's pretty hilarious if you need a laugh.

What I need is a secret identity.

That would make you a true superhero.

Indeed.

Srsly, tho. You need anything, I'm here.

Thank you Shar. xo

Come stay with me. I will shield you from the paparazzi.

I wish I could teleport.

I will buy you a ticket. I work in America, they pay me in American dollars. It's the biggest money of all the current currencies.

Aw, you're sweet.

Sweet has nothing to do with it. I'm serious.

I know you are.

I'm going to crash. Ttyl

Anytime. xo

Wanda turns off her phone. She lays her head on the cool pillow and shuts her eyes. They can call her when lunch is ready. Supper

too. The occasional sound of pans banging downstairs and movement outside makes her jolt, but she succumbs to sleep.

Mom cooks an early supper and she and Dad leave right after eating:
"Rest and eat, keep your strength up." They hug her before they haul
on their coats and she wonders if she smells like cigarettes. Wanda
peeks out the window as they scurry down the path. A camera flashes
and they're gone. Dad will call in a couple of hours to let her know
they made it back to Trepassey, something they do without being
asked, as if to point out that she should ask.

Ivan makes a pot of mint tea and brings it to the living room.
The coffee table is clear except for the two piles of cards and gift
certificates. "So," he says, "you know they want interviews, right?"

"Do we have to talk about this now?"

"No," he says. He fills her cup with amber liquid. The mint steam
tingles the air. "But if you step out the door, they'll want a statement.
Maybe you should think of what you want to say, or who you want
to talk to."

She warms her palms around the tea cup. Should she do
research? Find out everyone's angle? "Let's go with the CBC. Just
the single interview."

"Okay," Ivan says. "Their PR person contacted me; I'll call her
back."

"When you talk to others, can you tell them that? One interview
only."

"I will."

"Thank you for doing this."

"It's nothing." His hand on her back. "You just take care of
you. I've been going through the messages. I'll let you know anything important."

Later that evening, she checks his list. He has gone through the
phone calls, the emails, and produced a list of options. Her eyes
flick through the names. Look at all those acronyms. Their logos pop
into her head as she reads. She imagines their jingles, her name being
announced.

Before bed, she checks Facebook. One hundred and sixty-six
notifications. Messages and posts and tags, many from people she

hasn't seen in years, not since high school or even elementary. People she shared spaces with. *God bless you, Wanda!* From Melanie Ruxton, she taught biology two semesters ago. She liked to joke that Wanda had "resting bitchy face." And Reg Mitchen: *Wow, Wanda, didn't know ya had it in ya!* He sat across from her in grade ten. He would make preparing-to-hawk phlegmy sounds in his throat. Once, he got a hold of her math notebook and drew penises all over it.

Most of her memories of school interactions are similar. She had friends, but wasn't popular. To be popular, she needed big toys, a skidoo, a truck, something to go racing down the road in. No way Arnold and Jane Jaynes would buy something dangerous for their only child. When she thinks of high school, she sees herself as a floating apparition everyone was accustomed to seeing, but occasionally they remembered they didn't approve of ghosts. Like seeing dust in a sunbeam and realizing the place needs a good wipe-down.

And now, this is it. Her name highlighted for everyone out there, all the vicious people, all the stupid people, and all the vicious, stupid people. They ick her out so much and it's so hard to fight the ick. Wanda Jaynes and the Kneejerk Disdain. That would be her band name.

It's so hypocritical of her. Seven years a teacher and when asked why she chose education, she offers a cliché: a love of learning, a desire to help. Saying it's because she hates ignorance and stupidity is admittance of misanthropy. Sometimes, at the beginning of the school year when she's settling into the rhythm of classes and schedules, she wakes in the middle of the night frozen in fear of the possible random, idiotic acts that could be her demise. A drunk surgeon with dirty hands. A stack of 2x4s in the unlocked pan of a truck. A city council-neglected snowdrift-covered sidewalk in the middle of February, sliding off into traffic during a walk to the store.

And now, beaning someone with a tin can is the most she's done to combat stupidity—if stupidity is defined as senseless destruction. Or the result of overlooked, undiagnosed mental-health issues. Or a lifetime of abuse. Or the glorification of violence. There are so many flavours of stupid.

She writes a general status update: "Hi, I'm okay. Thanks everyone, for your kind words." She responds to an email from Ivan's sister, Sylvie, who writes she's "sending love from Alex, Fiona, and I." Fiona's birthday's coming up. She never got that card.

Wanda reads the words "I love you" and writes the same. She types the words "thank you," she returns compliments. Pat statements, but she doesn't have the energy to edit them. Ivan left half a Valium on the side table. That's a relief. He's good to her that way.

6

THE boom is a giant, dangling pussy willow, looming in the living room.

"I didn't expect the equipment to be so big," Wanda says.

"That's what she said."

"Oh, shut up, Ivan." Wanda rolls her eyes apologetically. Genevieve Davey smiles. Her presence in their house is surreal. Even with the CBC cameras and the microphones set up, Wanda is most intrigued by Genevieve's hair. It is a perfect, glossy blond bob that fills her with questions. What products does Genevieve use? Does the CBC tell her how to get it cut? Does she get her hair done every day at the station? Imagine, never having to do your own hair. Imagine being coiffed and presentable on a daily basis, in professional makeup and good clothes. Ivan can go on and on about how no one really needs to use shampoo because it's all chemicals, and natural oils give hair all the health and lift it needs. But check out this woman's goddamn dreamy hair. And really, all Ivan has to do is rinse and add a bit of conditioner once in a while, lucky frigger.

The CBC people want to interview her in the house, so she spent most of the morning tidying up. The place seemed pretty presentable, but now, compared with Genevieve Davey's immaculate self, everything they own looks slapped together: their wrinkled paisley-print IKEA curtains, the ancient coffee table peppered with scratches,

Ivan's old guitars mounted on the wall. Ancient water stains tinge the ceiling by the doorway and the screen door croaked and whined when the crew entered. But Genevieve is all gracious poise. She wears all black with colourful accents: sleek pants and a long-sleeved shirt set off by a vibrant sea-green silk scarf tousled around her neck. All crisp and impeccable against the chipped paint of the kitchen chair. Ivan sits to the side, legs spread, slouching in a faded plaid shirt. And plain Wanda Jaynes, in her business-casual khakis and sky-blue cowl-neck top. Dirty hippy Ivan and Sears Days Special Wanda.

"So, Wanda," Genevieve says, "as I said in the email, I'm going to first ask you a few questions about that day and what happened leading up to the incident with Edward Rumstead. We'll do it conversationally, so just speak openly and comfortably. This isn't a live interview, we're under no major time restraints. I also have a few questions about how things have been going for you over the past few days."

"You mean, since she became the new Chewbacca Mom?" Ivan says.

"Chewbacca Mom?"

"Or double-rainbow. Or Damn Daniel. Or cat video of the week." Ivan says. "I'm referring to her popularity on the Internets." He grins. What a knob.

"Ah yes," Genevieve says. "I'm hoping we can talk about that. But only what you're comfortable with, Wanda."

Wanda nods. Her damp hands rest in her lap. The sound guy, an older, bearded man with a barrel chest, holds the boom and looks straight forward with unreadable eyes. The director or assistant or something is a guy in his twenties wearing a blue ball cap with "LOCALS" written across the top in yellow letters. He holds a clipboard in one hand and texts constantly with the other.

Genevieve has quality posture and an ease to her limbs. When she leans forward, there is a soft scent of something deep and warm, a touch of cloves. "Let's start on the day of the shooting. What were you doing up until the incident?"

At first, Wanda plods through the events: it was a regular day, she was just trying to get in and out of the store. When she starts to describe how she saw Dr. Collier fall, her voice hits a snag. Genevieve nods and looks into Wanda's face, but not prying. Wanda finds herself matching Genevieve's posture, speaking into her open, up-turned expression. The words gain momentum and her hands pick up and move with her voice—she wants Genevieve to know, she wants her to take it. Like a kind of thrall, Genevieve's poised and willing countenance washes the words out of her:

"I see her, Dr. Collier, over and over. She wears a purple coat and she is running. When I saw her picture on the news, she just looked so…wise and knowing and together. I can't stop thinking about her." Wanda wants to say other words: the magnifying glass, the chicken, the annoyance, but catches herself. She forces her eyes down, slows her hands into her lap.

"A lot of people know your name now," Genevieve says. She gestures to the guy with the LOCALS cap and he hands her a clip-board. "Here are a few reactions—these are comments left on the YouTube video." She reads them out in a clean, neutral tone:

"'This is an intervention of God. God guided the hand of Wanda Jaynes to bring down evil. God bless you, Wanda Jaynes.' 'Wanda Jaynes stopped the devil.' 'From Acts 28:5. And he shook off the beast into the fire and felt no harm.'" Genevieve looks up. "When it comes to the moment where you threw the can, you've said it's unclear in your memory, that you just did it without thinking," she says. "In fact, Geraldine Harvey, the woman who Edward Rumstead shot at and missed, says that her survival and your act are proof that miracles exist."

"Really?"

"Yes, she's been quite vocal through social media. And many agree with her in believing something powerful was present in the store. What do you say to that?"

"No, I don't believe that. I mean, I don't believe in God, so I can't say it was a miracle. I can see how people want to think it was a miracle or magic or something, but you can explain it through science. The range of what you're capable of increases when you're pumped up with fear and adrenaline." She glances at Ivan. Huge grin on him. "I didn't feel anything different. I just…all that was in my head was *stop*. I just remember thinking *stop*."

Genevieve nods. "Have you spoken with any of the other

witnesses? We spoke with Liang-Yi Chen, the woman who was in the next aisle, and she expressed a great deal of gratitude towards you."

"Liang-Yi and I met briefly at the vigil," Wanda says. "I haven't spoken with anyone else really. I've just been trying to process everything. And spend time with my loved ones. I'm very lucky to have so much support." Also, lucky to have booze. Like the bottle of wine she drank last night. Oh, and cigarettes, smoked a pack with the wine. And speaking of loved ones, hoping to find a way to procure more Valium once Ivan's mom returns from Florida. Every little bit counts, Genevieve.

"What do you want to say to the many people who consider you a hero and want to thank you?"

"I don't really know what to say. I don't think I'm a hero. In fact, it was pretty impulsive and stupid, maybe? I don't know. I think a lot of people might have done the same thing or done something better. As I said, it was an act of adrenaline."

"But everyone in that store was afraid and full of adrenaline," Genevieve says. "Whether or not it was the right impulse, you are the one who acted. That is something to consider. That is something that you may feel proud of someday." She regards Wanda with somber eyes. Ivan nods in agreement. Wanda could burst into tears, lean forward like she's starting a somersault and rest her forehead on Genevieve's knees. She could shudder hot sobs into those expensive black slacks.

As the crew gathers equipment, Genevieve shakes Wanda's hand between both of hers. "Thank you. Thank you." Wanda says thank you as well and then you're welcome and they both laugh. She is reminded of a novel she read in high school, *The Giver*, about a society where the citizens had no memory of history. How cleansing to give these words to Genevieve, wouldn't it be nice if she could take it all away with her.

When the door is shut, Ivan does a little jig in the living room. "'A miracle or magic or something.' That was fucking gold," he says. "You've done so much for their ratings. Their viewers will have a lot to say about that."

"Shit. Your mom."

"Oh, pfft, don't worry about her."

"But, we've never *really* talked about it. Does she know we're atheists?" Mrs. Medeiros and the gold cross around her neck, the St. Christopher medal pinned inside her coat. The woman is disappointed enough that Ivan and Wanda aren't married. This will kick her hard in the faith.

"She knows on some level," Ivan says. "It's not like we ever go to church." He wraps his arms around Wanda's waist and pulls her to him. "You're so eloquent and straightforward and sincere. I'm so proud of you."

She nestles her face into the warm corner of his neck and collarbone. She lets her pelvis press into his. "How proud are you?" she says.

Something twitches against her chest. "Oops, sorry," Ivan says. "It's on vibrate." He releases one arm and pulls his phone out of his breast pocket.

"Who is it?"

"Message from Trish. Something on Imgur." He lets go of Wanda. "Ho-lee fuck."

"What is it?"

"You're a meme! No, plural! You are memes!" Ivan holds out his phone. The screen shows a picture of her, a frame from the YouTube video. It's her, standing alone with her purse and the can, her round head and blue coat. Above and below her are large block letters:

WHEN YOU SAY YOU WANT A GIRL WITH A CAN-DO ATTITUDE

Ivan slides to the next one.

GROCERY LIST: MILK EGGS BUTTER AND A CAN O'WHOOP ASS

And more:

EVERYONE'S TALKING ABOUT GUN CONTROL...
WHO'S GOING TO STOP THE COCONUT MILK PROBLEM

THIS IS WHAT HAPPENS
WHEN YOU'RE DISTRACTED BY A WOMAN IN YOGA PANTS

And two which include small, photo-shopped faces of Ryan Gosling:

HEY GIRL
YOU CAN HIT ME UP ANYTIME

HEY GIRL
YOU LOOK WANDAFUL TONIGHT

"Jesus," she says. Her stomach buckles, like it's hunching down to hide.

"It keeps reaching new levels," Ivan says. She hardens her eyes at him. "I'm sorry," he says. "But it *is* kind of amazing."

7

THE door rattles open, shoes clunk off, bottles jingle. "Hey, hellooo." Leo and Trish enter with wine, beer, and hugs. Leo is one of those huggers who really goes for it, a tight embrace with an extra squeeze. "Crazy time, Wanda Woman," he says.

Trish gives baby-bird hugs, her arms a faint suggestion of limbs. But both she and Leo are so warm and sincere that Wanda lets out an involuntary sob. Trish caresses her hair with her little sparrow fingers. "Oh honey. It's fucking brutally stressful."

The four of them sit at the dining-room table. Wanda is handed a glass of Shiraz and the temporary coziness and sanctuary of it and their friends are euphoric. She takes big sips and Leo tops her up without asking. They talk and drink. The Rogue Skaters might play a festival in Clarenville in August. Two of Trish's photographs are being published in some German art magazine. Leo is doing sound for a couple of bands this weekend; hopefully, they'll start before two in the morning.

Leo clears his throat. "So, you don't have to answer this, but do you worry about post-traumatic stress?"

Wanda swallows her wine.

"I mean, I'd be surprised if you didn't have it," Leo says. "Your life was in danger."

"Yeah, my god, I'd probably be in the psych ward," Trish says.

"I'm not sure how I feel," Wanda says. "I think I'm okay. But when I try to fall asleep, the sounds from the store come back."

"She's fretting in her sleep," Ivan says. "You tossed and turned last night."

"Did the cops give you any resources?" Leo says.

"Yes. I have a card for a therapist," Wanda says. "I mean, it's hard right now, but I expect that. I'm still processing everything. I don't know where I would start if I spoke to someone at this time." Processing. How many times has she repeated that word since Monday? Like she's creating cheese slices, wrapped in cellophane. Or a new kind of bologna.

"I checked out that therapist online," Ivan says. "Mixed reviews on ratemds.com."

"Leo's Gran had PTSD after her car accident," Trish says. "She said the worst was right before the other car hit her, the realization that she wasn't going to stop in time. For months, she'd be falling asleep and jerk awake. She got so jittery, she couldn't drive or even be in a car."

"Yeah, she's on Venlafaxine now," Leo says.

"I don't want to go on any meds," Wanda says.

"Don't worry about it for now," Leo says. "It takes at least a month of symptoms for them to diagnose you."

"Oh, they give you a month?" Ivan says. "You see a slaughter and you get thirty days before they act? And then they'll dope you up? So fucking backwards. Might as well keep calling it shellshock." He stretches along the table and rubs Wanda's shoulder, his guitar calluses chafe against her bra strap under her shirt.

"I wouldn't want to have anxiety and panic for thirty days," Wanda says. "But I'm not eager for drugs. And I wouldn't want to talk to just anyone." And, at this point, with over a million views, it's not like she could find someone in town who hasn't seen the video already. Or who wouldn't creep her online after she poured out her guts.

"Technically, we're self-medicating now," Leo says. He tips his beer at her.

"Good point, man." Ivan says. Wanda eyes him. He sprawls across two chairs. Double-seating. When they first started seeing each other, she noted how he didn't really sit, but would morph into his seat. His arms spread out over backs of chairs and booths, one knee might be nestled into his chest, the other might find a fit in the crook of the table or drape over an armrest. He fills all available spaces with himself, outstretched arms and appendages dangling and anything could come out of his mouth. Now here he is, leaning back in one of their matching chairs, toes tucked around the spokes underneath, and why does he sit like he has worms? *Look at me, I'm Ivan, I even sit unconventionally.*

Ivan widens his eyes at her. She realizes she is staring at him hard—her eyebrows are knit. She looks away. Her face is flushed with wine and annoyance. Everything is too warm.

Not surprising—besides the vigil, she hasn't been outside in two days. All she's done is eat, drink, and find distractions from the outside world: rom-coms she's seen before, binge-watching *Breaking Bad*. And here she is with her friends, cramped and contrary. "Back in a sec," she says.

In the kitchen, she sees Ivan has put away the pots and pans, wiped down the counters. He isn't doing anything wrong. All his quirks are things she loved, initially. He doesn't know how to act or react in this situation. And neither does she.

She opens the fridge. She should offer things, cheese, olives. There is a fruit tray and a platter of cold cuts from Mom. The crisper is empty except for a limp bunch of asparagus. No groceries, of course. *Of course.* She closes the fridge and rests her head against the cool, white surface, shutting out the glaring light on the products. Chips, there are chips in the cupboard.

Laughter pours in from the dining room. Ivan and their friends. Her friends for a few years now, since she and Ivan got serious. But the three of them—Ivan, Leo, and Trish—go way back.

When Wanda started dating Ivan, those three felt like an impermeable clique, gated with tall historic walls, strengthened with in-jokes and shared stories. Conversations would hitch into some shared memory and they'd be off. Like that time, it was ages ago, what was her name, Zoe, remember her, elaborate butterfly tramp-stamp tattoo, that's how Trish described it. Ivan and Zoe got in a fight. Later, Leo and Trish found her, loaded drunk and crying on the front step. She was eating ranch dressing straight out of the bottle with her index finger, shoving it into her mouth between sobs. Missus was lactose intolerant. What a state she was. And the story was over before they explained Zoe was an ex-girlfriend of Ivan's. They forgot Wanda didn't know, or didn't realize it might be a point she would need for understanding.

Or the summer Leo and Trish lived in Montreal. They were house-sitting for Trish's uncle, and Leo had a job as a security guard. Ivan came up for a visit. Trish and Ivan went to the Radiohead concert, Leo had to work a nightshift. When the show let out, the two of them came home to two German guys asleep in the main bedroom. When they tell the story, Ivan does a high voice to mimic Trish shrieking, *What are you doing in my bed?* And then they both say, *Dis ist your bad?* for the German guy's reaction. And then Trish describes him as covered in blond hair, like an albino Sasquatch.

Turns out, Trish's uncle had double-booked the house and completely forgot. Trish had to bunk with Ivan on the twin bed in the kid's room. Ivan jokes that Trish farted in her sleep, but Wanda suspects he's trying to take the curse off it. Trish and Ivan, parallel forms on a small mattress. Did they sleep on their sides? Back to back? Did they wake up touching? Questions she'd never ask, for these are *before* times, irrelevant history. Leo shows no sign of minding, why should she?

Those beginning evenings were like that, listening to the same anecdotes, well-told, embellished, successfully climactic. Wanda laughed and smiled. She even got in the odd joke. She carried on and shrugged off the awareness of how they rarely asked her about herself. Of how no new stories were created with her as a character.

Looking in from the kitchen, she can see Leo stooping over his rolling papers. Ivan arches his spine and stretches back his hand to reach an itchy spot between his shoulder blades. Trish reaches out and scratches the spot for him. They grin at each other without words, like kids passing notes in class. Wanda's eyes narrow. She grabs the chips and brings them in. Where is her wine? There it is. Her stomach tightens, but she downs the contents of the glass anyway and pours another. Leo peers up at her from under the sandy drapes of his hair. Ivan rants:

"I've got one. You're standing at an intersection. The light turns red and a monstrous Hummer pulls up and stops right in the middle of the crosswalk, you know, so you have to walk into traffic to get around it. The driver smokes a cigarette—no, a cigar, a big fat Cuban. In his other hand, he stuffs a huge, greasy Big Mac in his face. When the light turns green, he peels out and flicks the cigar out the window. And as the Hummer vanishes, in a puff of carbon monoxide and greed, you realize the driver is David Suzuki." Ivan picks up his beer to signify he's done.

"Oh, my God," Trish gasps. "That's the worst."

"What are we talking about?" Wanda asks.

"Ivan just asked what would be the most discouraging thing to see on the street," Trish says. "Like, something which would shatter your dreams."

"Well, homeless people," Wanda says. "That's kind of obvious."

"No, you're not allowed to say homeless people," Trish says. "We're talking discouraging, not depressing."

"I feel very discouraged when I see homeless people."

"Yes, we all do," Ivan says. "But that's a given and let's just acknowledge we're desensitized, shall we? What else would rattle your philosophy on life?"

"David Suzuki in a Hummer with a burger? That wouldn't discourage me at all." Wanda tops up her glass. "In fact, I think I'd feel relieved. If he's doing it, maybe it's not so bad for us after all."

"You know all that shit's bad for you," Ivan says. "David Suzuki doing it just means he…oh forget it."

"If I saw David Suzuki doing that, I'd go out and celebrate with a Quarter Pounder."

"I prefer Wendy's, myself," Leo says. He lights up the joint.

"Seriously though," Ivan says. "David Suzuki's been telling everyone for years that if we don't change the way we treat the environment, the natural world will be destroyed to the point it can't ever repair itself. And then, the end of the world will start actually happening. It's happening now, my love. If I saw David Suzuki behaving like that, to me, he's accepted the end of the world."

"David Suzuki eating fast food is one of the signs of the apocalypse?"

"Exactly."

Wanda nods slowly and pours more wine into her glass. Thick, hot irritation trickles though her. "Would it really be that bad, though? So, people die. We're the worst things to happen to this planet, anyway." Her words are greased and lubricated.

"Oh. Very well then," Ivan says. "End of humanity. Pass the nachos."

"Seriously, what does it matter? We're here, we don't care about maintaining things. Fuck the trees and the air and the water. Fuck all the species of bats and bees and…," Wanda clicks her fingers at Trish, "what are those little birds called? The ones that sit on hippos and rhinos, picking bugs off them?"

Trish bites her lip in thought. "Um, oxpeckers or something?"

"Cleaning symbiosis," Leo says.

"Yeah, oxpeckers. Fuck those helpful lil' birds. Who asked for their help anyway?" Wanda reaches for the bottle. Her fingers slide off the glass, sending it spinning. Shiraz sprays across Trish's shirt.

"Aw shit, I'm sorry." Wanda's face flames with shame. Leo hops up to get a cloth.

"It's okay, it's okay," says Trish.

"Come on, I'll clean your shirt." Wanda jolts up. Her chair topples on the floor. "Fuck."

"Okay." Ivan stands. "Let's give you a hand." He puts an arm around Wanda.

"No, I'm going to clean Trish's shirt," she says.

"Don't worry, my love, I'll do it." Trish pats Wanda's arm and darts to the bathroom.

Wanda looks down at the table. It fluctuates and gears, then starts a slow grinding spin. Damn. "Bed," she says. "Need to go to bed."

Ivan guides her upstairs. She lets him bring her in the bedroom and lower her onto the mattress. "I'm going to put a bucket beside you, just in case." He leaves the room.

She takes deep breaths. Pack off, spins. Voices reverberate outside, low and concerned. Whatever. She has witnessed every one of those people get messed up. She's cleaned up their puke, made them hangover breakfasts. What do they expect from her anyway? Especially now.

Ivan brings her the bucket.

"I'm sorry," says Wanda.

"It's all good," says Ivan. He kisses her forehead. "Sleep it off."

Wanda peers up as he closes the bedroom door. Trish gazes in from the hallway. She wears one of Ivan's shirts.

8

WANDA is in a pile all morning, but manages to arise before eleven. She tries not to move her head on the way to the kitchen. The dining-room table has been wiped down and the empties put away. Glad they had the sober consideration to clean up. Then she sees Ivan's note and the pressure in her head kicks in:

> W,
> Gone to the airport to get Ma. There are popsicles and Gatorade in the fridge. Tsk-tsk.
> I.

Oh dear Jesus, Mrs. Medeiros returns from Florida today. She grabs a Gatorade from the fridge and chugs. Her stomach gripes at first, but her parched bloodstream rings out in gratitude. Okay. Hydrate, Advil, shower, and warm up face for a day of polite smiling.

She rushes out of the shower to her phone going off. Maybe Ivan from the airport.

Text message from Nikki:

Hey Meme Dream.

Clever. Bitch.

How are you?

Hungover. And Mrs. M is on the way here.

Hoo Jesus.

Eeek.

I saw your CBC interview. You were great.

It's aired already?

Sharon sent it to me last night.

I didn't know. So out of it.

You've seen the other video, right? The Christian guy talking about the shooting?

What guy?

Ok. Damn. I'm going to send it to you.

www.workmanworkers.com/watch2?v

Sound of a car outside. She peeks out the window. Here they come.

Can't watch it now, Mrs. M is here.

Wanda rakes her fingers through her hair and watches Mrs. Medeiros approach the house. That woman has presence. Tiny, but her impeccable posture makes up for her lack of height. Her nub of a chin juts forward, a proud shelf for the soft, buttery folds of flesh underneath. From a distance, her eyes look solidly black, but when she faces you, their velvet brown emerges, like expensive chocolate with high cacao content. Eyes that can gash through your guilty conscience or make your childish heart swell. The media cleared off when Wanda committed to the CBC interview, but at this moment it would be entertaining to watch Mrs. Medeiros speak into a microphone, her responses polite, but scathing, the flash of shame on a reporter's face.

Mrs. Medeiros meets her with a hug and presses her cool cheek to Wanda's. "Oh my dear. I am so pleased to see you."

"You too," Wanda says, perhaps a little too loudly, in Mrs. Medeiros's ear.

The woman leans back and clasps Wanda's face in her hands. Her wrists emit Johnson's Intensive Care lotion. "Look at you. You're so white. How have you been eating? This stress can lower your immune system." Mrs. Medeiros's eyes scan Wanda's face. Does she smell like wine? Does her hangover hang over her?

Mrs. Medeiros looks back at Ivan. "Bring my suitcase in." Wanda meets his eyes in panic. Suitcase? Is she staying?

"But you're going home after supper."

"You park your car in the street, anyone can break into it."

"Okay, I'll get it." Ivan shuffles back to the car, hands stuffed in pockets.

"So many break-ins with people's cars," Mrs. Medeiros says. "My neighbour had his back window smashed in. He had left his backpack in the car. Nothing in it! They'll smash glass for nothing." She shakes her head. Wanda holds the door open for her and waits for Ivan and the suitcase. "I have some fresh Florida oranges in my bag," she says. "They'll be good for you."

"Again, Ma, really?" Ivan says. "You can't take fruit across international borders."

Mrs. Medeiros dismisses him with a wave and unzips the side of her suitcase. "Where are we going to get fresh oranges like these around here?" She pulls one out and holds it up to be admired. "They're falling off the trees in one country and you can't take them home to enjoy. It's not fair."

Wanda puts on the kettle while Mrs. Medeiros freshens up. They'll have tea and she'll feel jetlagged and want a nap before supper. They'll play down the shootings. They'll focus on putting her worries aside.

"Sylvie tells me you were on TV," Mrs. Medeiros says. She lifts the teapot lid and peers inside, adds another teabag.

"Yes, the CBC interviewed me yesterday morning. I think it may have already aired."

"It did. Sylvie says it's online. I would like to see this."

"Oh. Okay."

Shit. For over four years, she and Ivan have avoided philosophical discussions with his mother. Bowing their heads and remaining silent during grace. Simply saying "thank you" when she says she prays for them. Afterwards, when they're alone, Wanda usually says something like "Doing our part for peace," to which Ivan replies, "what-fuckin'-ever." For him, an evening where his mother praises the pope causes him to chew his tongue into a wad. If she donates to the Church, he flies into a tirade when she's out of earshot: "I guess those sexual-abuse lawyers need cash," he spat after Easter dinner last spring. "How can an intelligent woman not question an institution like that?"

Wanda brings out the tea tray and sets it on the coffee table. Mrs. Medeiros has sliced and proudly arranged one of her illegal oranges on a plate. Ivan sets up his laptop.

Genevieve Davey and Wanda appear on the screen. Wanda cringes as she watches herself. Her own voice is deeper than she imagined, with a tinny edge. She never realized how strong her dialect is. There is something loose at the corner of the opening to her shirt. The strap that goes over the hanger—the edge of it peeps out. "Why didn't you tell me that string thing was showing?" she asks Ivan.

"What string? You're the only one who sees that."

"String thing, no difference, you look good," Mrs. Medeiros says.

Questions about the day, the witnesses. Mrs. Medeiros nods approvingly through it all. And then the miracle issue.

"No, I don't believe that. I mean, I don't believe in God, so I can't say it was a miracle. I can see how people want to think it was a miracle or magic or something, but you can explain it through science. The range of what you're capable of increases when you're pumped up with fear and adrenaline."

Wanda is struck by how clear and convinced her words are. She imagined herself hemming and hawing, but she speaks with crisp assurance. Right into the ears of Mrs. Medeiros, who holds her teacup halfway to her lips. She lowers her eyelids and lays the cup and saucer down. She picks up a slice of orange and bites into it, soundlessly sucking out the juices.

According to Ivan, Mrs. Medeiros doesn't get angry. She dwells before she delivers. One story in particular stands out for Wanda: Ivan at eleven, the year after his father died. He and some other boys broke into a neighbour's shed. They stole a flat of Pepsi and cans of spray paint, wrote their names on the rocks by the highway in the haze of a sugar high. When his mother found out, she didn't speak or look at him. And she didn't go about her normal routine. She sat in the living room with the TV off, ticking through her rosary beads in silence. It went on for days. Ivan said he did everything around the house to show he was sorry: laundry, dishes, vacuuming, cleaning the gutters, painting the deck. He nagged her every day to speak to him. The silent treatment continued until he took up the seat beside her and prayed out loud for his sins to be forgiven.

Mrs. Medeiros mouths her orange slice. The CBC news continues; a story about the Muskrat Falls project will be up next. Ivan slaps his hands onto his knees. "Well, I was going to make a cake for dessert. What do you say, Ma, pineapple upside-down cake?"

Mrs. Medeiros nods slowly. "That would be fine. I'd like to take a nap before our supper."

"Of course," Wanda says. "The guest bedroom is all set up." Mrs. Medeiros nods without looking at her and glides off to the room.

"Fuck fuck fuck, fucking hell," Wanda hisses at Ivan.

"Please. She'll get over it." Ivan goes to the kitchen. She follows him and watches as he takes items from cupboards, a can of pineapple slices, flour. "This is what she does," he says. "She acts like she needs time to deal. What you're doing right now, worrying about how she feels, even though she hasn't told you how she feels? That's exactly what she wants."

"How can I be any other way? She's your mother. She terrifies me."

"What can she do about our personal beliefs? Are we supposed to apologize for not buying into the same doctrine as her? Or lie and say we agree?" Ivan twists the can opener around the pineapple can. "I spent my childhood being dragged to church twice a week. We had to say the rosary every other day. That's enough religion for one lifetime, thanks very much."

"Fine. Maybe she'll be better after her nap."

"Oh yes, that will happen."

Wanda busies herself with supper. Roast beef and mashed potatoes, steamed greens. Mrs. Medeiros doesn't come down until they call her. She appears with her hair neatly pinned up, like she was ready and waiting to be rung.

Mrs. Medeiros doesn't speak until she is about two thirds of the way through her meal: "This has been a horrible week for you, Wanda."

"It hasn't been easy, no," Wanda says.

"It was a great deal of fear you experienced. To see that man with the gun, to see people die." Mrs. Medeiros shakes her head. "It would be hard to keep your faith. But you may want to reconsider abandoning God." She gestures to the sky with her butter knife. "Sometimes it seems like He is not with us, but He is."

Wanda swallows. She glances at Ivan. He sips his wine. "I didn't do that," she says. "I mean, this wasn't a decision I made this week."

"How long have you felt this way?"

"Oh, I would say since I was twenty or so." Wanda busies herself sawing through her beef.

Mrs. Medeiros stares at her. "I see." Pause. She passes a fork through her mashed potatoes. Pause. Apologetic smile. "You must think I'm a foolish old woman."

"Not at all." Wanda says. "Why do you say that?"

"It's obvious. For years when we're together, I pray, I say grace, but it has meant nothing to you. Like a dance step." Mrs. Medeiros makes a small twirling motion with her butter knife.

"It's not that it means nothing. I was just being respectful."

"Dishonesty is not respect."

"I don't think it's dishonest." A lump starts its way up her throat. "I just…belief is private for me. I never told you because you never asked."

Ivan grasps the bottle of wine and pours himself another half glass.

"I say what I believe," Mrs. Medeiros says. "I expect others to do the same."

Wanda speaks slowly: "So, if I had said I was an atheist…," Mrs. Medeiros tenses up, "it would have been okay with you?"

"I've come to this house so many times, spoken about the Church. You've said nothing."

"Because it's my home and I want you to be comfortable. Talk about your church. Pray if it makes you happy."

"I don't understand why I have to find out this way. You tell the CBC and not me. The last to know." Mrs. Medeiros touches her napkin to the corner of her eye. Ivan moves the stack of serviettes next to her.

"It's just private for me," Wanda says. "I think belief is whatever gives you solace, gives you peace. And this is the only thing that has ever done that for me."

"It gives you peace? To think there is no God?"

"Yes. Very much so." Wanda pushes her greens with her fork. "Some people say everything happens for a reason, that God has a divine plan. Something awful happens and they say, 'God works in mysterious ways.' When I started thinking how maybe there is no plan and things happen for no real reason at all, I felt relieved. And that's what I believe now."

Mrs. Medeiros doesn't respond. She cuts her meat and puts a piece in her mouth, delicately, like it might crumble. She chews and swallows. "I can see how that would work well for you, especially now, after this horrible thing has happened. After Ivan's father died, everyone told me to talk to someone, get a shrink. So I sat in a room with a man for months, giving him money, watching him watch me cry. Always with a bad feeling about him. Something about the way he looked at me. And sure enough, he gets fired. Affairs with two patients at the same time. I said to myself, I'll trust my gut from now on. And I went to church. That felt better for me."

"That's terrible. About the therapist."

She starts to cut another piece. "I hope your belief has brought you solace this week."

Wanda sighs. "It has."

Ivan helps himself to more beef and douses it with gravy.

"You said nothing through all of that."

"Huh?" Ivan presses start on the dishwasher. Mrs. Medeiros has returned to her home out in Topsail. Wanda isn't touching a dish. Shag that.

"She talked about this with *me*. Like you and I don't share the same beliefs."

"I can't talk about God with her," Ivan says. "I learned that a long time ago. Believe me, that conversation went much better with you than it ever could with me."

"But we're together. It's like now you're the nice Catholic son and I'm the heathen atheist you fell in with."

"Please. She knows I'm far from that. And if I had jumped in, there would have been more tears than that little swipe-swipe." He mimics dabbing his eyes.

"Well then. Nice to know you've got my back."

"Wanda, it would have been wretched. Did I ever tell you what she did to Sylvie? She and her friend Tina got caught shoplifting when they were like, fifteen. Ma got it in her head that it was all Tina's fault, that she was a bad influence. Talked to a bunch of people about Tina, collected gossip, made a list of other 'bad things' she'd done. Presents it all to Sylvie and forbids her to see Tina ever again. Sylvie argued it up and down, said Ma was a hypocrite because she's Catholic and doesn't practice forgiveness. Ma wouldn't budge. She can't let stuff go."

"That's within your family though. I'm your partner."

"Seriously, honey, it would have amplified everything," he says. "I know my mother's neuroses. I know her triggers. It would still be going on. You handled it beautifully."

She glares at him. The anger prickles like a rash that burns to the bone. She cuts a big square of pineapple upside-down cake and leaves him to the pots and pans.

Before bed, she gets more cake and checks her email. Still trying to trim her inbox down to a reasonable number. Ivan has left three tabs open on the computer: one is a short article about her in *The Telegram*. It includes a quote from Dad: "Wanda was always brave, but she could never hit a target. She'd miss the dirt if she threw herself on the ground." Gee, thanks, Dad.

The Twitter account for a Geraldine Harvey is open. Genevieve Davey mentioned her, the woman who Rumstead shot at and missed. The thumbnail shows a woman with long red pigtails, a royal-blue ball cap. @GeraldineHarv1968 has only tweeted thirty-one times, but most are from the past few days. Three have been retweeted over twenty times each. And today, she's having a fight:

Geraldine Harvey @GeraldineHarv1968
Feeling blessed 2 b in the world. Thanks to Gods intervention for sparing my life!!! Tell yr family you love them. #praisebe

DCleal @reasonseason111
@GeraldineHarv1968 Have some sensitivity for families who lost loved ones. Not everyone is feeling so blessed.

Geraldine Harvey @GeraldineHarv1968
@reasonseason111 Im not saying im more blessed. But i know a miracle when it happens!!!

DCleal @reasonseason111
@GeraldineHarv1968 So you believe God saw YOU were in trouble & came to save YOU, but not Darcy, Ella or Michael? #saytheirnames

Geraldine Harvey @GeraldineHarv1968
@reasonseason111 I dont claim to know the mystery of Gods ways & u r rude 2 think u know! Theres no way its not a miracle!!!!

DCleal @reasonseason111
@GeraldineHarv1968 I call out smugness and lack of compassion when I see it.

Geraldine Harvey @GeraldineHarv1968
@reasonseason111 Well @JNWorkman agrees w me! We r strong & united! #workersformodernchristianity

Workman. That name was in the link Nikki sent. She fishes out her phone for the address and brings it up on the computer. The link is to a show. Wanda reads the description: "Selected clips from Joseph Nigel Workman's channel, *Keeping in Touch*. Live stream worship every Sunday!" The episode Nikki sent is from last week. Wanda clicks play.

A man stands on a stage with sleek, varnished floors. His black hair is cut in a high swoop, Jerry Lee Lewis style, a headset keeps his hands free. A large TV screen behind him displays the frozen image of Wanda standing in the aisle. It seems he has just shown the video of Edward Rumstead's takedown. The audience cheers. Joseph Nigel Workman struts back and forth in a smart, blue suit. He runs his hands through his floppy hair: "People of America, if you find yourself in doubt, if you find yourself wondering, feeling hopeless and questioning where God is in these dark times, I implore you to watch this. Just this week in a town in Canada, a miracle! You can see it!" He shakes his open arms at the screen behind him, at Wanda's face. "God answered the prayers of the people in that store and acted through this woman."

"Holy shit," Wanda says. The cake glues itself to the roof of her mouth.

The right side of the screen shows a ticker feed of tweets, both from and to the website.

> Sallysally55:@keepingintouch Joseph Workman is 2 harsh
> this wk 2 say she's conceited. But I do feel sorry for her.
> God's love's everywhere & she doesn't want to feel it. ☹

Conceited? A new video has been posted within the last two hours. She clicks play. It starts with the clip from the CBC interview: Wanda responding to Genevieve's question about miracles. It shuts off when she finishes. Deep, low booing from the audience. Joseph Nigel Workman paces the stage in a lean, pinstriped suit. "People, I know how you feel. It's like giving someone a diamond and they respond that they prefer plastic. It's like cutting down roses to hang paper flowers. It's sad and it's the sickness of promotion of the self over God." He presses his hand to his heart. "This conceited woman, Wanda Jaynes, was given the power of good. Yet, she cannot bring herself to acknowledge it. Shame."

"Shame, shame!" says the audience.

"Shame on this modern, apathetic, atheistic world," Joseph Nigel Workman says. "But we know better, don't we people?" The audience whoops and claps.

Wanda clicks pause with her shaking hand. Why does this man

have to focus on her? Why can't she be left alone? More and more all the time. Her eyes drop to the comments section.

DCleal55: So, let me get this straight. Even though Wanda Jaynes doesn't take credit for being a hero, she's conceited because she doesn't credit God? And no one has any problem with worshipping a conceited God who needs to be credited for all good things in the world? It's hypocrisy, people.

Thatguy980: I think people can believe whatever they want, but it doesn't seem rite to just say it's not possible that it was a miracle. It's like people who think aliens don't exist. The universe is huge, who can say we're the only life in it?

Bobothebo: @DCleal55 God is not conceited! Read your bible, without him you would have nothing! We praise him because he is deserving.

Saborsun7: This woman is a hero and I think it's great she's not afraid to speak her beliefs. F&%k Joseph Workman, he's a right-wing pig.

Iwalkwithhim3: It saddens me that we live in a world so jaded and godless that an obvious glorious act like this can be shrugged off as nothing. Atheists, feminists, and homosexuals are ruining this country.

DCleal: Really, @Iwalkwithhim3? This wasn't walking on water, this wasn't transformation. It saddens me we live in world so blind and fearful it's afraid of scientific explanations.

Iwalkwithhim3: IT IS YOU WHO ARE BLIND!!!!!! HIS JUDGEMENT WILL STRIKE DOWN THE CORRUPT AND THE DOUBTERS!!!!!!!!!!!!!!

Wiscousinpies: @Iwalkwithhim3 Religious people like you give the rest of us a bad name. I don't blame people for becoming atheists when religious fanatics spout hate like that.

ShellMcBee: She worships $$ and the CBC paid her for this interview. Get rid of both of them.

Thatguy980: @ShellMCBee The CBC don't pay anyone, their f%#king commies.

DCleal55: Wow, the remarks towards atheism range from condescending to violent. Real critical thinkers, the lot of you.

Cowboylove1974:@ DCleal55 this is a site 4 Joe Workman what u expect.

A whirlpool churns in Wanda's belly. She fits as much cake as she can into her mouth and bites down.

9

TREVOR Dowden has said that Wanda can take as much time as she needs, but on Monday morning, she returns to work. Ivan disagrees with her decision and Mom is skeptical, but being at home feels like hiding. She's drinking like it's Christmas break: Baileys in her coffee, a beer with lunch, a mid-afternoon cocktail. And if she's watching something lame on TV or Netflix, she orders from Eddie's Pizza and lights a dube. And there are so many stupid things to watch. There are so many stupid things.

It's wet out and she predicts the rain will crank the volume on the "It's Monday" complaints. Which can make for small-talk filler, and really, it would be nice to hear talk of something else, something boring and benign. She throws on her black trench coat and flicks up the hood. "A Grim Reaper Named Wanda," Ivan says. He plants a kiss on her cheek, he smells of soap and toothpaste. "Text me when you get to work," he says. Like she's headed overseas.

The sound of rain peppering her hood reminds her of childhood camping, some memory of lying in a tent, knowing she's not supposed to touch the edges when it rains, but pressing one fingertip to the canvas wall, receiving a drop of water, like an offering. Today, she'll get back into productivity, into comfortable, nourishing habits. Today is a fresh start.

Pascale Aggressive sets blue recycling bags by the curb. Her yellow rain slicker is zipped over her chin and her dark eyes expand at the sight of Wanda. Pascale raises her hand and opens it in a slow wave. *Here is my open palm. I come in peace.* "Good morning, Pascale," Wanda gives her a wide, empty grin. Pascale nods, waggles her fingers, and scurries back to her house. Thanks, Pascale. Way to make someone feel like the neighbourhood sex offender.

She starts the car and pulls out into the street. A woman walks by with an umbrella and a golden retriever. A guy in full rain gear jogs along. No sign that last week a man's mind turned on itself and convinced him the most sensible thing to do was gun down strangers in a grocery store. She turns up the radio. There will be piles of things to do at work, assignments to mark, exams to prepare. Distractions like a tray of appetizers offered at chin level.

The campus is on the outskirts of town and although the drive goes against traffic, it's still busy. Suburbia fans out over this tiny peninsula. She read somewhere that, currently, there are more people in Conception Bay South than Corner Brook. A new sprawling housing division on the way, named after a former premier's mommy. Her lane has low traffic, but the opposite side is full, a moving wall of bumper to bumper vehicles on the other side of the yellow line.

Even though she has the right of way, she finds herself braking for a red pick-up truck merging into her lane. He zooms his way in. How easy it is for someone to run her off the road, especially with so many people driving big, aggressive trucks and SUVs. Bullymobiles. They say these large vehicles will save them in an accident, but they probably just want to look menacing. Oil money and oily influence.

The red pick-up's brake lights jolt her into awareness—was she daydreaming? What's going on? People in hard hats along the highway, construction signs. She slows, 60 km/hour, 50 km/hour. A figure in an orange vest takes long slow steps in the distance ahead. A hood hides their face and they carry something long and black in both hands. She grips the steering wheel. The figure pushes the hood back with one hand—a young face, a woman's face. She adjusts the shovel in her hands. Wanda exhales and loosens her fingers on the wheel.

A black SUV monopolizes her rear-view mirror. Right up her ass. Hey mister, there's no room in front. She stares at the back of the red pick-up. The pan is down and it's pristine inside. Why do you have a pick-up truck if you don't use it? She feels like taking a photo. #trophytruck #wasteofspace. But if she posted it on Facebook, guaranteed some acquaintance will have to defend their tastes, preach the virtues of their favourite brand. She could just send it to Sharon and Nikki. They could have their own private snark fest.

A blaring horn behind her. The red pick-up truck has dashed on ahead leaving an expanse of emptiness. She presses the gas, but must cram the brakes as the SUV swings out around her with aggressive impatience. Asshole. She only paused for a second. Or five seconds. The time lapse is fuzzy. That pick-up must be floating.

The traffic on the other side of the lane has lessened and there is room to pass. A transport truck ploughs by, submerging her windshield with a wave of rainwater. She is blind. She switches the windshield wipers to top speed and they sweep rivers of water away with frantic little swipes. A high-pitched beep from inside the car makes her jump. Her eyes scan the dashboard for warning lights— is it the engine? Is she out of gas? Then she remembers: her phone, it's an email notification. She changed it last night so work emails would come straight to her cell. Scared by her own phone, the little frigger.

She shudders. Breathe, Wanda, just breathe. Check mirror. Breathe. Check side mirror. Breathe. Check passenger-side mirror. Breathe. 10 km under the speed limit. Breathe. Just let them pass. Breathe. By the time she reaches work, she is sweating. Her hands gloss the steering wheel. She parks her car in the first available spot.

The main hallway has the Monday smell of lemon floor polish and coffee. Her shoes squeak the tiles. Students stand chatting around open lockers. Some do a double-take as she passes. She focuses on her posture. This is where she works, this is what she does. She's a grown-up college instructor, walking to her office. She says hello if there's eye contact.

The staff room is empty except for Mona who sits at a lunch table. Mona's head is down and she mutters to herself. She's armed with a stack of papers and a highlighter. The seniority list. Still looking to secure a spot.

Mona looks up. Her papers and highlighter lower to the table in unison and she rises to hug Wanda: "Wan-da, my-god, it's so good to see you. I didn't think you'd be back already. My-god, my-god, I can't imagine what you've been going through at-all." She steps back to regard Wanda and her hand rises to her string of pearls. When she plucks at them, they leave a slight indentation in the folds of her neck.

"Well," Wanda says, "I was told I could take all the time I need, but I think it's best if I get out of the house." A patch of sweat taps her just below her bra strap and begins a slow trail down her back.

"I can understand that. Oh Wanda. What a nightmare. We were going to go visit you this week, but we figured you needed time." Mona nods at her own comment. The curls of her white hair sway in agreement.

Wanda also nods. Lots of nodding, let's all nod. There is a shuffling behind her—Andrea and her loping steps. Wanda feels a hand on her shoulder and turns with a prepared smile.

Andrea gazes down at her with grinning scrutiny. "You're a sight for sore eyes." She clamps her hands on Wanda's shoulders and yanks her forward. Wanda gets the full brush of the blond frosted tips along her face. Andrea's head smells like some kind of fruity candy. Skittles? Jolly Ranchers.

"Yes," Mona says. "I'm surprised she's back already. Some good to see her though."

"Sure, Trevor emailed everyone to say she was coming back," Andrea says. "We've all been dying to see you."

Trevor Dowden emailed them. Gotta prepare the masses. What directives did he give? Sensitivity and decorum, people. Put on your kid gloves.

"Such a terrible thing," Andrea says. "Stuff like this makes you think about the big picture." A frozen look floods her face. "And here, everybody's still bitching and moaning about the cutbacks. Same old, same old. Guess you can't take it too seriously, right? Not going to get out of it alive." What platitude will she utter next? You win some, you lose some, my dear.

Andrea flops on to the couch and stretches out her long legs. The cuffs of her brown slacks rise up to reveal white sport socks and clunky black sneakers. The woman has a permanent job, is married to a successful engineer, lives in a big house on Forest Road, and her wardrobe originates from the bargain bin.

"So," Mona says, "how are you doing? My God, it's been all over the news."

"Yes, students have been asking about you," Andrea says. "Will you have to go to court?"

"You didn't have to identify him did you? My God, the picture of him on the news. He's terrifying."

"Court, yes," Wanda says. "Eventually. Depends on how he pleads. No identifying, no."

"Whew!" says Andrea, "Well, I guess we can all thank G— I guess we can all be relieved about that."

Andrea saw the interview. Whatever. Wanda gestures at the seniority list on the coffee table. "How are you doing with that, Mona? Any changes?"

"I'm done like dinner. The only way I can keep my job is if I move and start over at a rural campus."

"Terrible." What to say? How many kids does Mona have? Grandkids? Does she support them? Wanda should know this.

Mona gestures to a name on the top page, highlighted in yellow. "That one? She won't leave. I can't see her wanting to bump and move in here. There's enough work at that campus for her to switch. All the ones at the top will have the option to stay or go." Mona looks up at Wanda. "Have you checked the list yet? You might be able to bump."

Wanda shrugs. "That's for permanent staff." They've already been over this. They never remember she isn't like them. "I don't expect they'll know if there's anything left for months."

Mona nods. "Well, you can join me down at the harbour, teaching the sailors a thing or two. Gotta have a fallback career, you know." Mona laughs and Andrea joins in. Their chugging laughter like a cold engine, turning over. The perspiration on Wanda's back makes another move south.

Wanda rises. "Really gotta get back at it," she says. Yep, yep, so much to do. If she gets out of the staff room quickly, she won't catch their voices lowering as they speak whatever's truly on their minds.

Inside her office, she fires up her computer and wipes dust from the monitor. There's an envelope on the floor. Inside is a card with a picture of a seaside scene. No inscription, but it's been passed around and signed. How does one pick out a card for this occasion? "You survived! Congratulations!" Her co-workers have written things like *Thinking of you. Be well. You are amazing. I'm glad I know you.* It's heartfelt. She tears up a little. Then she checks the back of the card, to make sure it's not from Dominion. Does Dominion even make cards? She hiccups in laughter at the absurdity—what if it was? What would that mean? Why is she looking for a moment of possible tactlessness?

She filters through her inbox. It's calming to delete old, irrelevant messages, to set her mind back into prioritizing what needs to be done or remembered. There's a request from a student for a make-up test. A session on insurance from the union. Reminder for the monthly staff meeting. Corny jokes forwarded to her from Dad in the form of a list of misspelled and/or poorly thought out announcements from church bulletins: *A bean supper will be held in the church hall on Tuesday. Music will follow.*

And one email from an unfamiliar address. Holdenshat@ mail.com. The subject header says "last week's lessons." Maybe one of her students. They often use a different email address than the one the institute assigns them. She clicks on it.

To: JaynesWanda@nlil.ca
From: Holdenshat@mail.com
Subject: last week's lessons

U r both brave and bold.

One line, no signature. People are creeps. Creeps who can't spell. She aims the cursor at the delete button, but reconsiders. They can trace these things if there's a record. That's what the cop said last year at the Cyber-Bullying Information Session. Up yours, Holdenshat. Holden Shat? Blech.

Her stomach fluctuates with unease. Calm down. It's not difficult to get her work email address—she gives it freely to her students.

This is to be expected, she's all over the news. When you're on the Internet, the forecast calls for trolls. She closes her email and retrieves her lesson planner. Today is English 3201, Student Development, and one-on-one work with ABE students in the Learning Centre. Enough variety to keep her busy, enough individual students with issues to absorb her.

Her ABE classes are slightly behind. Throughout the day, students give her closed-mouthed smiles and raise their hands instead of calling out. It feels like the first day of school. She hopes it doesn't stick— it's hard to have open discussions this way. They need to work on their final projects: comparison essays, oral presentations. The principles of descriptive writing: subjective and objective approaches. How to organize an essay—they'll need to write one in their final exam. She clicks through Power Point slides, draws out suggestions for visual organizers on the board. Look, a Venn diagram, good for compare and contrast. Look, a fishbone timeline, good for cause and effect. Questions? Just trying to cause an effect on you, you silent mouthed motherfuckers.

She reminds herself to be patient. The ABE students come from a spectrum of need. Some are here voluntarily, some are forced, and most are funded through social assistance. They need to finish the program with an average above 60, get through the high-school equivalency, get into a program where they can take real post-secondary courses. That gets said a lot, *real* courses, where they can learn something technical or money-focused and never need to write an essay again.

She stays busy and on task. The day flies and she's back in the car. The highway is clear on her ride home. She turns up the radio, presses the gas. This is how her commute usually goes, this is her normal. The sun fights its way through a slice in the clouds.

The trees close to her house carry the fresh-lime tint of new buds. Arguably, the best shade of green. Maybe after supper she and Ivan can go for a walk. Rennie's River Trail would be nice. Or around Quidi Vidi.

The kid appears in front of her like he dropped from the sky; he must have dashed out from between the parked cars. Her foot drills into the brake. The car lurches and screeches to a halt.

The kid stares wide-eyed at her. He looks about six years old, mussy hair, the stain of something pink and punchy on his lips. Then he strolls across the road like nothing happened. Wanda leans forward and rests her forehead on the top of the steering wheel. "You stupid, stupid little bastard," she says. She could park the car, stride down the sidewalk, find the child, and bend him over her knee, right out in the open. Hopefully within sight of his house. She'll utter a word with every spank: *Didn't. Your. Goddamn. Parents. Teach. You. How. To. Cross. The. Fucking. Road.* How many is that? Twelve. An even dozen is a good number for spanks.

The blare of a horn jolts her spine straight. The driver in the car behind her waves his hands around his head. He mouths words. Something like, "What's wrong with you?" And, by the way he bares his teeth, something with bitch in it. She releases the brake and presses the gas gently.

By the time Wanda arrives home, a new knot has fastened itself onto the back of her neck. She checks her phone. One new text message.

> I thought you were going to text me when you got to work? I assume everything is okay cause you liked my Facebook status an hour ago.
> CHECK YOUR PHONE SOMETIMES, MISSUS. xo.

"Give me a fucking break," she says to her phone.

She fumbles out the contents of the mailbox. Takeout menus, flyers, a bank statement. A postcard from Sharon in New Jersey with a picture of a brewery: The Cape May Brewing Company. "Thinking of you." Wanda smiles at Sharon's round handwriting, her loopy *O*s. She unlocks the door and lays the contents of the mailbox down to remove her shoes. A pamphlet slides out of the pile. Yellow lettering, a photo of a man in a suit, cheesy smile, but familiar. She squints at the words while she loosens her laces. *Workers for Modern Christianity.* That religious group. She scoops up the pile of papers and moves to the recycling bin. The pamphlet lands face down. Markings. Her name scrawled on the back.

Wanda picks up the brochure. The cheesy guy in the photo is Joseph Nigel Workman. He beams at the camera from under his sculpted, limber hair. On the back, someone has written her name in black ink: *For Wanda Jaynes.* Inside is a bible passage with several lines highlighted:

> *"Lord, if it's you,"* Peter replied, *"tell me to come to you on the water."*
>
> *"Come,"* he said.
>
> *Then Peter got down out of the boat, walked on the water and came toward Jesus. But when he saw the wind, he was afraid and, beginning to sink, cried out, "Lord, save me!"*
>
> *Immediately Jesus reached out his hand and caught him. "You of little faith,"* he said, *"why did you doubt?"*

She rips the brochure in half. Then rips it again and tosses it back into the recycling bin. Good luck with your promotional flyers, Workers for Modern Nagging or whatever the fuck. Maybe you should print some coupons. Get saved and save 50%.

The knot at the back of her neck twists and hitches. Shag this. She'll lie down and smoke up until Ivan comes home. She'll text an apology. Although, what does he expect? It's her first day back at work. She'll watch something mindless. Maybe they'll order a pizza. The bong and baggie are on the coffee table. She stuffs the bowl, sparks it, and inhales. The water bubbles and the puffs of smoke are a salve.

What was it Leo said? The doctors give it a month before they diagnose PTSD. What's a month, really? It will be summer soon. Work will be done, and although future employment is bleak, there will be a break from its obligation. There will be time to relax and get on with things.

It was this time of year when she finished her Bachelor of Arts degree, and that was a pile of stress. She had no job or idea of what to do. She had applied to study Education and hadn't made the cut; the letter said she was on the waiting list. She kicked herself over that for weeks. Why hadn't she worked harder? Why hadn't she done an Honours Degree? She could have handled it if she had her shit together. She had tried volunteering in different places to pad her résumé, but nothing stuck: the university paper, the art club, the different societies. Each one had its respective clique, people who knew each other for years and monopolized the interesting stuff. She remembers going to a party, a mixer for English or Anthropology or something. Having a great chat with a classmate, Jean something, who invited her to a house party. But she was the only one who was new and Jean's friends sat around listening to Roxy Music and telling stories from their summers together. Some guy mocked her because she didn't know who Bryan Ferry was.

And Simon Moriarty, four months of sleeping together and he went back to his ex-girlfriend. "I can't stop thinking about her," he said. "I like you, but this has never gotten more than casual, right?" Her sleeping patterns erupted. She lost seven pounds by the end of May. When it reached three months with no periods, she went to the doctor. The pregnancy test was negative. "Any stresses in your life right now?" the doctor asked. Wanda listed them off. As her voice cracked on "waiting list," she pulled a Kleenex from the offered box. "My dear," the doctor said, she was blond and chipper, "you have enough going on for three women to miss their periods. Just relax. Be nice to yourself." And a week later, she got into Education. And her period returned and hung around twice as long as usual.

So wait it out. Once the term ends, it will only take a couple of weeks to feel sane. She can sleep in. She can get out of town for a few days. She and Ivan can have more sex.

She takes another puff from the bong. Maybe some music. Ivan left his iPod in the stereo. She presses play. Wax Mannequin pours out: *You've got to tell the doctor to believe me.* The record shelf is white with dust. Has she ever seen Ivan wipe the place down? He doesn't seem to ever notice. The oblivion of the Y-chromosome: can't see dust or grime, can't clean a toilet. The face of the little boy on the street, with his fruit-punch mouth. Can't wash off their sticky faces.

She goes to the kitchen cupboard for the Pledge spray. Small, black specks at the bottom of the cupboard. Goddamn mouse turds. How long have they been there? If they're in the cleaning supplies, they're everywhere. Her skin crawls. Why is it so hard to have a clean, vermin-free house? She brings the spray and a cloth to the living room. Wax Mannequin continues:

He's got a gun
bang bang bang bang
gun gun gun gun gun

She is panting. Her heart is a swinging door in a windstorm. Go to the stereo. Change song. Something else, now. Her thumb fumbles through the menu and presses random. The intro to a Wilco song plays, acoustic guitars, a cheerful build. There. She goes to the couch and lies down. It's okay. It's like in high school and she and Paul Strowbridge broke up and she couldn't handle hearing Pearl Jam for months because that's all he listened to in his car. This is to be expected. "War on War" plays:

It's a war on war
There's a war on

You're gonna lose
You have to lose
You have to learn how to die

She swallows. She cannot hear anything but different kinds of endings. She closes her eyes, but cannot will her mind to stop. The supermarket lights, the screams, shots, streaming eyes, the red truck blazing in from the merge lane, sentences in all-caps—I'M GLAD I KNOW YOU. CHECK YOUR PHONE SOMETIMES, MISSUS. HE'S GOT A GUN.

The couch lowers itself into the floor. It sinks into the dusty rug, into the hardwood, into the nests of mice and whatever else is beneath the surface. Is this how it feels to go crazy? When you lose your mind, can you sense it happening, like watching a ball of string unravel? Can she sense actual synaptic snaps and the deterioration of grey matter right now? This is it, she will be terrified for the rest of her life, crouched in whatever dark corners she can find or invent. Dusty corners full of fear and mouse shit. This is it.

"You at?"

Ivan stands over the end of the couch. He peers at her, holding his phone flat down in his palm, like a waiter with a tray. "You look like you're having a hard time."

Thank fuck. "I need you to sit down and talk to me."

"Got right baked, did ya?"

"Please. Tell me a story. I need to keep my brain together."

"You're just really high. It'll pass."

"No. It's not. I'm losing it."

"This happened before. Remember the time in Outer Cove, you got all trippy about the ocean. 'It's all vast and unknown, man. We don't know what's in there.'" His fingers waggle in the air. "I'll get you a snack. You can eat your stone."

"This is different." She sits up and rocks back and forth. "I don't think I can drive to work tomorrow."

"Okay. Carpooling is better anyway."

"How long do you think it would take me to get a bus out there? Fucking hell."

"You'd have to get up at six, I'd say. Call Andrea, she doesn't live that far away. She'll drive ya." He smiles at his double meaning.

Wanda rubs her forearms. "She was checking for germs. The Professor. Ella Collier. She was checking the chicken. She loved her life and her health so much she took the time to inspect raw meat for germs." She scrapes her fingers through her hair. "She knew about the inadequacy of humanity, she wasn't going to take any chances with dodgy poultry kept at the wrong temperature, wrapped with dirty fingers." The speed of the words makes her gasp. "And then she's gunned down by a complete chemical disaster, by an unclean mind. If that means anything. What's a clean mind? Mine isn't. Hooooo fuck, it won't stop."

He sits beside her. "This will pass. You smoked up alone when you're not in the right mindset."

"What if it's not? What if I'm losing my mind?"

"Let's go outside. Change of scenery. C'mon." He guides her up.

"What the fuck am I going to do, Ivan?"

"You're going to go outside and breathe fresh air. You're going to admire the trees in the backyard."

They go out the back door in the kitchen and sit on the step. He pulls her onto his lap and nuzzles the back of her neck. "I'll call

Andrea. You can get a ride with her. For tomorrow, anyway. Or not. You can still tell Trevor you need time off."

She closes her eyes. Gettin' drove by Andrea. What a way to die. She can see it—Andrea driving and jabbering on, turning to make sure Wanda's listening, careening into a transport truck. Wanda sucks air through her teeth.

"It will get better." He pulls her to him. "You'll see. You're an Amazon."

"I'm a monster."

"You're my Amazon goddess."

She stares at the maple tree. What if the wind picks up, snaps one of those thick branches at the top? It could come through the bedroom window. The wind sways the branches towards her, like weak grasping fingers. There is a gentle patter in her pocket and she pulls out her phone. An email. A distraction. She taps the screen.

To: JaynesWanda@nlil.ca
From: Holdenshat@mail.com
Subject: today
That blue jacket u wore in the grocery stores nice but I like the black one u wore today too.

10

ON Tuesday morning, Andrea's white Rav 4 rolls up to the house at seven sharp, about thirty minutes earlier than Wanda usually goes to work. The horn honks merrily. Wanda locks the door behind her and slogs up the path. She can hear the music emanating from the vehicle. "Su-su-sussido." Andrea is blasting Phil Collins. *No Jacket Required.* Here we go.

"Good morning!" Andrea says. She flicks down the volume as Wanda puts on her seatbelt. "I picked up coffee and bagels. I wasn't sure how you like your coffee, so I got double-doubles." Andrea's short hair is swept back, helmet style. She wears aviator-style sunglasses and a polyester tracksuit in industrial pink. The sleeve rasps as she passes Wanda the cup.

"Um, black, but this is fine. Thank you." Wanda takes a sip. Holy sweet. Andrea's half-eaten bagel rests on a napkin in her cup holder. Wanda gets a whiff of onion. An "everything" bagel first thing in the morning. With sickly-sweet coffee. Gross toast.

"How are you doing? You sleep well?" Andrea bites her bagel and lays it back in the cup holder. She licks her fingers and pulls out into the street, her wet fingertips daintily raised off the steering wheel. "You look tired."

You look like the 80s version of Anne Murray on her way to coach basketball. "I've been having broken sleep," she says. "I might try melatonin tonight. I hear it works." Or pop another of Mrs. Medeiros's Valium, a handful of which was wordlessly left in a dish in the spare bedroom. The pot knocked her out last night, so she didn't take one, but she didn't stay asleep. Instead, she woke at 2:47, 4:06, 4:53, the digital clock branding numbers into the darkness. She focused on relaxing separate body parts, pictured herself in calm places—North West Brook in Trepassey, a waterfall, a beach. Sleep crept in, but tripped up on thoughts.

Andrea clucks her tongue. "You have to watch some of those supplements. They can mix badly with your body chemistry. I like warm milk before bedtime. And sometimes a turkey sandwich." She chortles. "I'm terrible, I am." She looks down to retrieve her coffee. Wanda sucks in her breath. Stay relaxed, stay chatty.

"Yeah," she says, "you might become a tryptophan addict."

"Trip what now?"

"Tryptophan, it's the chemical in turkey that makes you sleepy. You know, like after Thanksgiving and everyone's tired."

Andrea frowns. "Yeah, but that's from eating a lot. My family always does a ham."

"No, but, if you're having a turkey sandwich before bed-time—"

"Oh, I love this song." Andrea twists the volume knob. The tinkling synthesizer in the opening of Phil Collin's "Take Me Home" flows from the speakers. "*Take that look of worry, I'm an ordinary man*," Andrea sings along.

Wanda takes a big sip of her coffee and stares out the window. Ivan called Andrea last night and lied, told her they were having car trouble. Andrea insisted she could give Wanda a ride every day, no problem. It's very kind of her. And it's most unfortunate the woman makes her feel like a cat having its fur stroked backwards. Three minutes in the Rav 4 and she's already mussed and indignant.

Andrea belts along with Phil and stops hard at every light. "How are things going anyway?" she says.

"Oh, not bad. Gets better all the time." There's an itch in her chest to discuss the email, to verbalize it: *Can you believe this shit?* But the fewer people who know, the better. She showed the messages to Ivan yesterday evening and they called Constable Lance. He came by the house, all concerned forehead, lots of product in his hair. "It is alarming for someone to comment on seeing you," he said. "But it's not an overt threat to your safety." Not a threat at this point, you saucy youngster. He asked her to list all the places she went yesterday. Outside of going back and forth to work, she hadn't been anywhere—limiting it to the twelve hundred-odd people who occupy campus every day, plus anyone who saw her en route. He gave her his email address and instructed her to forward any new messages to him. Don't delete anything or block anyone for now.

"Overt threat to your safety, my hole," Ivan said once Constable Lance had left. "Cops, I don't trust their priorities. Leo knows about tracing emails. There's nothing to stop us from checking ourselves." Wanda was too tired to argue. If Ivan and Leo want to pretend to be private investigators, they can fill their boots. Ivan Medeiros and the Internet Detectives.

But what if they trace it to work? It's probably a student. Or, one of them took a picture of her, walking in or out in her black coat. They could have shared it on Snapchat or whatever the fuck. Anyone could have seen it.

Who else might have written her? Wanda thinks of Pascale Aggressive, her startled eyes and hidden mouth in her yellow rain slicker. She may resent them. Maybe she gets off on spooking people. Pascale, peering out her front window, watching her get in with Andrea, making note of the car, the time. From now on, Wanda will keep track of her interactions, note who's around, who can see her.

The day passes uneventfully. Linda, a twenty-two-year-old single mother of twins, brings her a latte for their one-on-one lesson and speaks softly to her. But then she gets flustered when Wanda points out that she didn't reference her sources in-text.

In her regular classes, attendance is high, higher than before the shooting. Maybe this is a positive outcome. Her notoriety will result in higher GPAs all around.

At lunch break, she sits with Mona, Andrea, and Samantha, one of the French instructors. Andrea leans in to examine what Wanda's eating. "What's that? Looks like curry."

"Butter chicken."

"Where'd ya get that?"

"Ivan made it."

"You can get that sauce in jars at Sobeys," Samantha says.

"He made this from scratch," Wanda says. Samantha raises her eyebrows. It's a fact, not a brag, Wanda feels like saying.

"She's always got something different," Andrea says. Her eyes shine in approval at the novelty of Wanda's lunch. Mona wrinkles her nose.

She takes long slow chews to fight a sarcastic response. Look everyone, look what Wanda brought to school today. Holy fuck, that's not ham and cheese. She stirs her food while Andrea takes gummy bites from her sandwich and talks and talks. Three times, she brings up how she drove Wanda to work this morning. Someone wants a sticker.

At the end of the day, they meet in the parking lot. "I have to run a quick errand on the way home," Andrea says. "Just have to stop by a pharmacy." Wanda nods. She should get some melatonin. Good idea to not rely on Valium. It will run out way too fast.

In Shoppers Drug Mart, Andrea grabs a cart and pushes it up the first aisle. She scrutinizes a display of reduced-price Pringles. Quick errand, indeed. The pharmacy stereo plays Tina Turner's "Simply the Best." Maybe adult-contemporary music trails Andrea like a will-o'-the-wisp. Wanda scans the aisle signs for vitamins and supplements. You'd think the woman would be a little sensitive about bringing her into a store after what happened last week, but you know, gotta buy chips.

"You're her."

The voice is right behind Wanda, a bug in her hair. She wheels around. The man is short and rotund. He stands close enough that she can see the dust on his glasses—they're quite filthy, actually— thick lenses over greyish eyes. A smudge of a moustache ridges his upper lip. His hairline is making a run for it, receding up a stretch of shiny forehead.

"You're Wanda Jaynes," he says. He has a lisp and "Jaynes" comes out with a little squish at the end. *Jaynish.*

"Yes, that's me."

"Karl Prendergast." *Prendergash.* He extends a hand and Wanda shakes it. His hand is hot and damp. She fights the urge to twitch. He pumps her arm. "I jush want to shay, thank you. I think you are very brave." He pushes up his glasses with his other hand and keeps pumping. "Ish a real pleashure."

"Thank you, Karl."

"I…I wrote the mayor about you," Karl says. "I shaid you should have the key to the city" *Shitty*. "The lash time they gave away the key, it wash to shome hockey playersh." Karl shakes his head with vigor. "Why a bunch of overpaid atheletsh should have it and not you confoundsh me." He holds his elbow into his side and as he bops her arm up and down, Wanda has to lean forward into him. There's something sour on his breath, some intestinal disagreement.

"Wow, thanks," she says. "Everyone loves hockey, though."

"What ish your ward?"

"Excuse me?"

"Which ward do you live in?" There is a formation of spittle in the corner of his mouth. And another smell, something musty and pungent about him. Mothballs in a bag of old sneakers. She keeps her face neutral. His eyes swarm behind the filmy lenses. They slide down to her chest, widen slightly, then jerk back up to her face.

She gently pulls her hand out of his and resists the urge to wipe it on her pants. Also, to check the top buttons on her blouse. She pulls her jacket together. "Which ward?" Hospital ward? Psychiatric ward?

"What area of Shaint Johnsh? I'll write your shitty councillor to put the presshure on."

"Oh, um, ward two."

"Ward two." His eyes shine. "That's alsho my ward. Downtown to Georgetown and around Shaint Clare's, that's all ward two. I live by Bannerman Park."

"Oh, that's a good area." Wanda says.

"It's pretty good I guesh." Karl tilts his head slightly. Like it's her turn. Now she's supposed to give her address. Good luck with that, buddy.

"Ready?" Andrea appears by Karl's shoulder and barges her shopping cart between them. Wanda has never been so happy to see her.

"Sorry, I have to go," Wanda says. "Nice to meet you, Karl." She gives him a little wave and walks down the aisle with Andrea.

"Niysh to meet you too. I'll keep talking to the shitty!" Karl says. He continues standing in the aisle, watching them leave.

"Hey, you got quite the fan base," Andrea says. "Ha, don't mind me, I'm some bad."

"You really, really are," Wanda says.

At home, she finds Ivan and Leo at the computer with Trish standing over them. She wears a black, silky, off-the-shoulder top and it sags enough to expose a polka-dot push-up bra in soft pink. "Hi Wanda!" Trish says. She dashes over for the hello hug. Wanda's hands have nowhere to go but Trish's hips. Does she rest her hands there? Give them a squeeze? She gives Trish's narrow hips two quick pats.

"Hey baby," says Ivan. "Leo is the man. He's been digging around on that email."

"Yepper," Leo says. He grins up at her and taps the empty seat next to him. "Come see."

She sits down in the leather office chair. Trish stands behind her and inserts her fingers in the hair at the nape of Wanda's neck. "Did you get your hair done lately? So nice." It's like being massaged with a garden tool.

"So, there are websites that run services called *Who Is*. It's a way of finding out ownership of an IP address. I used one on the address from the email and it belongs to the university."

"Really? Do you know where in the university?"

"No. The university buys their addresses in bulk. You'd need to talk to an administrator to find out the specific computer used," Leo says, "but it's a start if you want to nag the cops about it."

So, it could be anyone. Students from both the institute and the university share apartments, houses. Many study at the university library. Biggest university east of Montreal, thousands of people.

"Jesus," she says. She leans against the desk, away from Trish's touch. There is a note pad next to the monitor. Ivan has made a list.

Options/Offers
Hero-vs-Hero—reality TV show. "Real-life heroes face off in
a variety of challenges" (CTV).

Weekly/Biweekly blog? Huffpost can pay by popularity.

Rick Mercer Report—can she meet Rick? Can they go shopping together or something?

Interviews—most Canadian media won't pay, but British media does. Email back Sam at the BBC.

Buzzfeed Listicles—a real quote from Wanda? They can pay.

Big Brothers/Big Sisters—can she throw out the first softball of the season?

"Real Life Lucky"—Bio, interview, and re-enactment of "Dominion Day."

Interview requests from Juanita at The Reason Rally, canadianatheist.com, atheistalliance.org.

CBC, CTV, VOCM want W's response to Joseph Workman statements.

T-shirts? Threadless.com wants permission, maybe signature on grocery store meme shirts and merchandise

Check domain names: wandajaynes.com, wandajaynes.ca.

The list goes on to the next page. "What is this?" she says.

"Those are your offers!" Trish says. "Can you believe it?"

"Offers?"

"They've been coming in since last week," Ivan says. "It's a long list."

"They've been coming to you?"

"Well, the media outside our door had to be funnelled somewhere." He brings his knee up and hugs it into his chest. "Where did you think all your celebrity enquiries were going?" He smiles at her. If she put both her hands on his knee and gave one hard push, the chair would topple backwards. Hovering Trish would take a tumble as well.

"Hero-vs-Hero? What does that entail? A three-legged race?"

"They say it's a variety of challenges involving real people who have committed acts of bravery."

"So, what, like, Trivial Pursuit with firefighters?" Wanda says. "Or a scavenger hunt with some kid who saved a drowning cat?" Her voice is edging up. Trish's gaze switches to the computer monitor. Great, Trish and Leo get to witness a Wanda meltdown for the second time this week. "Anyway," she says, "we can talk about it later."

"K," Ivan says. His eyes flick away from hers. He clicks the mouse and stares at the screen.

She walks to the kitchen, pulls a beer from the fridge, wrings off the cap, and pours most of it straight down her throat. A long list. How much help did he have making that? She flings the cap towards the garbage can. It hits the edge with a ping and bounces on the floor. "For fuck sakes," Wanda says. She bends and hooks the cap off the floor with her fingers. Her eyes heat up with tears. She can't make the shot when she wants to, of course. So stupid.

The fridge door smacks closed. Leo opens a beer for himself. "Hey Jaynes."

"Hey."

"You alright?"

"I'll be fine."

He reaches out and takes the cap from her. "You don't have to be."

"Offers and options? Like I won the jackpot or something."

"I know," Leo says. He takes a sip. "Some pretty crazy things on that list."

"I can't believe they've actually been written down."

"Well, everything seems more important when someone writes it down. You teach writing, you know that."

"I know. I just...what am I supposed to do with this?"

"I don't know. But people are talking about you anyway. If you can get comfortable with it, why not turn it to something positive?"

"Reality TV? I don't think so."

"Yeah, it's so cheap. When reality, real reality, is not." He reaches forwards and clinks his bottle against hers. "I think Wanda should take care of Wanda. And we'll all take care of Wanda too." Half his mouth shrugs up in a smile. His hair, the colour of wet sand, hangs in his face so only one blue-green eye is visible. It shines at her with affection.

"You're sweet, Leo."

"I try my best."

Laughter ripples out of the next room. Wanda and Leo go to the doorway and glance in. Ivan and Trish are watching a video on the computer. Their voices match each other in pitch and enthusiasm. Wanda takes the final swig from her beer and regards the empty bottle.

11

To: JaynesWanda@nlil.ca
From: Holdenshat@mail.com
Subject: Just thinking

U might not believe in god but u r an angle weather u believe
it or not.

PACK right off. Wanda narrows her eyes at the screen. Angle
indeed. Feeling pretty obtuse at the moment. This message and
another Workers for Modern Christianity brochure in today's mail.
This one includes a cartoon titled "The Descent of the Modernists."
The picture depicts men descending a staircase, each step labelled
with a foreboding statement: *Christianity* at the top and down to
Bible Not Infallible to *No Miracles* to *No Resurrection* to *Agnosticism*
to the bottom level of *Atheism*, written in a black scrawl on the floor.
And now, their address has been printed on a sticker and attached to
the back. Shit gets official when people make labels.

Ivan comes in from the kitchen with a plate of cheese and
crackers. Over two hours since Leo and Trish left and he's been
puttering around outside, raking things, chatting with neighbours.
Doing the avoid-dance. Stir some soil, cha-cha-cha. Chat with
neighbours, chat-chat-chat.

"I got another one." Wanda points at the screen.

He leans over her to read. "Nice spelling. Think it's a student?"

"If it is, it could be any of them. No one can spell anymore."

"I'm surprised you haven't received more stuff like this. There were over a thousand references when I Googled you last night." Ivan stuffs a wad of cheese in his mouth.

Wanda watches him chew. His skin glows from outdoor exposure. He always radiates health. Has he ever had a zit? Even his good looks are annoying, especially since they haven't had sex since the week before the shooting. Over two weeks now and he's only interested in probing her online.

"Why were you Googling me?"

"Curiosity. Gauging the climate."

"Climate of what?"

"The climate around you. You know, what people are saying."

"What difference does it make?"

He sighs. "I know you're annoyed with me about all this. But some of these offers might be good for you."

"Like what? Some cheesy reality TV show? You hate that shit. We watched *The Bachelorette* once and you said you could physically feel your IQ decreasing."

"It doesn't have to be a reality show." Ivan points to the list. "Look. People want to interview you on their podcasts. Or, you could blog. You teach writing, you're good at it. You'd be better than most of them out there, for sure."

"What would I write about? 'Hi, I'm Wanda. I threw a can once. Now I can't drive my own car to work.'"

"Why not? You think you're the only person to ever feel this way? Lots of people can relate to what's happening to you."

"How can you say that?" she says. "I did one interview and was called names."

"By a few wacked-out evangelists. Ninety-eight percent of the stuff out there on you is really positive."

"But the two percent is terrifying. And organized with their propaganda and ominous emails."

"You could write about that. You could talk about that." Ivan points to the bottom of the sheet. "Look at the organizations who want to speak to you. *Jezebel Magazine*. You read it all the time."

She picks up the list. *Jezebel*, holy shit. "Their reach is huge," she says.

"It is. It could really be something."

What approach would *Jezebel* take? What if she stuck her foot in her mouth and it was retweeted into infinity? There would be shitty little analyses of her looks, her dialect, her lack of cool. And then, a backlash against the criticism of her, accusations of misogyny towards those who would break her down into elements. After all, she's a fucking hero.

"I explained what happened in the CBC interview," she says. "People should be concerned with more important things. No one asks about the people who were actually fucking shot."

"You're right. And you could do that, point that out to people. And people would listen."

"But I'm nobody."

"But that's just it. That's why you're interesting, it's why they want you."

Wanda contemplates Ivan with his snack plate balanced on his palm. One cracker hovers on the edge looking suicidal. It probably just voiced how it feels like nobody and had its partner agree.

"I want to show you something," he says. He rests the plate on the desk and leans over her. He opens up YouTube, types "grocery shooter" in the search engine and brings up a user profile. The channel belongs to someone called Pikeitalot. "Grocery Shooter Take-Down!" is first on the list. It's been viewed over two million times. Pikeitalot's profile photo shows a pale-faced man in a black toque, arms crossed menacingly, but flexed. He has facial piercings and a neck tattoo. She squints at his face. The neck tattoo reads *infinity*. He's the Dominion deli guy she asked for help finding the can of coconut milk. The most recent video he has posted is titled "Me being interviewed—what it was REALLY like that day." 3263 views so far. Ivan clicks play.

Pikeitalot/*infinity* strolls into a living room—beige couch, brass lamps, family pictures on the wall. The voice of Genevieve Davey narrates: "*Darryl Pike worked in the deli section of the now infamous Dominion store. He was on shift the day Edward Rumstead entered* and opened fire on staff and customers. When the shooting began, Darryl, like others, found a place to hide. He locked himself in an upstairs security office with a small window overlooking the store. But before he hid, he held his phone in the window and, this way, filmed what is now the famous video of Wanda Jaynes stopping Edward Rumstead in his tracks."

Darryl Pike sits with wide-open legs. Major manspreading. He wears slouchy blue jeans, a tight white t-shirt, thick gold chains and a backward ball cap. He scratches his chest absently as he speaks:

"When I heard the shots, I wanted to run for it, but the exits was blocked solid with people. So I said to myself, Pike, you gotta get high up somewhere, keep an eye out. So I run up to the security room. Blocked myself in and got down on the floor. That's how we used to do it for lockdown procedures back in high school."

"What made you decide to film what was going on?"

"Well, I didn't want to look right out the window in case I was seen. So I turned on the camera on my phone and keep my eyes on that. And I said to myself, Pike, b'y, this might be it. This might be the end. Might as well press record." Darryl Pike looks into the camera and grins.

"Okay, so he's a skeet," Wanda says. "What's your point?"

"Just watch," Ivan says.

Genevieve's narration continues. "Darryl says he is deeply saddened by the shootings and the death of his friend and co-worker, Michael Snow. However, the video has changed his life in many positive ways."

"Yeah, so I've been a YouTube member for a few years, right? Me and my buddies are always filmin' videos of us skateboardin' or rap songs we make up. So with this one, once it got over so many views, they started payin' me. There's been a few offers. Commercials, things like that. But I want to give something back, you know? To the victims. To the memory of Mike." Pike drops his head at this. He regards his clasped hands with their thick chunky rings.

Genevieve's voice trails off. "Darryl Pike plans to use some video proceeds for a fundraising concert to raise money for victims of violent crime. He says his own group, the hip-hop band Infinite Finds, will headline."

Ivan presses pause. "So. What do you make of that?" he says.

"Gross toast. That's what I make of that."

"Why?"

"He decided to be reckless and make that video—a video which could have ended up showing me getting my brains shot out—and he's profiting." She exhales. Fucking idiots everywhere. "And promoting his 'music.'"

"Oh, he's a bottom feeder, for sure." Ivan reaches out to touch her shoulder. She leans away.

"It's blatantly opportunistic, Ivan. Either that or he's about to get sued for posting the video and this is how he's paying his lawyers."

"I agree with you. But, and I'm just being straightforward here, it's working for him. He's making money because of you." He selects a slice of cheese from the plate and cracks it in half. "If you were to, say, join YouTube, start a video-blog, people would watch anything you put up."

"A video-blog. Yeah, I'll set up the webcam and wear something low cut."

"I'm just giving YouTube as an example. Wanda, you've said before that you got into teaching because you wanted to help people do something with their lives. The position you're in lets you really *do* something."

"Oh yes. Finally."

"You know what I mean. It's rare to have a spotlight. You've been given this. It's literally fallen in your lap."

"This isn't a gift. And you're misusing the word *literally*." She could bounce his cheese plate off the wall.

"You're an educated person who educates. People will listen to you. This shit happens for a reason."

"Since when? I thought believing in a plan was part of the problem."

"Ugh, I don't know how else to say it. You know what I mean," he says. He bites into his piece of cheese.

"Why is it so important I do this?" she says. And then, carefully, "What else is there to get out of it?"

"Well, the money of course."

"Of course."

"Wanda, you're laid off in a month. We're doing okay, but I go contract to contract too. We're not much more than hand to mouth here."

"So, I should do this to survive?" She pushes the chair away from the computer. "I mean, I can't even drive. Or sleep."

He leans forward to touch her and his arm brushes the plate, knocking the cracker off the edge. It lands on the hardwood and shatters. "I understand," he says. He squats and starts sweeping the pieces into his hand, head down.

"Do you?"

"I do." He keeps sweeping. "And what you're feeling, it's natural. Fuck, I wouldn't want to be pressured into being a role model or something." He looks up at her, his face frank and composed. "I know you're stressed and everything is hard right now. But you know, you're handling it all beautifully."

Wanda looks down at him. "Thank you." She strokes his hair. The thickness of it always feels heavy and satisfying in her hands. His eyes are dark and pleading. "I'm sorry," she says into them.

"Don't be sorry." Ivan lays the plate on the floor. His hands clasp her knees and run up her thighs. "You're the most impressive person I've ever known."

Wanda leans down and kisses his mouth. He returns her kiss, his hands spreading over her hips. Their lips break and he rests his head in her lap. "I would never suggest you do something you can't handle."

"But you understand I can't."

"Of course." He squeezes her around the waist. "Right now. I understand the big picture is hard to visualize."

Her hands freeze in mid-stroke along his back. She straightens and starts to stand.

"What? Oh, come on," he says.

She pushes herself out of the chair and steps around him, inadvertently kicking the plate as she goes. Crackers skitter across the floor.

She shuts the bedroom door and sprawls sideways across the bed. For the first couple of minutes, she listens. But the knob doesn't turn;

there is no click and whisper of the door opening. She realizes she is holding her breath. He's not coming. The small embroidered flowers on the comforter start to embed themselves into the flesh of her cheek. She tucks her arm under her head and lies on her side, making sure to face away from the door. If he does come in, he won't get to read her expression right away.

She stares at the wall-hanging installed over the bed, a souvenir from their trip to Nepal. From a distance, it looks like a quilt, but close up, the details come out, the beading and stitching, an abstract painting done in textiles with patches of silk and satin. They were together for a little over a year when they decided to go on the trip. And it was so cool they had that in common, that Nepal was on both their bucket lists. For months, her parents fretted about it. Mom forwarded articles on disasters and depressing Nepalese statistics. One of the eighth poorest countries in the world. One of the only places where men outlive women. But they were going.

They decided on a trek through the Annapurna mountain range and found a group called Three Sisters who train women to be guides, as a way to create independent female workers. They hired two women, a guide and a porter. Each night, she and Ivan had their own guesthouse room where the power shut off at eight o'clock. They took quick showers and lay together in candlelit darkness. He would massage her tired legs, long strokes from hip to ankle. Even after hiking all day, she couldn't control herself, looking up at him looking down at her, the pleasure in his eyes from touching her, his smooth warm hands, his fingers long enough to wrap around the base of her calf, the pale tan line from his wristwatch shining in the dark.

She shifts into her regular side of the bed. She closes her eyes and listens. There is a distant, faint sound of tapping and clicking, the keyboard, the mouse.

Around eight, Ivan leaves to "jam with Leo." Which means he'll be back late. Leo and Trish and Ivan, up 'til three, J-A-M-M-I-N-G. What will they talk about? Will they dissect her lame dismissal of celebrity? She finds distractions around the house, she reorganizes the pile of Tupperware containers so they match up with lids, she wipes down the inside of the fridge. She stops several times to reread Holdenshat's emails. What students write this way? What about coworkers? She considers other instructors on campus, people she passes every day in the hallways. People she's never interacted with beyond polite greetings. That wiry woman in the chemistry lab who never smiles. The maintenance guy with bulging eyes who smokes by the parking lot. Andrea, so very aware of Wanda's proclamation of non-belief, the way she makes a point to skirt around it.

She opens her Facebook account. Thirteen friendship requests. She fixed the privacy settings so she can't be found in an Internet search, but it doesn't stop friends of friends from adding her. There have been at least a hundred friend requests since the shooting and she has dismissed most of them. Who's on the list today? Morris Jaynes, her great-uncle. Just joined Facebook. Sure, why not. Eight students from the college. Not a chance. Andrea's husband, Boyd. Ugh. She can add and unfollow him, perhaps.

Geraldine Harvey. The lady who was shot at, who played dead. Her cover photo is the Workers for Modern Christianity banner. Wanda squints at her profile picture. She is the red-haired woman who passed out brochures at the vigil. Nope, not connecting with this one. Although maybe her feverish faith is new, a result of surviving that moment. Everyone's having a lot of feelings these days.

Another one. Karl Prendergast. She stares at the name until it comes to her. The cootie machine from the pharmacy. How did he find her? She checks their mutual friends. There are two: Rose Mahon, a local photographer who adds everyone in hopes of building business, and a woman named Helen Marsh, who she can't remember meeting. She clicks on Karl Prendergast's profile. The cover photo is a sunset. The profile picture shows him holding some kind of placard. She clicks on it for a closer look. It's a giant novelty cheque—he raised money for the local children's hospital. Good for you Karl, you're the besh. She clicks through his profile pictures. Karl holding a tiny Pomeranian, the dog looks deliriously happy: "*Me and my adopted baby.*" Karl on a beach, sprawled underneath palm trees, brandishing a tall, fruity drink: "*Life is good in Jamaica!*" Karl wearing a red-and-black-checkered deer-hunting hat, staring at the camera with unsmiling intensity: "*This is a people shooting hat. I shoot people in this hat.*" She recognizes the quotation immediately. Photo posted January 27th, 2010.

There are a number of comments. A Jay Simms says, "*Dude, that's creepy.*"

Karl's response: "*J.D. Salinger died today. He was the author of my favourite book, 'The Catcher in the Rye.' I wanted to do a tribute to him.*"

Jay Simms: "*Still, dude, pretty creepy.*"

She knows, but for some reason still needs to confirm it. She copies and pastes the quote into a Google search. Spoken by Holden Caulfield, protagonist of *The Catcher in the Rye*, to his roommate Ackley in a discussion about his red-peaked hunting cap. Ackley calls it a deer shooting hat:

"'*Like hell it is.' I took it off and looked at it. I sort of closed one eye, like I was taking aim at it. 'This is a people shooting hat,' I said. 'I shoot people in this hat.'*"

Holden's hat.

She's taught the novel in ABE courses as a high-school English credit and she's had class discussions about the shooting of John Lennon, of Mark David Chapman's obsession with the book. Holdenshat@mail.com, of course. It's lamely obvious. Naive of her to not pick up on it earlier. And here is Karl in his stupid hat, the gawky vehemence in his eyes, and she feels like she did when she was eight years old and found all the Christmas presents "from Santa" hidden away under her parents' bed. Of course. Of course it's you.

But this is just one thing and it's weak and flimsy. Circumstantial. There are lots of Salinger fans out there. She clicks through the rest of Karl's profile pictures: Karl with an elderly woman: "*I love my Nan!*" A blue Nissan Versa: "*Fresh from the dealership!*" Karl in a Santa hat. Nothing else screams stalker. Whatever that means.

She goes to the "About" section of his profile. Male. Single. Works at Memorial University. Those first emails came from the university. She scrolls through his timeline. He keeps a lot open to the public. His last status was this morning: "*Nothing like a fresh cup of coffee and a carrot muffin!*" Earlier in the week: "*Hope I don't*

get this flu. Everyone at work has the sniffs!" Last week: "*TGIF!*"
Holy boring status updates. There are a few "likes" and comments.
Boring social-media poster + being kinda gross = unfollowed by
most "friends." But maybe deep down, he thinks they're phonies.

She continues scrolling. Karl shared Darryl Pike's video the day
it went viral. On the post, he wrote, "*The victims of the shootings and
their families are in my prayers. And thank god this Wanda Jaynes
was there!*" Thirty likes. Six comments, one from Helen Marsh, one
of their two mutual friends: "*Wanda is wonderful! She goes out
with my friend's son and is a nice lady.*" That explains how Karl found
her on Facebook and how she knows Helen Marsh. She vaguely
remembers an introduction at a Christmas party—Helen is Mrs.
Medeiros's friend from church. Helen added her on Facebook and
Wanda unfollowed her from her newsfeed because all she posts are
inspirational quotes and recipes.

She clicks on Helen's profile to see how she is connected to Karl.
"See friendship." Helen works in the university archives. So they
probably work together, somehow.

Wanda starts an email to Mrs. Medeiros, but deletes it. Mrs.
Medeiros would want—would respect—a phone call. And after
everything that happened last week, it would be good to have a solid
chat with her. She picks up her phone. Maybe she should text Ivan
first to let him know what she's doing. But he won't think it's a
good idea. "It will just get her worked up," he'll say. "She looks for
reasons to be paranoid." And he's been condescending enough today.
She pours herself a glass of wine before calling. This conversation
will take a while.

Mrs. Medeiros's voice rises several notches when she realizes it's
Wanda. "Oh, I thought you were one of those awful sales callers.
They always call when it's dark out." Mrs. Medeiros asks where Ivan
is and goes on about how nice Leo and Trish are as friends: "But
they're too thin. They never stop running around." They discuss the
weather, the cost of fresh produce in town—Mrs. Medeiros is almost
out of her smuggled oranges.

Wanda takes a deep breath, "I was wondering, do you talk to
your friend Helen Marsh often?"

"Oh yes, I see her at least once a week."

"I met someone the other day who might work with her." Keep voice neutral. "Karl Prendergast."

"Oh?" There is a metallic rattle in the background, pots bubbling on the stove.

"Yes. I was wondering if it's possible…just to bring it up to Helen, that I met this guy. He added me on Facebook and I'm wondering what he's like."

"Yes, I can ask her." There is a pause and shifting, she's puttering around the kitchen. "Can I ask why?"

"Well, I've been receiving some strange anonymous emails lately. Nothing to worry about though."

"Oh Wanda," Mrs. Medeiros's voice shivers with sympathy. "I'm so sorry. You don't deserve this. You deserve good things to happen, not nasty strangers. There are so many people out there with evil secrets. And you know this too well now. Oh, it makes me sick." There is a short click, the shutting of a pot lid. "It's not fair you have to have this extra stress. It can wear you down. When Ivan and Sylvie's father died, I thought I was going to have a breakdown from the stress. I was all alone and they were so little."

"I can imagine."

"And all my family is so far away. You know, you get married and start a family and build this life together. And then he's gone and all you have left are memories. And you have to do everything for your children. Keep them safe. Thinking about what might happen to them, all the dangers of the world, it kept me up at night. All I could think about were my own limits. How I could only do so much."

"I'm so sorry you went through that." Pots rattle in the background. Mrs. Medeiros, alone in her house. They need to go visit her.

"It was a long time ago," Mrs. Medeiros says, "but I still have trouble sleeping, sometimes." Yes, yes she does. Thanks for the Valium, by the way. "So these messages," Mrs. Medeiros continues, "do you think it might be this Karl?"

"Well, I just want to be sure. The emails come from the university and that's where he works. And there's a photo on his Facebook profile which kind of connects to the email address." She's such a Sherlock. So fucking lame.

But Mrs. Medeiros makes soft gasps and clucks her tongue. "I will ask Helen what kind of man he is. Don't worry, I'll be discreet." The pots and pans sing out and Mrs. Medeiros curses under her breath in Portuguese. "I should see her tomorrow. I'll give you a call."

They say their goodbyes and Wanda pours another glass of wine. She considers a bath. If she bathes now and gets ready for bed, she'll be asleep when Ivan gets home. Or she can pretend to be.

12

THE clock radio reads 9:19am. Wanda's lips are gummy with wine tannins. Ivan is deposited on top of the comforter next to her. He managed to get his pants off, but everything else is intact: black t-shirt, black socks, and black boxer briefs. His jaw is slack and parted and his curls stick straight up. Like last Halloween when he dressed up as Kramer from Seinfeld. Her hand floats up to touch them, but stops. He rubs his face in his sleep. The imprint of a stamp is still inked on the back of his wrist. Black letters: CBTG's. He shifts and gives a whisper of a snore, she catches the faint scent of something sweet and boozy. Rum or whiskey. Jamming no doubt.

She slips out of bed and snatches her bathrobe on the way to the door. Downstairs, she gets a glass of orange juice before checking Facebook. Let's see if Karl posted anything new.

Karl Prendergast: *Nice mild day today! Great day for the Dog Walking Club on Rennie's River Trail!*

Posted ten minutes ago. The orange juice bites a path through her food pipe. Where would he go after walking his dog? Straight home? If he is watching her, wouldn't it be good to be aware of his routes? Figure out how he knows about her?

She tiptoes back through the bedroom to grab some clothes. Ivan has shifted into an X pose in the bed's centre; arms and legs spread wide to monopolize both sides. Good thing she didn't plan on returning to bed.

She slips into jeans and her navy-blue hoodie. She scribbles a post-it note and slaps it on the refrigerator door: "Gone for a walk. W." Outside, the overcast sky is thick and full, gauze over a wound. She puts on sunglasses anyway. Check out Wanda, so incognito.

She takes lengthened strides, jerky with nerves. The entrance to Rennie's River Trail is about a four-minute walk from her house, three if she hurries. The brisk air fills her lungs and she tugs the cotton hood around her chin. It's just going for a walk. It's good exercise. If she sees Karl and learns something, that's a good thing. She's not crossing any lines by going for a walk.

She spots him as she comes down the hill. A lucky break. He is at the bottom, crossing the street with a fluffy Pomeranian on a neon-green leash. A stocky woman with short, cropped grey hair walks beside him leading a beagle puppy which constantly lurches to escape. Both Karl and the woman wear burgundy fleeces, the woman's sneakers are breast-cancer-awareness pink. Looks like they are the only club members who showed. Must be hard to plan an early walk on a Saturday morning.

Karl half turns in her direction as he maneuvers his puff of a dog over the curb. Wanda pushes her sunglasses up the ridge of her nose and hunches down in her hoodie. She takes short steps to slow down, but her momentum wants to pitch her down the hill. At the bottom, the trail diverges into two separate paths, one on each side of the river. She staggers onto the side opposite them and hovers behind a patch of alders. Something on the ground moves towards her. She yelps. A duck, scampering away. Karl and the woman continue walking without looking back. They haven't seen her.

Their stroll idles and meanders; they pause and point at things in trees, they feed treats to the dogs. A couple with two little girls stop and fuss over the puppy and Karl's excited ball of fluff. Wanda congratulates herself on having the common sense to bring her phone. She stops for minutes at a time, pretending to text people.

Karl and the woman leave the trail to climb the steep path back to Georgetown by the brewery. From Fleming Street, they walk up Bonaventure Avenue and cut by Holy Heart Theatre to the Sobeys grocery store. She watches them pass Sobeys and enter a blue house across the street on Newtown Road. Who lives there, Karl or the woman? He said he lives by the park, so it's probably her. Wanda scowls to herself. The whole morning, wasted. Or she could wait for him to leave. She could go into the grocery store and wander around, give them some time. Then hover outside like she's waiting for a ride until he leaves.

The store entrance leads into the wide, bright produce section and the automatic doors whisper closed behind her. She glances around the space before her. Displays of grapes, sliced cantaloupe in clear plastic. She steps forward and a force presses her chest. It squeezes her ribcage. She gasps for breath. A thick, dry presence fills her windpipe.

"Miss? Are you okay?" A soft-faced young man in a Sobeys apron. He grips something black and metallic, he aims it towards her.

"Get that away!" Her voice scrapes. "Don't hurt me."

"This?" He holds it up and looks at her. His shape blurs and swims in the sharp florescent light. "It's a pricing gun."

She turns and scatters towards the automatic doors. Outside, she leans against the brick exterior. Deep breaths. She bends her knees and slides into a sitting position. Where is her phone? Please, Ivan, be up. It rings three times and answers.

"Hello there." Not Ivan, but completely familiar.

"Who's this?"

"It's Leo. Ivan forgot his phone here last night."

Of course he did. Not the first time. She groans slightly.

"You okay?"

"No. I just…had a panic attack or something. I think."

"Where are you?"

"Sobeys on Merrymeeting."

"Are you hurt? Do you need to go to the hospital?"

"I need a ride." Her legs feel light and hollow, like plastic straws.

"I'm leaving now."

In what seems like ten seconds later, Leo's red Tercel pulls into the parking lot. Thank fuck he's alone. Couldn't deal with questions from Trish right now, all wide concerned eyes and bitten bottom lip. Leo parks the car by the curb and sprints out. She starts rising, but he scoops her up effortlessly and carries her, baby-style, to the car. He lays her softly in the passenger seat. The car smells like pine air freshener and the dashboard is glazed with dust. Leo closes his door and turns to her. "Hospital?"

"No, I'm okay now."

He stares at her blankly. "Really, I'm okay," she says. "It was just a few seconds."

"What happened?"

"I don't know. I walked in and couldn't breathe."

"Fucking grocery stores." Leo shakes his head. "It's too soon for you."

"I thought it would be okay. I was in a Shoppers Drug Mart this week, it was fine."

"All these grocery chains design their stores the same way. This one looks like the other one. Guaranteed to bring it all back."

"Great. I can never take advantage of double Air Miles points again."

"It's to be expected. And I doubt you're the only one."

She gestures to the far side of the parking lot, facing Newtown Road and the blue house. "Can we just park over there for a few minutes? I think they ticket you if you stay in front of the entrance like this."

They park at the edge of the lot. She can see the front door of the blue house. The light flickers in the window, like someone shifted the curtain to look out. She pulls her hood over her ears.

"Are you sure you're okay?" Leo says. "I think I have some water here."

"I'm okay." She notices the CBTG's stamp on the back of his hand. "Have fun last night?"

"It was okay. Some band from Corner Brook," Leo says. "I only had a couple of beer. Ivan got on the rum and cokes though. Trish too. I had to take care of both of them."

She steadies herself from flinching. *Both of them.* Out on a tear with Trish. Good ol' Trish, so much fun. Never says no to things. Maybe they can start their own YouTube channel.

"Yeah," she says, "he was out cold when I left."

"Did you walk here?" Leo asks.

"I needed some fresh air." The door to the blue house opens and the Pomeranian pops out followed by Karl with the leash. Here we go. "Leo, I need you to do something for me."

"What?"

"See that guy?"

"Yeah?"

"I think he's the one who's been emailing me."

"The poodle guy?" Leo squints at him. "How do you know?"

"It's a Pomeranian. Can we follow him, please? I just need to see something."

Leo blinks at her and starts to say something, but stops. He watches Karl make his way down the street. "We'd have to go pretty slow."

"We can just hang back." Karl and the dog cross Newtown Road and continue down Merrymeeting.

"Okay. Wanda Jaynes and the Secret Agents." Leo starts the car. They wait until Karl is almost out of sight to leave the parking lot. By the time they get to the bottom of Merrymeeting, he is heading towards Military Road.

"He said he lived by the park."

"Are you stalking him? This is fucked up."

"I met him a few days ago." She tells him about Karl's *Catcher in the Rye* picture. They follow Karl for five minutes or so, pulling over twice when he crosses the street and when he stops to talk to a man with a golden retriever. Finally, he ducks down Knight Street. When the car reaches the entrance to the street, they catch a glimpse of Karl closing the door of a house at the end.

"So," Leo says, "you meet this guy, he adds you on Facebook and his picture might connect to the email address?"

"And he works at the university, where the emails originated. I know it sounds stupid. I'm just trying to know for sure."

"Almost everyone has read that book. I had to do it in grade twelve. It's in the curriculum."

"I know. But it's all I have right now."

"K." Leo's mouth broods. "Be careful. Just be clear-headed about this, please."

"I am careful. I'm trying to be. I don't even drive right now."

"I think you should talk to somebody. The shooting alone is enough to have to deal with, let alone the media scrutiny. It's like I said to Iv…I think you should take it easy."

So they did discuss the offers last night. What did Ivan have to say? Enough to make him want to get loaded and forget about it for a few hours. "Thanks for understanding," she says.

"It's nothing." Leo smiles with warmth and, in spite of herself, a sprout of goose bumps manifests on her arms.

"Why don't we take you home?" he says. "If Ivan wakes up without his phone, he might go into withdrawal."

The house smells like pizza. Neko Case plays on the stereo.

"Hey, baby." Ivan sprawls on the couch, damp hair, pajama pants, pizza slice on a plate balanced on his chest. In a Google search of "comfortable," he'd be a stock photo. Meanwhile, Wanda's hangovers can render her immobile in bed, all day.

"Good walk?"

"It was alright." The smell of pizza triggers her empty stomach. She hasn't had anything besides orange juice all day. Which probably contributed to the dizziness in the store.

"Was that Leo's car outside?"

"Yes. Here's your phone." She walks to the kitchen. The Eddie's Pizza box is on the counter. She tugs off a slice and finds a plate.

"Who's Karl Prendergast?" he calls. She freezes as she lays the plate in the microwave.

"Huh?"

"You left your Facebook open on his profile. He looks like one of the Addams Family."

What to say. Who is Karl? Is he a stalker? How insane is she for following him around all morning? "I met him a couple of days ago and he added me on Facebook. He seems a bit spooky." She presses the start button and watches the plate rotate inside the microwave. Forty-five seconds. She brings the hot plate to the living room and sits beside him.

She's about halfway through when he takes a deep breath and begins. "So, I was talking to Trish last night about things, you know, these offers and stuff."

Of course you were. She fixates on her slice of pizza. Bite marks like half-moons.

"She has this idea for an art project," he says. "Photographs of real heroes. She's already recruited some local activists to pose. You would be great in it."

Wanda takes a bite. Chewing is soothing to her stomach.

"She has some good ideas," he says. "And it's not like you'd be working with some ambitious journalist who might take any angle."

"Sure," she nods and swallows. "I'd just be helping advance Trish's career. Who isn't ambitious at all."

"Well, yes, it would be helping her. She's your friend."

"Uh-huh."

"And I think it would be good for you, too."

"How is modelling good for me?"

"Art can be very therapeutic."

"If you're making it. It's her photo project, not mine."

"But, by contributing, you're part of the process. I play with other musicians all the time. You get into other people's ideas, you see how they think. It's been really inspiring for me—"

"Can I just eat my goddamn pizza?" She lets the crust drop to the plate in a weak plop. "Jesus Christ, with the sermon."

He stands and hikes up his pajama pants. "Just putting it out there." He strides to the bedroom and shuts the door behind him.

She spends the rest of the day watching reruns in the living room while Ivan naps in the bedroom or putters around, sending a hundred thousand text messages. Neither of them cook supper; they graze on leftovers and snack food. Mrs. Medeiros calls her that evening. Her voice is hot and hushed in Wanda's ear. "Helen and I talked this afternoon about that man. From what she says, I think he is very strange."

"What did she say?"

"Two years ago, he was at a staff Christmas party. It was the library employees and he was invited because he helped set up some computer program for them. There was a young girl there as well, a student, she worked in the archives part-time. Very pretty girl." Mrs. Medeiros pauses to breathe. Ivan is at the computer upstairs. Wanda moves into the kitchen to make sure she's out of earshot.

"Anyway, this young girl drank a lot of wine and got silly. She danced with everyone and kissed this Karl man under the mistletoe. He walked her home after the party. Something might have happened. Helen doesn't know. But the girl wasn't interested in him, you see. The next week when everyone was back at work, he asked her out. She said no. But he didn't stop asking. For three months, he emailed her all the time. Messages, stories, pictures he took. He wrote her poems. She said no again and again and then stopped responding. He kept going, on and on with the messages. Who does that? Who writes over and over when someone has already said no? When they don't say anything back?" Mrs. Medeiros clucks her tongue. "Very strange. And now, you get emails and you don't respond and they keep coming."

"I agree, that is odd." The stairs creak. Wanda looks up. Ivan walks to the front door in his jeans and a fresh shirt. He puts on his jacket.

"Thank you for letting me know," she says. "It's nice to know you care."

"It's my pleasure to help you," Mrs. Medeiros says. "Anything for family."

"I feel the same." She watches the back of Ivan's jean jacket vanish out the door.

13

WANDA takes a deep breath before she clicks the link. Another video clip from Joseph Nigel Workman's show. He struts across the stage before his frothing audience. 50,896 views so far.

Workman makes a sweeping Vanna White-style gesture towards the screen behind him. Four pictures line up. "*Here they are, fellow Workers. The famous atheists. They write slander, they scoff and mock those with faith. They brag about their best-selling books and their number of Twitter followers.*" Booing ensues.

Ivan's voice floats in from behind her: "What are you watching?"

"Mystery emailer sent me a Workman video." She swivels back to see his head in the doorway. "I think whoever is writing me is some kind of religious Internet troll." Ivan cranes his neck to see.

Workman strides with hands on hips. The lapels of his suit buckle out like wings. "*Don't be upset, everyone. Think of other things our society considers cool.*" Images flash on the screen: lines of cocaine, a bowl of multicoloured pills, broken glass bottles, vomiting teenagers, syringes, Ellen DeGeneres, Caitlyn Jenner. "*Shame! Shame!*" from the audience.

"*We know better, don't we people?*" says Workman. The screen flashes and the face of Richard Dawkins appears. "*God delusion? Your confusion, Dawkins.*" A red line slashes through the picture of his face like a no-smoking sign. The audience whoops.

The next photo pops up: comedian Ricky Gervais. "*Praying is hilarious? Your fame is nefarious.*" A red slash and more cheering. Next, Christopher Hitchens. "*Hitchens said 'Jesus Christ is Santa Claus for the adult.' And Hitchens was the misleading minister of the atheist cult.*" Pounding applause, wails of delight.

"*And then, we have our jaded hero.*" The screen flashes and Wanda is confronted with a freeze frame of her own face, taken from the Genevieve Davey interview. They chose a moment when she wears a rather sheepish look: eyes peering up, mouth in a crooked smile.

"Oh, fucking hell," she says.

"*Wanda Jaynes.*" Deep guttural booing. "*Not a word from her since her Canadian interview. Why is that, do you wonder?*" Chaotic cries of random words: "*Liar! Blasphemy! Coward!*"

"*Now, now, now,*" says Workman. "*I want to believe in Wanda Jaynes. I want to believe this silence is contemplation. I want to believe this silence is about coming to recognition. I want to believe that this woman, whom God chose to stop evil, to stop murder, will come to her senses.*" The audience explodes in cheers, stamping of feet. "*Re-cog-nize, Wanda Jaynes, recognize the truth.*"

"Ho-lee fuck," Ivan says. "There are some batshit people in this world."

"I think they're all in that room with him."

"The audience? Half of them are there for the circus. He's the Jerry Springer of religious fanatics."

Wanda swallows and rubs her arm. A patch of dry skin above

her elbow decided to flare up this morning and beg for contact. All day, she's been fighting not to scratch it and now it's become a cluster of fierce red bumps. Perhaps this is what Joseph Nigel Workman does. He inflicts minor skin infections on those who don't respond to his tirades. His vigilant followers pray around the clock for a scourge of psoriasis to descend on the unfaithful.

Ivan examines her elbow. "That looks itchy. I can run out and get you some chamomile lotion if you want."

"It's okay. I just need to leave it alone."

"Well, keep an eye on it." He strokes her shoulder. "Make sure Mom doesn't see this Workman madness when she comes over. I can't handle her fretting right now." His hand drops from her neck and he ambles off to the kitchen.

Sunday dinner with his mom: she almost forgot. At least she and Ivan made up last night and the tension in the house has dissipated. Yesterday, he left without speaking, but returned in brighter spirits. He hugged her, kissed her face. "Come on. We've been spending too much time in this house." She changed her clothes. They decided on The Ship for nachos. Ivan sent a text message for Leo and Trish to meet them.

Trish and Leo were there when they arrived and had claimed the table in the corner by the payphone. Trish scrambled to her feet to hug Wanda. Leo had already bought them pints of Guinness, the rims of foam on the top nicely settled. Leo gave her a wink. No sign he had mentioned their morning tracking session to anyone. They all chatted about who did what at the show last night.

After the nachos were devoured, Ivan and Leo popped outside to smoke a joint. Trish leaned in close to her. "Did Ivan tell you about my idea for the photo shoot?"

Wanda nodded. "Yes, he mentioned it earlier."

"What do you think?"

"I think it's an interesting idea." One which almost put her off her pizza. "I'm sorry, I haven't thought it through yet."

"Oh, God, no pressure. Take your time to think about it, mos def." Trish gave Wanda's hand a quick pat. "And if you don't want to do it, I totally understand."

"Okay."

"And if you do say yes, it's going be so classy. You will look beautiful. No posing, just you in your natural glory. I'm really excited to do the shoot. A portion of the money made from the sales will go to this charity I found. They raise funds for victims of gun violence and their families."

"Really? Huh." Wanda surveyed the room to avoid Trish's beseeching gaze. Two elderly ladies sat at the bar. They sipped white wine from orb-like glasses. One made a low comment in the other's ear and, in response, she threw her head back and belly-laughed, her shock of white hair flashing in the warm light. A thick sliver of guilt rent its way into Wanda's chest. Lots of academics and artsy types hang out at The Ship. Dr. Collier might have been a patron. She might have lay her purple wool coat on the window ledge and ordered a drink. She might have joked with the bartender.

"Well…if money can go to some of the victim's families, I'd be interested," Wanda said. "I think it might help."

Trish clasped her hands over Wanda's. "Oh, I'm so happy! It's going to be great!" She looked up behind her at Leo and Ivan, returning from outside. "Wanda said yes!"

"Did you propose?" Leo said.

"That's great!" Ivan said. "Having Wanda in the show will totally bring in donations."

"Oh, mos def!" Trish said.

"I hope so," Wanda said.

The remainder of the night continued with a celebratory air. They even went dancing afterwards. When they got home after three, she hoped her and Ivan would have sex, fully seal the deal. But he wanted to order another pizza, the Hawaiian this time. And afterwards, they were too full and logy to do anything but sleep.

Wanda looks at the clock. 4:33pm. She forwards the email with the links to Constable Lance. None of the messages have been overly stalker-like since the one about her jacket, so it's doubtful Lance will get right on them. She makes sure to close her email account and the link to Joseph Workman's show, although it's unlikely Mrs. Medeiros will be anywhere near the computer to see it and worry. Ivan is ever vigilant for his mother's triggers.

Being widowed with two young kids must have been traumatic,

but Wanda suspects worrying and the inability to resist expressing is a universal part of parenthood. Her parents are worse, really— Dad's reminders to put the snow tires on in November, Mom forwarding virus warnings, inspecting expiry dates on condiments. Ivan brushes it off as parental love, but for her, their anxiety means her obligation to soothe it. And it can feel so heavy. And it's increasing—Mom and Dad seem to collect worst-case scenarios as they age: *Make sure you leave a light on if you're going away. I read an article about identity theft, they get at you through your social media. I read an article about criminals posing as police, make sure you always ask to see their badge. Do you keep a first-aid kit in your car?* Like she's too naïve to understand danger exists so they circle every hazard with red ink.

Mrs. Medeiros said she wants to make a chorizo bake. Wanda lays out the ingredients she needs: green onions, cornmeal, eggs. Preparing like a good Girl Guide. It all feels like work. She is solidly tired, as if tired could take a concentrated form, like carbon or cubes of chicken stock. She is constructed from a thousand building blocks of tired.

But maybe she's just hungover and feeling negative about the ritual of Sunday dinner, the pressure to have light, yet interesting, conversation. Then bed and an early rise and more of the same during the commute to work. Wanda the strapped-down, but grateful, passenger. Andrea, hot-boxing the car with hooting laughter. And then into the classroom to stand before the glum, burned-out student faces as they compare their results to their expectations. And the faces of her coworkers, people she may never see again when her contract tickers out.

A slight flitter of delight echoes through her at the thought. No more Andrea, no more safe, boring exchanges about families and pets while waiting for the photocopier, drinking sour coffee. No commuting. But that's how things are, they become annoying when a reprieve is in the mail.

She plods through the kitchen, laying out tools, a spatula, a mixing spoon. Meanwhile, in some room, a thousand miles away, Joseph Nigel Workman scapegoats her lack of belief for a hundred hyper-faithful. And somewhere in Halifax, Edward Rumstead is hidden and analysed. Maybe watching TV. Maybe sitting down to a hot, industrial-looking meal.

Ivan opens the door and Mrs. Medeiros trundles in with bags of groceries. Ivan rolls his eyes at Wanda from behind his mother. Here we go, parents and food. Mrs. Medeiros pulls a loaf of bread out of one: "Whole wheat." She passes it to Ivan.

"Thanks, Ma," he says. He tucks it in the freezer where at least two other loaves live.

Mrs. Medeiros's eyes shine at Wanda with eager knowingness. She surveys the ingredients. "Do you have hot peppers?"

"Yes, Ma, we have a jar of them here," Ivan says.

"No, no, I need fresh ones." She scrounges in her purse. "Can you run to the store and get some? In the produce section." She shoves a five-dollar bill in his hand. He opens his mouth to protest, but changes his mind. "Sure." He puts on his jacket and touches the pocket with the pack of smokes.

Mrs. Medeiros turns to her as soon as the door shuts. "Helen sent me some things. You need to see them." She pulls folded papers from her purse. "These are his emails to that girl, the one I told you about." She lays them on the table and flattens them with the bottom of her hand. "She and Helen are friends. For a while, the girl was considering making a complaint about Karl. She sent the emails to Helen to get her advice. But, in the end, she didn't go through with it."

"Did she say why she didn't go for it?"

"Helen said she found the whole thing really embarrassing. And since he didn't come around her, she didn't want to make a big deal."

"Still, you'd think a guy who works at the university would understand cyber harassment."

"I don't want Ivan to see these," Mrs. Medeiros says. "He'll think I'm being nosey. Or he will get angry about this man. He always has such strong reactions."

Yes, it's hereditary. "I understand." Wanda flips through the pages. The emails are plentiful and regular, sometimes three a day. No responses from the girl, amandapb@mun.ca.

"What do you think?"

"His spelling and grammar seem pretty good. Not like the Holden's hat emails."

"But look," Mrs. Medeiros says. "As time passes and she doesn't write back, his writing gets worse." She pulls out some pages at the bottom and jabs her index finger at words. "*Their* instead of *they are.* No apostrophe in *it's.* And here," she yanks out one sheet, "he starts with the poems, good Lord." Karl's poem is entitled "The Math Angel."

At every angle, you're an angel
Every angle absolute
If an angle was this angel
It would definitely be "a-cute."

Wanda snorts and covers her mouth with her hand. Oh my, poor Karl. What happened between him and Amanda? Maybe she woke up with a stinging hangover and a starry-eyed Karl in her bed. Maybe she couldn't remember him. Maybe she gave him her email address so he'd get out of her house and avoid an uncomfortable breakfast. And he didn't take the hint.

The stack of emails look like harassment. He'd argue it wasn't, but unintentional harassment is still harassment. Or would it be, if they didn't directly work together? And Karl doesn't get it. Some people lack the ability to pick up on subtle signals, either low emotional intelligence or poor communication skills—she's talked about it with students. There was Karl's persistent handshake in the pharmacy, the way he didn't notice she wanted him to let go of her hand, the way his eyes slunk to her chest. All her negative nonverbal cues bounced off him. And here's Amanda, she never responds and it takes him months to stop trying. And now, like Mrs. Medeiros says, Wanda doesn't respond to Holden's Hat and the emails keep on keepin' on.

Wanda's phone beeps. A text message from Ivan at the store. "Ivan's on his way back," she says.

Mrs. Medeiros scoops up the papers and taps them into a neat pile. She hands them to Wanda. "Here, put these somewhere, she says. "Compare them to your emails, see what you can see." She grabs a knife from the rack in front of her and attacks the green onions in a flurry of little chops.

It isn't until supper is over and the dishwasher is humming that she remembers. She opens her work email account and rereads the email from a few days ago.

You might not believe in god but you r an angle weather u believe it or not.

It's commonly misspelled; angle/angel gets messed up in autocorrect all the time. And Karl doesn't misspell it. But he thinks about angels and angles. When the counterarguments form in her mind, they take on Constable Lance's voice, his apple cheeks moving up and down as he speaks: *This is not enough to go on. We can't arrest someone based on mild coincidence. You didn't acquire his emails to Miss Amanda Whatsherface with permission.* All she can do is wait and see.

The next day feels like three. During their morning drive, Andrea rattles on and on about a bake sale she participated in where four people donated coconut-covered snowballs: "A list was sent out, why didn't they read it? More than enough snowballs. It was like winter carnival, there were so many snowballs. Ha-ha-ha-Ha! I'm some silly."

While Andrea describes baked goods, the coffee in Wanda's belly summons all its laxative powers and by the time they're in the building, she has to scurry to the nearest staff bathroom which is, unfortunately, the unisex one near the cafeteria. She hates the doorknob with its subtle lock, the kind that has to be pressed and twisted slightly to work. Whenever she uses it, she imagines the door will fly open to the surprised face of some male colleague and a cluster of passing students.

When she hits the flush, the water swirls, but gives up the gusto. She considers telling maintenance, but it all seems too embarrassing, so she ends up using a small plastic garbage pail in the corner of the room to pour water from the sink down the toilet. She removes the black garbage bag, empty except for one wad of gum stuck inside, fills it with water from the tap, and pours it into the toilet. The contents finally disappear. She washes and dries her hands, flushes the toilet with her foot on the lever one more time for good measure. When she opens the door leading to the offices, the doorknob is cold and wet. Sparks of hot aggravation: *dry your wet slimy hands, adult coworkers.*

At the end of her last class before lunch, she spends an extra ten minutes with a student who claims he has all his assignments done, but can't access them because he and his girlfriend are fighting and she won't let him back in the apartment to get his tablet. "And they're all there, Miss, they're all on the hard drive. But she won't let me in and I lost my key."

When Wanda returns to get her lunch, the intense smell of fried chicken throbs out of the staff room and her empty stomach moans in response. She remembers now, the memo on the bulletin board; the union is buying lunch for all staff today. She walks in, smiles in greeting at her coworkers, and takes a paper plate. There are low murmurs: "Uh-oh. Oh jeez, Wanda, are you only getting here now?" Empty boxes stained grey with grease clutter the counters. All that's left are ketchup packets and plastic forks.

"Oh my god, did no one leave any food for Wanda?" Mona says. "We're only supposed to have two pieces each."

"That's it, my dear," Andrea says, "gotta get here early to score any food with this crowd. They're a bunch of gulls."

"Well, I'm definitely filing a grievance," Wanda says. This gets a few cackles. She turns and strolls out, trying to affect an air of nonchalance and not display her hangry annoyance. Keep your fried chicken and permanent jobs. She makes a silent wish for their increasing cholesterol.

On the ride home, Andrea's voice is background static. As they approach the Basilica, Wanda says, "Could you let me out here? I really feel like going for a walk." The idea is immediate, her tongue's decision working independently from her brain.

"Oh. Okay then." Andrea pulls over. "Enjoy your walk, lovely day for it." She smiles wide as Wanda gets out, lips peeled back over gums.

Wanda waves goodbye from the sidewalk. Yes, indeed, a random choice to walk home. And it feels good to be outside, far from work. Her shoes keep a beat on the pavement. She feels more awake than she has in days.

When she reaches Knight Street, her heart wants to heave itself out of her body in protest. *Come on now*, her brain says, *we're here because of Karl. And really, this is just walking home. Checking out a side street which has nothing to do with the route home isn't a big deal.* She tucks her chin and mouth into her collar and turns down his street.

If it wasn't recycling day, the houses would seem abandoned. Curtains drawn, clapboard siding chipped and faded. But a blue bag waits by every house. Wanda holds out her phone like she's reading a text. The house Karl entered is the last one down. She glances around. No sign of anyone, no cars. She reaches his front door. Her heart hammers in her chest. Karl's door is painted a soft yellow, a ripe banana. The rest of the house is bright blue clapboard, robin's egg. Looks like a recent renovation. Her eyes scan the windows. No sounds from inside. Curtains closed. Her eyes drop to the transparent blue bag on the pavement. Empty two-litre bottles: Pepsi, Pineapple Crush. A few cans. Something small and orange: a pill bottle with a label. She picks up the blue bag.

Irate squeals blast from the house. The curtain swishes. She freezes. The animated foxy face of the Pomeranian pops up in the window and berates her with a machine-gun rattle of barks. She bolts to the end of the street and down a path. When she reaches a graffiti-coated wall, she slides to a stop. Where is she? Behind an elementary school. School is out, no one around. Her heart pounds. She takes a deep breath that backfires into coughs.

She squats to examine the bag's contents. Plastic salad containers, more pop bottles. She works open the knot at the top and pushes the pill bottle up from the outside of the bag to avoid touching Karl's recycling. Her hand clasps over the top of it like a claw crane. She shoves the canister deep in her pocket.

The path leads out to King's Road and she takes it up to cross over the intersection and walk home down Monkstown Road. People get their recycling taken all the time, especially with the refund for cans. This economy? Happens all the time.

14

THE studio contains long strips of windows and flattering light. Which is a relief.

"A good day for photos," Trish says. A bright light is suspended above Wanda's head. "I want the suggestion of a grocery store, but it can't be overt, you know?" Trish flits around the space, her hands light on random objects and areas; she straightens a bottle of foundation on the make-up table, she lays a hand on the back of a large lamp. She knows the owner of the cafe downstairs ("Oh, we go way back, I sang at his wedding") and they have use of this loft-style room for the afternoon. Hardwood floors, white walls, high ceilings, and a wall of windows. "I'm so excited for the photos," Trish says. "You will look totally radiant in this room. This light could flatter anyone."

Anyone indeed, no matter how homely. Wanda looks to Ivan, but his eyes are busy taking in the space. "Wow," he says. "I bet the acoustics are amazing."

"Oh, they are," Trish says. "I caught Justin Rutledge's show here. He was splendid." She angles her elbows at her hips and wheels around, to showcase it all. "Anyway, we have an hour before the next portrait shows up." She ruffles the back of her white-blond hair. "I've been in a tizzy all day. I look like carnage."

Wanda eyes her. Trish wears a burgundy shorts-jumper with navy tights and neat black flats. Her cropped locks are perfectly

145

dishevelled. If that's carnage, it was with malice aforethought. In contrast, Wanda feels prim and stilted in her tailored black business suit which hitches in her waist and runs rigid down her legs. Trish said Wanda should "dress sharp, something with clean lines, no patterns." The only thing that seemed fitting was her job-interview suit, but wearing it brings stressful associations. Any second she will have to explain her strengths and weaknesses, why she wants this job. Her hair is freshly straightened, make-up's on thick. Trish brought a pair of cherry-red stilettos and Wanda perches precariously in them. "They'll bring out the lines in the suit and make you look super sexy-powerful," Trish says.

"If I had to walk any distance in these, I would break my face," Wanda says. Nice complaining. What an old fusspot.

"Oh my god, me too," Trish says. "Those shoes aren't for walking. They're Oprah shoes. Remember how you'd never see her walk in her heels? They laid them on the stage and she just stepped into them before the cameras rolled."

Ivan chuckles. Like he ever watched Oprah. "Great idea for the backdrop, Trish. Where did you get all this?"

Trish has constructed a wall of cans of coconut milk, the same brand as the notorious flung can with the green label and the brown coconut husk. "Costco and donations. I have to return most of it." She gazes at her handiwork. "I guess I could have just copied and pasted the images and created a paper backdrop, but it wouldn't have the texture, you know? Plus, I like the Warhol allusion it creates."

Mass shooting as pop art. Wanda imagines the cans crashing down, domino style. A red stiletto flung across the studio, impaling in something.

"Anyhoo," Trish says, "I think it will look beautiful. And if you don't like it, it won't get used. You have the last word." She fiddles with the tripod. Fine, let's do it.

At first, it's hard to relax and compose her face, but soon, Wanda finds herself letting go. Trish plays music in the background, all stuff she likes. Ivan makes a few jokes. They both gush compliments: "Oh, that's nice. Great smile. You're a natural." Trish gives lots of suggestions: "Gaze out the window. Turn slowly. Don't smile until you face the camera." Twice, she pauses to show Wanda the photos and even though it's hard to tell in the small digital image, they do look good, the black suit and red shoes sharp against the cans.

Afterwards, they decide to grab a coffee downstairs. The cafe is busy and the crowd is mostly young people: college students with black-rimmed glasses and various forms of facial hair. The tables and chairs are a mish-mash of funky unmatched furniture. The barista is doe-eyed and cartoonish with fake eyelashes and heavy bangs, her lips a red bow. Wanda orders a cappuccino. "What kind of milk do you want in that, two percent, one percent, skim, soy?"

"Two percent is fine."

The barista stares at her. The red ribbon of her mouth parts slightly as recognition sets in, but she says nothing. She turns to Ivan and Trish and her big eyes sparkle. "Hey, you two. What will it be?"

"What do you think?" Trish says to Ivan.

"I've had enough coffee today," Ivan says, pondering the menu board. "A chai latte, I think."

Trish stares intently at the coffee menu on the wall above, blinking with deliberation. "That sounds good. I'll have one of those too," she says.

A tall, lanky guy in a baker's smock passes behind them. He punches Ivan in the shoulder. "Hey man. Hey missus," he nods to Trish. "We'll have those chocolate scones tomorrow."

"Oh, I'm definitely gettin' some of that!" Trish says. The guy grins down at her and saunters away.

"You guys come here often?" Wanda says.

Trish looks at Ivan and shrugs. "Two or three times a week probably."

"Huh." Must be nice. Wanda looks to Ivan. He thumbs through his phone, eyebrows slightly raised. She turns from him and stares straight ahead. The barista clangs metal taps and gadgets. Wanda works her right hand into her left sleeve and digs her nails into the rough bumps above her elbow. The more she scratches it, the better it feels. When she removes her hand, her nails are ridged with scabs and a little blood.

Trish pulls out her own phone as soon as they sit down. "Lydia just texted me. I don't have much time."

"When do you think the photos will be ready?" Ivan asks.

"Oh, pretty soon. There's already buzz about the show."

Wanda stares into her drink. The barista placed the foam on top artfully, in a little leaf pattern. She raises her mug to her mouth and her napkin flutters to the floor. When she ducks down to pick it up, she glances below the rim of the table. Trish's knee in her navy-blue tights presses into Ivan's. Trish's knee jerks away.

At home, Wanda yanks her coat off and flings it towards a hook by the door. It lands on the floor. It can stay there. Ivan comes in behind her. He plunks his keys in the dish by the door. "We both work and live downtown. What, you thought I never got coffee with Trish?"

"I guess because you've never mentioned that you have coffee with Trish every day, no." She stayed silent through the journey home, until stomping up the path and hissing at him: "*You and your shitty little secrets.*"

"What's to mention? It's coffee."

"It's not coffee. We have goddamn coffee here at home. You're not hanging out with each other to refuel on caffeine."

"Jesus Christ. Trish is my friend. I've been friends with her since before you and I met."

"Yes, and you've been having regular coffees with her since forever, and I'm only finding out about it now."

"Holy fucking shit." Ivan stares at her. "We have coffee and talk. What do you think, she blows me under the table?"

"For all I know, it's another detail you've failed to mention."

"You're…I can't talk to you when you're like this." Ivan zips his coat up. "Take some time to calm down." He walks towards the door.

"Are you serious? You're just going to leave?"

"I'm not having a discussion with you when you're being irrational."

"You sit and talk with another woman every day and never, ever mention it." The frustration is so fierce, she might start panting. "I ask you how your day is, you say fine. I ask you what you did. You say 'not much.' Never a word. Never a word about her."

"There's nothing to say!"

"Bullshit! If it's nothing, you'd mention it. 'Oh, you know, same old same old. Did some work, Trish and I got our special French-press coffee and we shared secrets.'" Wanda stares at him, arms folded, fingertips clawing the spot over her elbow. "Does Leo know you two hang out all the time?"

"Probably. Or maybe not. Because he wouldn't give a fuck. Because he *trusts* us." Ivan shakes his head. He zips up his jacket to his chin.

"No, *I'm* leaving." She passes him, grabs her coat from the floor. "You don't get to run away." She throws it on and leaves with a slam. Her black dress pants swish together as she stamps up the path to the sidewalk. She almost knocks over Pascale Aggressive who carries large brown paper bags in her arms. Pascale hops out of the way like a startled cat. Look out for Wanda, she might lay you out with a can or fly into a jealous rage.

After the photo shoot, she replaced the red stilettos with her regular, chunky-heeled black shoes, but they'll prove uncomfortable soon. And she wants to walk a long time, wants to run, pump her arms, speed past everything. She should have grabbed her sneakers on the way out. She reaches into her sleeve to scratch and the flesh stings and she jerks her hand out. Her fingertips are red with her own blood. She searches her pocket for a tissue and finds something plastic and conical. The pill bottle. She placed it in her pocket yesterday with plans to look up the medication. She pulls it out. Karl V. Prendergast. Zyprexa. Take 10mg/day. Rather stunned of him not to remove the label before chucking it out.

Her elbow throbs. It's about a ten-minute walk to Churchill Square. She could get some band aids and lotion at the drug store. She could wander around the aisles to consume time and sort out her thoughts.

Why doesn't he understand? Ivan and Trish, sipping their coffee in their element, surrounded by hipster chic. People seeing them, people remembering them: *Hey, you two*. Trish and Ivan, down at the coffee shop. Trish and Ivan, hanging out at a gig.

Wanda used to go to his shows in the early times, before they were official, when they were still being aloof. He'd invite her to where he was playing, usually somewhere dim with cheap cover at the door and graffiti in the bathrooms. Places where no one got carded and teenagers frolicked in front of the stage in black boots and too much eyeliner. Sharon and Nikki came with her those first times and she felt powerful beside them on the walk to the bar. Nikki made sure they timed it so they showed up in the middle of the set: "Don't be eager. These musicians get laid too easily. It goes to their heads."

They'd arrive at the show while the band was playing. Ivan up front on stage, but she'd resist looking right at him. She'd make sure he saw her get a drink at the bar. She'd take small, insouciant sips and pretend to be enthralled with whoever she was speaking to. When she finally let her eyes meet his, usually during the chorus, he would smile right into her from under his valance of black curls. And then her heart was a helium balloon quivering against the ceiling. And she'd smile back and when there was a break between sets, he'd keep his arm around her waist and slide his hand up the back of her shirt. His fingertips stroking her spine, playing a song about the promise of later.

And now, him and Trish, in their special spot, being cool. Trish and her wandering touch. How many times have her hands stroked his hair, his legs. She thinks of Ivan's legs, lean and toned, the way his legs feel on her legs. It's been weeks now. And he hasn't made her laugh in so long. Why does Trish deserve it? Petulant fury escapes in a hot sob. She rubs her face with her cuff.

In the Churchill Square plaza, she first goes into the washroom to check herself. The blood from her fingertips has left a smear on the side of her nose. Her hair, made neat and straight for the photo shoot, is now windblown and rumpled. As she washes her hands, her eyes land on a handwritten sign taped above the sink. "Careful Hot Water." She stares at it until someone enters and the squeal of the door breaks her trance.

She meanders around the drug store. A middle-aged couple nudge each other as they pass by in the Skin Care aisle. Whispers like cobwebs on the back of her neck. She tosses two kinds of soothing oatmeal-based lotions into her shopping basket. In a corner of the store is a small kiosk, "Your Medication Information Station." The screen says to enter the name of the medication and a handy information table will be produced. There is also a downloadable app.

Wanda peeks at the canister label to check the spelling. She types "Zyprexa."

Zyprexa (olanzapine) is an antipsychotic medication used to treat the symptoms of psychotic conditions such as schizophrenia and bipolar disorder (manic depression) in adults and children who are at least 13 years old.

Side effects may include weight gain, high cholesterol, high blood sugar, slow reaction time, and some dizziness. Alcohol should be avoided when taking Zyprexa.

Whenever she comes across the word "schizophrenia" she thinks of that old black-and-white movie her mother rented, where the main character had multiple-personality disorder. What was it? *The Three Faces of Eve*. It's an unfair association, but it's where her mind goes. One of those broad-reaching disorders encompassing all kinds of misery. And bipolar disorder—she had a bipolar student last year. He told her about how the serotonin in his brain peaks and burns out. He was doing well, then stopped showing up, then reappeared with a doctor's note and apologies. "I just can't get the right meds, Miss." She gave him an extension on his assignments.

So Karl takes Zyprexa. Mental illness on top of his myopic eyes and speech impediment, sitting alone in his house, drinking pop, writing desperate emails to a young librarian who never responds. Like Holdenshat@mail.com , maybe he lives in his own little world. Wanda touches the X icon and closes the window. She squints as her eyes adjust from the dark screen to the astringent light of the store.

Her phone dings. A new text message from Ivan. He can wait. She strolls through every aisle. In the magazine section, she reads headlines and judges celebrity hairstyles. New Spring Fashions! Summer Skin! The front page of *The Telegram* shows a photo of an elderly woman getting out of a police car. The headline reads "Mother of a Maniac: Grocery Store Killer's Mother Harassed." Wanda leans in to grab the paper so quickly she forgets the shopping basket in her hand. It bounces off the shelf, barking her shin.

At the checkout, the cashier scans the lotions and the newspaper. Her eyes travel to Wanda's face and hesitate, hazel eyes with deep eyelids full of sudden knowledge. Wanda jerks her fingers through her dishevelled hair and tries not to snatch the receipt. "Thank you," she says to the cashier.

"Oh no," the cashier says, "thank you." Have a dollop of extra warmth. Wanda nods and exits the store.

She crosses to the Tim Horton's next door. It's quiet, she can sit and go over the article. She buys a coffee and a blueberry muffin, cracks off a top section and chews it as she reads.

> *The Royal Newfoundland Constabulary was called to the home of Frances Rumstead on Monday evening to investigate an act of vandalism. Cans of food were thrown at Mrs. Rumstead's house, breaking two large windows.*

> *According to the RNC, the cans were wrapped in paper and contained threatening messages and insults. Mrs. Rumstead told* The Telegram *she has also received harassing phone calls: "I am scared to go out alone. If this continues, I will have to move. My heart is broken about what Eddie did. He always had problems. I did the best I could."*

> *Edward Rumstead is currently in custody. His defense states he is pleading not guilty on basis of insanity/mental illness.*

Cans of food. They made a plan, they were symbolic about it. She stares at the picture of Frances Rumstead. She has short, dark curly hair and a stricken expression. Her face turns towards the camera, her eyes black and lost. Edward has his mother's eyes. Wanda sees those eyes seeing her, haunted but decisive.

Her mouth and throat are suddenly dry. A morsel of blueberry muffin sticks to the top of her palate. Her stomach lurches and she covers her mouth with a napkin and spits out the muffin bite. Did anyone see that? A couple of teenage girls perch at a table by the window. They text and show each other the little screens on their phones. Both have long hair with the tips dyed in jewel tones. Behind the counter, a plump woman in a hairnet and too much blue eyeliner moves coffee pots onto burners. Everyone in their own little worlds, consumed with their immediate realities, attention sunk into their devices, into their many little tasks. None of them are aware of her. Less than a month since the shooting and Wanda, too, stays in her own little world, filtering what comes in and out. People know her name, know what she did. She will be linked to Edward forever, her and Frances. Wanda takes a swig of her coffee. It leaves a dull queasiness in her belly.

There's free Wi-Fi in the cafe. She brings up Google on her phone and types in "Edward Rumstead." Just seeing his name is an internal nudge, like a prodding knee under a table. Just fucking take a look already. She touches the search icon.

The results are massive. Her eyes flicker through the list and land on a link that includes Frances's name: "Killer's Mother Discusses Disturbed Son."

Frances Rumstead describes her son as a simple soul, plagued throughout his life by academic struggles and health problems. His father died when he was an infant, and as an only child, he was shy and preferred to play by himself. In childhood, he scored 75 on an IQ test. He missed a lot of school due to severe allergies and asthma. He was held back twice and continued to have trouble maintaining his grades.

At fifteen, Edward dropped out of school and took a job cleaning warehouses at night. He lived at home, although Frances states it didn't feel like a permanent situation back then. In his mid-twenties, he developed severe sleep apnea and had difficulty sleeping for more than thirty minutes at a time. His mother says at this time, he was unable to work and became more reclusive. He lived at home with her, assisting with small chores around the house and retreating into his room for hours at a time, watching TV and searching the Internet. His main responsibility was the weekly grocery run. We interviewed the visibly distraught Mrs. Rumstead and she described a prior incident with her son and the grocery store:

"Eddie loved getting the flyers every week. He would go over the specials to see what we needed in the house. That was his job, ever since he was in high school. He loves a bargain. He'll walk all over town to get a deal: go to Pipers for eggs, Coleman's for potatoes. Always a help to me. We never had much money and he was proud to be able to save me some."

"A month or so ago, there was a mistake in the Dominion flyer. When he didn't get the price he expected, he got upset. The cashier got scared. She called security. That night, the store manager called me and said they didn't call the police, but Eddie wasn't allowed in the store anymore. Eddie was very upset about that. He didn't speak for days."

According to Chris Channing, the manager on duty at the time, there were signs posted around the store's entrance, correcting the flyer error, but Edward Rumstead did not see them. When the cashier tried to explain, Edward Rumstead became so irate, he had to be forcibly removed from the store.

All of the guns found on Edward Rumstead were originally from the collection of his father, the late Benjamin Rumstead, who died of a heart attack when Edward was a few months old. The collection remained in the house for years, registered to Frances Rumstead. Edward Rumstead is currently in custody where he is undergoing psychiatric evaluations. When arrested, he was carrying a backpack containing extra weapons and ammunition. It is still unknown whether he intended to commit suicide, as has been a pattern with other mass shooters.

No diagnosis, no autism or mental illness. Or at least no evidence he was ever tested. How many people fall through the cracks like that, still? At least Karl has prescriptions. She should look up current statistics.

The bottom of the article contains the usual ferocious rash of comments:

Does this woman expect people to feel sorry for her son? Sad excuses from a terrible mother.

Another sad soul falls through the cracks of the system, God help us all.

Oh yes, sounds like they're both simple souls to me—pure stupid and evil.

One more murderer for the taxpayer to support.

This is another example of how undiagnosed mental health

issues are rampant in this country.

Get this pathetic woman some help and bring back the death penalty for her wack son.

People, don't have guns in your houses! It shouldn't be this easy for nutbars to get weapons.

Crazy breeds crazy.

"Hullo there."

Wanda starts. A woman stands beside her, red bucket hat crammed on head, fringe of grey hair underneath.

"You look lost in thought," the woman says. She slurps from her takeaway coffee cup. Familiar face. Who is she? She was at the vigil, her name was a place in the States. Dakota. No, Dallas.

"Dallas Cleal," Wanda says.

"Good memory on ya," Dallas says. "Good mind and good arm." She licks her lips. "I saw the video the next day and I said, sure, I was talking to her. If I'd known what you did, I would have bought you dinner." She looks at Wanda's partly eaten muffin. "Too late to even get you a snack now."

"Oh, there's no need of that," Wanda says.

Dallas blows into her cup to cool her drink. "How have you been holding up?" she says. Her eyes were swollen when they met and they are still small, like black pearls. She squints tightly at Wanda, scrutinizing. Maybe she needs glasses. Or it's an assertive manner she's developed. Dallas reminds Wanda of a teacher from grade eight, the woman could hear whispered conversations from the back of the room while she was at the chalkboard: "*You two can wait 'til class is over to talk about the weekend.*" She said it wasn't because she had sharp ears; it was that they had ruined their hearing with walkmans and ghettoblasters: "*You children have no concept of how loud you are.*" Which was probably true.

"Okay, I guess."

"Look at this unfortunate creature," Dallas says. She points to the newspaper's photo of Frances Rumstead.

"Yes. It's sad. And people are targeting her."

"Everyone loves a scapegoat." Dallas shakes her head. "And now, she'll never be free."

"Well, he'll be in prison his whole life, I'd say. Or institutions."

"Will he? And technically, he was already a life sentence for her," Dallas says. "Can you imagine? He never left home. No job, no social connections, no romance." She sips her drink and grimaces. "If he was dead, if he had done all he was going to do and killed himself, or if he had been brought down by a cop, his mother would be free. Now, you see, she has to deal with him and the tragedy he caused."

Wanda nods. What else to do while this woman gets to her point?

"But, you know, after the trial, he'll be gone," Dallas says. "She could leave, start fresh somewhere else. Reclaim her maiden name. I did that, before I started teaching at the university. What a feeling." Her small eyes shine at the memory. "Because she'll always be *the mother*. She'll be forever told she didn't do her job right." She jerks her head, like she forgot she was there. "Listen to me ramble. I do that sometimes. I try to dig myself into the shoes of other people." She clamps a hand on Wanda's shoulder. "You take care of yourself. All this hoopla. Don't let it get to you."

"Thank you."

"And avoid those religious fanatics. Anyone who thinks they have all the answers is dangerous." Dallas wrinkles her nose. "I've been in an ongoing Twitter racket with Geraldine Harvey for ages now. It's too much fun. Hope she doesn't block me." She walks away, tipping her cup into her mouth.

The phone in Wanda's hand vibrates. Two text messages from Ivan now:

> Where are you?! You're making me worry. Not cool.

> I'm sorry, ok? I shouldn't have got mad just coz you were mad. Please tell me where you are. We can talk it out.

She takes a deep breath and all her aches tingle in response, her stinging elbow, the bruise forming on her shin, her toes pinched in her clunky shoes. It's an apology. It's a start. She allows herself to feel mollified and takes a big bite of the blueberry muffin. The top is satisfyingly crunchy and she finds herself appreciating the damage she has done to the dome shape. Take that, muffin. She presses reply:

> Churchill Square Plaza. Pick me up?

She presses send. A moment later his response appears: "OMW." She cracks off another piece of blueberry muffin and chews.

15

IVAN's fingers run the edge of the kitchen table and pause to circle a knot in the wood. "I'm sorry."

"What are you sorry for?" Wanda folds her arms from across the table. She still wears her black interview suit, like a scolding bank executive.

"I'm sorry you didn't know I had coffee with Trish that often. I guess I thought you knew." His fingers continue to etch the knot. "If I found out you were always hanging out with someone and you never mentioned it, it would throw me for a loop as well."

"So, you understand how I got upset."

"Yes. But you know, it's just Trish. It's just all of us." His eyes flicker up to hers. "I guess I don't draw boundaries. I think of us all as close." He brings his hands together and interlocks his fingers. "A solid mass. You, me, Leo, Trish, we're a family." He shakes his intertwined hands, like he's about to roll dice.

"But you can't assume everyone feels the same way."

"I can assume mutual trust though, can't I?"

She sighs. Can they stop talking now? The relief of his apology has sunk in and she is heavy with it. She reaches across the table and covers his joined hands with her own. "It's also because you've known her for so long. You have all these memories together. I want more of my—of our own, I guess."

"Memories? We live together. We make daily memories. We

have this whole life."

"Yeah, but I'm boring common-law wife. My novelty is gone."

He furrows his brow at her. The same expression he uses when he programs the remote control. She lets go of his hands and moves to his side of the table. "Get up."

He stands. She runs her palms up his shoulders and rests her cheek against his neck, presses her lips against the space where his jaw meets his earlobe. She kisses under his ear and down his neck. He runs his hands lightly down her back, dusting his fingertips along her spine. She presses her hips against his and brings one arm down from his shoulder, tucks it around his waist. She pulls his hips closer to hers. He cranes his neck while she continues to kiss it, still stroking her spine, letting her hands run over him.

His hand under her blazer. He tugs her blouse up a few inches for entry. His fingers jumble around the back of her bra. "It opens in the front," she says into his ear.

"Well, then," he says, "let's turn this thing around."

Her skin sings in relief once free of the suit. She undoes his belt and he unhooks her bra. They are adept with each other's contraptions. He holds her close, but she needs to see him. She looks into his face as her fingers smooth over his cock. He closes his eyes and exhales. He cups her breast, his fingers are cold on her nipple, but she leans into them. They fall into their steps: he likes to be sucked before he goes down on her; she likes it when he removes her underwear himself. They make the circles and strokes the other knows and likes.

She comes first, but he finishes about a minute later. She is on top and keeps riding him until he's done, his hips thrusting up to her, his eyes squeezed together. She stares at his face, his clenched teeth and crinkled eyelids.

Afterwards, they lie naked, side by side. Wanda lays her fingers on his wrist and leans over to rest her cheek on his bare shoulder. "Almost simultaneous," she says.

"Yes," Ivan says. "Good at closing, we are."

He kisses her on the forehead. "I think we need a snack." He bounces out of bed. "Stay there." He walks out of the room, wearing only his socks.

Wanda gazes at the ceiling. In the dim light, it looks blank and flawless, a clean sheet of paper. Her hand skims along her arm to the itchy scabs over her elbow, but she stops herself. Let it heal. She props herself up and inspects the afternoon's damage. A toonie-sized bruise, eggplant colour, has formed where she smacked her shin with the shopping basket. A bubble of a blister ridges the inside tip of her big toe, another small one on the back of her heel. She checks her hands. The fingernails on her right hand are dingy with leftover blood from scratching her arm. Blueberry muffin crumbs too. She has to take better care of herself. She'll go back to running. She'll update her résumé, put out some feelers for jobs. Maybe she should take a short drive this weekend to test her anxiety level. Ivan can come with her.

Ivan returns to the bedroom with a tray. Two glasses of red wine, a plate with slices of cheese: gouda and old cheddar. A small glass bowl of Kalamata olives. She sits up and accepts her glass of wine. Ivan pops an olive in his mouth.

"Thank you for the bed-picnic."

"You're very welcome."

"We should go for a real outdoors picnic this weekend. Maybe out to Clarke's Beach."

"Well, we might not have time, with my niece's thing," he says. He raises his eyebrows at her blank expression. "Forgot about that, did you?"

"Jesus. I did." This Monday is a stat holiday. May has blurred by. Ivan's sister Sylvie has planned a barbeque and a belated birthday party for her daughter, Fiona. The party was supposed to happen three weeks ago, but she postponed it because of the shooting. Now it's merged with the Medeiros's family barbeque which always happens on the May 24th weekend. Every year, they drive out to Topsail and spend the day at Ivan's childhood home. Mrs. Medeiros cooks her face off for relatives and family friends.

"I mean, we'll go if you want to," Ivan says. "If you don't feel up to it, we don't have to go."

"No, no, it will be good," she says. "I just forgot. It'll be a laugh." Ivan munches another olive. They finish the food and the rest of the wine while watching TV, they order Chinese food for supper. That night, she falls asleep feeling comfortably full and tipsy.

The next morning, Andrea rapid-fire beeps her horn to the "shave and a haircut" rhythm. Wanda scrambles up the pathway and into the Rav4. She senses the curtains in Pascale's front window shift as they pull out onto the road. Perhaps she's composing a note of complaint already: "*I was disturbed this morning by YOUR driver blaring their horn to get YOU. Perhaps YOU could tell them not to do that or be on time for YOUR ride.*" Wanda puts on her sunglasses. The morning sunlight pings off some spot in her frontal lobe where the wine kicked extra hard.

"How are we doing this morning?" Andrea says. "You look like you had a good night last night."

"Oh, I'm fine." Wouldn't it be lovely to have a silent ride? Some cab company offers that in their cars, it's printed on placards: *You are entitled to a silent ride.* Must take the car out this week. After work even.

"I hear you're going to be a model."

"Hmm?" Wanda peers at her. Andrea has broken out her summer wardrobe. She wears a mint windbreaker and white cotton capris with several million wrinkles in them. Like a tube of toothpaste that's been squeezed too hard.

"Oh, the word is out, my dear. Boyd follows your friend, what's her name, Tessa? On the Twitter. She's an artist type."

"Trish?"

"Yes, that's her. She was tweeting about a photo shoot with you in it." Andrea turns away from the road to give her an ample-toothed grin. "You're some famous."

Wanda fishes out her phone to check Trish's Twitter. There are several tweets discussing yesterday's photo shoot.

Trish Samson @trixiethepixie: So blessed 2 be surrounded by courage & beauty all day! @lydiasimms & @JJWoods. Photos r gorge! #localheroes #WandaJaynesNLhero

Trish Samson @trixiethepixie: Can't wait 2 start picking the choice photos! Will be a challenge. #localheroes #beauty #bravery #WandaJaynesNLhero

She knows Trish is trying to build momentum, but is it good form to brag about a project before it's done? What if it's total shit?

She scrolls through several more tweets written in the same vein, many retweeted and liked by others.

> Trish Samson @trixiethepixie: @Pikeitalot I think that's a great idea! PM me.

She taps Pikeitalot's profile to see his side of the interaction.

> Pikeitalot @DarrylPike: @trixiethepixie Great project sista! U should set them up @ my show in June.

Retweeted fifteen times. #heros #hergoddamnnameinahashtag. Darryl Pike and his self-promoting "hip-hop" festival thing. How absolutely tacky. Wanda turns off her phone and shoves it deep in her coat pocket.

"So what are the photos like?" Andrea says. "Gonna be any nude ones?"

"Only from the waist down," Wanda says. She stares out the window while Andrea whoops with laughter.

When Wanda refreshes her computer on her prep period, there's a new email from Holden's Hat.

> To: JaynesWanda@nlil.ca
> From: Holdenshat@mail.com
> Subject: pictures
>
> I hope if anyone takes photos of u, they show your inner beauty and not some magazine girl image. There is too much of that in the world, of people making others see others in only one way. U r better then that

How does Holden's Hat know to follow Trish's account? Through the hashtags? But that would be a lot of tweets to survey. Would that come up in a Google search on her name? Wanda forwards it to Constable Lance's email address. No reply from him on the last three messages. C'mon Officer, sort this stuff out.

She checks Karl's Facebook profile. About an hour ago, he joined an event: *Karl Prendergast is going to St. John's Festival of Healing.* Wanda clicks on the link.

> *St. John's Festival of Healing: An Outdoor Festival of Music and Art*
>
> *Event created by Pikeitalot (Darryl Pike)*

June 11th, 12:00 PM, to June 12th, 1:00 AM.

A day and night of music, dancing, art, games, food and drink, community spirit and merriment! Proceeds will go to The Newfoundland Coalition against Violence and to the families who lost loved ones in The Grocery Store Shooting.

Musical performances by Pikeitalot and DJ Spikeitall, Deep Turtle, and Case and the Tickets. Other bands TBA.

Healfest is excited to host the opening of the latest photo exhibit of local artist/musician Patricia Samson entitled Heroes in their Element.

Daytime activities include games of chance, crafts, and lots of food! Beer tent opens at 4:00 PM.

Healfest? Sounds like an advanced form of athlete's foot. A festering little blister on her heel. She checks the "Going" list. The event was posted this morning and over 200 people have added it already. Trish hasn't wasted any time signing on. She did say that Wanda would have final say on her image. So, if Trish isn't stupid, she hasn't made any promises to Darryl Pike that the woman in his video will be there in art form.

Wanda continues to scroll down Karl's profile page. No new status updates or pictures, but he subscribes to pages that keep track of what he's read and post for him.

Karl Prendergast read an article on NPR: Joseph Nigel Goodman, Evangelist or Hatemonger?

Karl Prendergast read an article on The Weekly News: Modern Mass Shootings, How Real is the Fear?

Karl Prendergast watched a video: Interview with Frances Rumstead: Being a Murderer's Mom

She clicks on the video and plugs her ear buds into her computer. Genevieve Davey stands in a parking lot with the Dominion store behind her. The parking lot is empty, the store's windows darkened. Genvieve's gleaming hair ruffles in the breeze, she wears a fitted moss-green jacket belted at the waist, a scarf tucked in the collar, burgundy and gold tones. Wanda wants all her clothes.

"On April 27th, Edward Rumstead opened fire in a grocery store, shooting four times, killing three people before he was stopped by Wanda Jaynes. What do we know of this man? What possessed him to commit such a heinous act? We spoke with Frances Rumstead, Edward Rumstead's mother, in hopes of shedding light on what the shooter was really like."

The next shot scans across a living room: dark wood paneling, a small shelving unit covered in ceramic miniatures. The camera zooms in on them: little cows, a teddy bear, an angel. A boxy grey sofa rests against the wall. Frances Rumstead sits with her hands folded. She wears a prim white blouse with a lace-rimmed collar buttoned to the neck. Something Trish would wear ironically, but on Frances, it reflects some desired sense of propriety, of what she believes "classic" looks like.

Frances speaks with a crackling fry, the echo of roll-your-own smokes and chronic hardship. *"He was always a good boy. He tried hard. He never got to understanding how to be good at school."* She picks up a framed photo. The close-up shows Edward Rumstead as a gawky young boy with a cowlick and braces. *"He was very shy growing up, didn't make friends easily. A couple of times, he came home with bruises. Nowadays, you'd say he was bullied and ya might do something, but he just took to stayin' away from other kids."*

Frances's lips button at the thought. Her flesh is ashy, her eyes lost in age like grease stains in paper bags. She looks like she's been old for a long time. Maybe she has a vitamin deficiency. Or maybe this is what happens when you have to raise a psychopath.

"Did you ever think he might do something violent?" The camera stays on France's face to get her reaction.

"No, I never thought that. I knew he wasn't happy. He would have liked a different life. But you do all you can, you know." Her voice shivers, a dry branch in the wind. *"You never think your son could do that."*

"How did he get the guns?"

"Those guns were his father's. They were in the basement for years. I never thought about them, honestly." Frances's gaze returns to the pictures beside her. *"Everyone had guns in their houses when I was*

growin' up. You never thought nothin' of it."

The camera returns to Genevieve, now walking slowly down the sidewalk outside the store. *"A quiet man who struggled and kept to himself. A description clichéd today when we learn of men who have committed similar, violent acts. As Edward Rumstead awaits trial where he will plead not criminally responsible on account of a mental disorder, his mother wishes for a quiet life. Frances has become a victim of violence herself, through the backlash against her son."*

The scene returns to Frances on the couch. *"Broken windows. Nasty calls all the time, I had to change the phone,"* she says. She wets her lips. *"It gets so you're frightened to go out."* She draws her hand over her eyes, her fingers unmoving in a twisted, arthritic claw.

"You're scared all the time, now?"

"Yes. All the time. I'm sad or I'm scared. There's no in the middle anymore."

Genevieve's voice flows out as the video shows Frances slowly stacking the picture frames up beside her. *"For Frances Rumstead, the journey may just be beginning as she awaits her son's trial. For CBC News, I'm Genevieve Davey."*

Wanda sinks in her office chair. Perhaps she should take a stroll to clear her head. Behind her door, Andrea's laugh rings hard in the hallway. Perhaps she should stay in her office with the door closed.

Alright. Get on with it. She needs to settle down and finish some marking. Just do it. There is a stack of assignments to be graded and more projects to come. After the long weekend, there will be three weeks of school left. She gets a little tingle thinking about it. Free. September may bring poverty, but free for now. She moves one stack of assignments to the far side of her desk. Two colourful pieces of paper fall onto the floor and stare up at her.

One she recognizes as a Workers for Modern Christianity brochure. The logo uses gold letters framed by cartoonish rays of sunlight: *The Good News for You!* Below the logo is a photo of a woman with a despondent expression, staring out a window with her chin on her hand. *"Have you lost your faith? Advice for rediscovering the joy of God's word in your life."* Wanda scoops it up and examines it. No note or signature.

The other is a colour printout. One of her Internet memes, the shot of her right before she throws the can. Whoever printed this out has added their own words to the image: I DON'T ALWAYS BRING DOWN MASS MURDERERS, BUT I WHEN I DO, I RELAX BY GIVING MY STUDENTS A BREAK ON THEIR ESSAYS. No signature or note. A joke. It's meant to be cute, like drawing a little cartoon on the bottom of a test. She tells herself this as the paper shakes in her hands. She wads it up and flings it towards the garbage can. It pings off the rim and rolls back towards her.

A tap on her office door. Her office is small enough, she can wheel her chair over a few inches and open the door. One of the ABE students, Evan McKinnley, peers in wide-eyed. Last week he was having issues with obtaining his assignments from his angry girlfriend.

"Yes? You can come in, Evan." She opens the door wide and wheels back. He takes a short step inside.

"Miss? Did you get my assignment? I left it in your mailbox." His fingers play with the cord on his brown hoodie.

Wanda flips through the stack of papers. "Here it is." She plucks it out and waves it at him.

"Ok, good. I wanted to make sure you got it." He scratches the back of his neck with twitchy fingers. "Are you going to take marks off for lateness? Cause I had it finished, I just wasn't able to get at it."

"According to the course requirements, I take off ten percent for every day late up to three days. Then it's a zero," she says. Evan's face starts to turn pink. "But seeing as things may have been out of your control, I'll reconsider," she says. His shoulders sink with relief.

"Oh, thank you so much, Miss. You're the best."

"That's okay, Evan."

"And Miss? Check it out." Evan unzips his hoodie and holds it open. Underneath he wears a grey t-shirt. Printed on his chest is a round-headed figure in blue and black, holding a green blob. It's her in the grocery store once again, the Internet meme from the video, the same one she just threw in the garbage. White capital letters above the picture: WHEN FEAR SAYS YOU CAN'T. And on the bottom: YOU "CAN."

"What do ya think? Pretty deadly, wha?"

Wanda glances up at Evan's beaming, expectant face and down

to the image again. "That's something all right." Her teeth gnaw the inside of her cheek as she scans her mind for some kind of calm reproach.

"My buddy made it." He zips up his hoodie. "I'd better go. Thanks a lot for your help, Miss."

"No problem," she says. Evan trots away with inflated steps. Wanda shuts her office door. She lays Evan's paper on her desk and selects a red pen from the mug by the monitor. She bites the top off and writes on his paper with a flourish: "Late paper. No excuse. 0%."

16

WANDA holds the cupcake tray steady on her lap as Ivan jolts over another speedbump.

"They'll get squished against each other."

The car jumps again. A pothole this time.

"What odds?" He grins. "She only eats the tops. She's an icing junkie."

"Fine uncle you are." She runs her hand over the top of the container as if to soothe it. Last night was spent decorating each cupcake, squeezing pale-pink buttercream through the star tip of the icing bag, making thick, gooey swirls. Afterwards, she peppered them with silver ball sprinkles. "When I was a kid," she said to Ivan, "I would hold these against my teeth and pretend they were fillings." "And as a result, you needed fillings," he said.

He flicks through the radio stations: "Fiona won't care if they're a bit squishy. She'll be too busy being a hyperactive banshee."

Wanda smiles out the window. Everything is blue skies and sweet air and three days 'til work again. The road narrows as they get closer to the water. Everything is ocean and trees and sloped green lawns and people puttering around their sheds. All things are fresh and productive.

Yesterday, she waited until the end of the last class to pass back her students' papers. She left right away, Evan's falling face a sliding door in her peripheral vision. She walked straight to Andrea's car, got home, poured a glass of wine, and made cupcakes from scratch. Her mind stayed on the task at hand: flour level against the measuring-cup line, dry ingredients sifting together, butter and sugar fluffing under the fork. Now the cupcakes sit patiently in their dome-like carrier, each one a pink, pristine offering in its own round divot. Those cupcake fads of a few years ago have died down a bit (hipster donuts are the new cupcakes, Ivan says), but maybe she can still get in on it. She could make up new flavours. Baileys and chocolate. Rum and butter. Wanda's Booze Cakes.

They turn up the driveway. Mrs. Medeiros had the house painted last spring and went with a creamy-lemon shade of yellow with white trim. The red tulips in her small front garden stand on ceremony. Party is on and in full force. Children spill out of the front door and tear off behind the house. Neighbours and guests sip beverages and watch the kids run. One woman looks down at a child clinging to her leg, another crouches in front of an animated little boy. Clusters of men, clusters of women.

They park and head to the picnic table. The cut grass is spongy under Wanda's canvas shoes. She moves a stack of paper plates and lays the holder on the table beside an assembly line of condiments. In the center, a two-layer cake decorated colour-by-number style with pointed icing dollops in the image of Hello Kitty. Plastic pitchers of red, punchy-looking liquid perch along the edge of the table, three large camping coolers line up beside the barbeque where Alex, Ivan's brother-in-law, holds court with a long, metal spatula. Two low, yellow plastic kiddie tables have been set up: one for eating, the other with toys and games—Jenga, Uno, Snakes and Ladders. Mrs. Medeiros likes to have something for everybody.

Ivan's sister, Sylvie, gestures them over. "Kids are gone mad on a scavenger hunt," she says. She punches Ivan in the shoulder. Wanda gets a one-armed hug while her other steadies a red plastic cup. "It's all about keeping them busy so you can have a drink," Sylvie says. She gazes into Wanda's face. "You look good." Sylvie is radiant herself, her ink-black hair swept over her shoulder. The outside air makes apples of her cheeks. "Jesus, did you make all those cupcakes? You have more patience than I."

"Did you put all this together?" Wanda says. "It's you with the patience."

"If you can buy it at Dominion, that's the extent of my effort," Sylvie says. And her face flushes. "Aw, shit. Sorry, Wanda."

"It's okay," Wanda says. C'mon, Sylvie, don't tiptoe.

"Wanda knows Dominion exists. You can acknowledge where your groceries come from," Ivan says.

"You're an ass." Sylvie slaps Ivan's arm. "I can't help it, though. I feel like there's this new apprehension in the air. I'm constantly looking behind me whenever I go out. And all I did was follow the story on the news. I can't imagine it, Wanda, I really can't."

Wanda shrugs. Yes it's horrible. Pass the ketchup. "How's Fiona doing?"

"Mom keeps giving her everything she wants. I said to her, you know, spoiled actually means gone *bad*. But she won't listen," Sylvie says. "If we lived close by, Fiona would be a real arsehole by now." She points to a gaggle of little girls running by. Fiona in the middle of them, her dark hair tied back in a ponytail.

"Fiona! Come and say hello," calls Sylvie. "Your aunt and uncle are here."

"Oh Mom!" Fiona puts her hands on her hips, her face crumpling into a ball. "We're two from finishing." Her shrill voice stabs the air. Ivan winces in response.

"It's okay," Wanda says. "She can come over after."

Sylvie mutters something about manners and moves towards the nearest cooler. Wanda turns back to the picnic table and opens the cupcake holder. She finds a large plate and gingerly lays each pink cupcake out, in a circular pattern. Ivan puts a cooler-wet bottle of beer beside her and gives her bum a light pat. She smirks to herself. It's good to be outside. The sunshine on her face and arms breaks through some force field. Colours are more vivid. Everyone's eyes dance on each other, on the children, on the freshness of everything. She licks a smear of pink icing from her little finger: buttery and sharp with sweetness.

Ivan looks off above the picnic table and waves one hand high over his head. She follows his eyes. Arriving from the path at the end of the yard is a couple, a man and woman and as soon as she sees the flash of platinum hair, something small and sturdy inside her withers a little. Of course, Trish and Leo would come. Mrs. Medeiros makes a point to invite their friends every year. Sharon and Nikki came out when they lived here. Ivan made fun of how Sharon referred to Topsail as "the bay." Trish and Leo didn't make it last year because there was no room in the house and it was too cold to camp. And neither of them wanted to drive and not drink, so that ruled out going home afterwards. There must be room this time.

Trish sees them and gives a little hop and wave. She carries her shoes in her hand and pads across the lawn barefoot. Leo follows with his hands in his pockets.

"Yay, May two-four!" Trish skips towards them. She holds up her empty hand and flashes two fingers, then four. "Two-four, two-four."

"You guys just get here?" Leo sidles up and gives Wanda's shoulder a squeeze.

"Yep, just parked," Wanda says. She makes sure to smile. Is her residual guilt apparent? Less than a week ago, she had a jealous hissy fit over Trish. About drinking coffee. Now, it feels like something she watched happen, like a scene in a bad soap opera, the kind that ends with someone getting a martini flung in their face.

"We went on a nature walk," Leo puts his hands on his hips in mock pride. "It's really nice down by the brook. You should go check it out." A robin lands on the grass beyond him and hops about, as if to prove his point.

"I'm going to settle in by that food trough and guard the beer cooler," Ivan says.

"And not help your mother or sister with anything," Trish says. "What an ingrate." Ivan mimics delivering a roundhouse kick at her.

Trish touches Wanda's shoulder and strokes downward, like she's spreading butter. She stops by the red blotches above her elbow. "Oh, sweetie, what happened?"

"Oh, it's nothing. Eczema," Wanda says. She fights the urge to cover the spot with her hand.

"Is it painful?'

"Sometimes. More itchy than anything else."

"Maybe you should give up dairy. It can be an irritant."

"Oh, yeah, maybe. Or just my spring molting."

She waits for Trish to laugh, but instead, she looks at Wanda with big eyes. "Okay, so I have something I'm dying to show you. I'm so excited. Come over to the car with me." She tosses her shoes down and scoots her feet into them. "C'mon!" She grabs Wanda's hand and heads towards the driveway.

Trish skips to the back of the Tercel, gravel spits under her feet. She pops the trunk, ducks inside, and remerges with an envelope. "It came out so beautifully. You're gonna shit when you see it." She pulls out a large, white rectangle and hands it to Wanda.

It is her photo, an 8" x 10", glossy and pristine. Wanda holds the edges daintily and regards her own image. She stands straight, but one leg bends slightly so her hip juts out. Her arms are bent so she's cupping each elbow—not folded and authoritatively posed, but a little self-hug. The suit is crisp and clean, the red pumps shiny and playful at the bottom of the frame. She smiles with her lips slightly parted, like she was just laughing. Wanda feels pleased to see her hair has movement, it flares out a little, as if in a breeze. She was scared her hair would look either messy or some kind of glossy helmet. Her backdrop, the wall of cans, resembles a retro 1960s wallpaper; the mass of them not recognizable as cans of coconut milk until they are considered separately.

"You look so hot," Trish says over Wanda's shoulder. "Powerful, but natural, comfortable. And a little demure. Do you like it?"

Wanda nods. It's the best picture of herself she has ever seen. She realizes she doesn't want to pass the photo back to Trish. The wind kicks up and tugs at it in her hand; she pinches the edges tighter so it doesn't blow away. "Yes. I love it," she says. She smiles into Trish's beaming face. "Thank you."

"Oh, no, thank you!" Trish's arms loop around Wanda from behind. She pats Trish's wrist without taking her eyes from the photo.

"So, originally, the opening was going to be at Eastern Edge. But, Darryl Pike, the guy organizing that festival? He proposed I show the pictures there."

"Oh yeah?" The Twitter proposal. The thought of the photo in an art gallery, a clean white space, is appealing. But Healfest. Ugh. What kind of art does Darryl Pike have on his walls? Something that heals him, for sure.

"Yes, he's got some great ideas for how to show it. There's going to be a tent and people can walk inside and around the pictures. I haven't decided if I'm going to set them up along the walls or kind of stand them everywhere so you can walk around them, you know?"

"Huh. Like a maze, kinda."

"Yes! Exactly. I really like the idea of it being outside, but inside, you know?" Trish gestures in circular motions to illustrate outside and inside. "And also, with that venue and a music-festival atmosphere, there will be people who don't usually go see art. A different audience for sure."

"Yup, should be good," Wanda says. She takes a small step back to indicate she wants to return to the party.

"You'll be there, yes?" Trish says. She clasps her hands in front of her chest and widens her eyes at Wanda.

"Oh, you know, that whole thing. I don't know if I can make it." She keeps her eyes down. The dust on the gravel bakes in the sun. "You know, crowds. And the overall theme."

"I know it must be hard for you," Trish says. "God, all those people who know who you are. Overwhelming."

"Yes." Is it hard for Trish to think of all the people who don't know who Patricia Samson is? "It stresses me out. With the weird emails and everything."

"Me too. Ugh, it's going to be so emotional." Trish steps forward and places her hand above Wanda's elbow, on her itchy patch. If she's aware of the scabs, it doesn't register on her face. "But it would mean a lot to me if you came."

"We'll see."

"And, I'm sorry if I'm overstepping, but it might help you a bit. Like, I know for myself, I have to face the things that stress me out. It took me a long time to overcome stage fright. Leo really helped with it. He'd talk me into singing a song with the band, here and there. Anyhoo. It's totally worked for me."

Trish stands close enough that Wanda can see a tiny blob of something black—mascara or eyeliner—in the tear duct of her eye. She speaks to the black blob: "I think I'm doing fine at the moment."

"Oh, you are! You're doing great! God, I'd hate to see how I'd be doing. I'd be a state. Just, you know, think about it." Trish runs her hand down Wanda's arm and squeezes her hand.

"Sure." Wanda squeezes Trish's hand in return and drops it. "By the way, you have something right here." She points to her own tear duct. She walks away as Trish rubs her eyes.

Back at the picnic table, she retrieves another beer from the cooler. Ivan and Leo hover by Alex at the barbeque, chatting about something technical. She feels a tug at her shirt. Fiona's round face is flushed and sticky with crumbs. She wears a peach t-shirt emblazoned with the words "Birthday Girl" in gold letters.

"Thank you for the cupcakes, Aunt Wanda. I ate one already."

"I can tell. Are you having a good birthday?"

"It's my belated birthday. Yes, it's lots of fun." Fiona sticks her bottom lip out and blows upward so her bangs puff out. "What does the word *gaudy* mean?"

"Gaudy? Well, if something is gaudy, it's like it's decorated too much. Like, too busy? Too much of something." Wanda tries to think of an inoffensive example. Mrs. Medeiros's Christmas tree and her tradition of coating it with at least three boxes of silver icicles comes to mind. Not a good sound bite to plant in the child's mind and mouth.

"Okay. So if something is ungaudy, it's a good thing then."

"Ungaudy? I don't think that's a word."

"Shelby's mom thinks it's a word. Shelby said her mom said you are ungaudy."

"Really?" Maybe it's a compliment? Like 'classic style.'

"Yes, she said she saw you talking on TV and that it's too bad you are an ungaudy Steven."

"That's a strange thing to say. Is Shelby's mom here?"

"Yep. She said you were the eightieth one." Fiona points to a tall blond woman in a yellow sleeveless blouse and jeans about twenty feet away, talking to two men.

"Eightieth?"

"Yep, she called you the eightieth ungaudy Steven. I gotta go, we're playing freeze tag." Fiona runs off, her ponytail waving goodbye behind her.

Shelby's mom looks over at Wanda and wrinkles her nose. The woman's hand moves up to her neck where she fingers a large gold crucifix on a chain. Their eyes meet. Wanda tips her beer at her. Shelby's mom looks away.

Eightieth ungaudy Steven. Wanda takes a large mouthful of beer and lets it fill her cheeks, chipmunk style.

As the shadows lengthen, the parents and kids dissipate. To Wanda's relief, Shelby's mom disappears right after the cake is cut, dragging the pouting Shelby, a tiny, blonde child dressed entirely in purple. Alex and Ivan get a blaze going in the fire pit at the far end of the yard. Mrs. Medeiros brings out a collection of collapsible camping chairs.

When the temperature drops, Wanda goes to the car for her sweater. Walking away from the chorus of boozy laughter is a long exhale. She takes her time getting the keys out of her jeans. The toe of her shoe stubs on something and she stumbles, but catches herself. She's drunker than she thought. When she goes back, she should eat something. Avoid being hungover at tomorrow's breakfast table— like this Christmas. Mrs. Medeiros served apple-cinnamon pancakes, thick and cakey and the fermenting apple mush made her gag. Oh, the shining holiday moments.

She takes her sweater out of the trunk and pulls it over her head. The neckline on this one is a bit tight. As she struggles with it, she hears rapid crunching of gravel, rushed steps coming towards her. Her hands scrabble at the neck. She plunges her face through the top with a gasp.

"Dear God, did I scare you?" Mrs. Medeiros stands before her, hands clasped at her chest. "You looked like you were being born out of that sweater."

Wanda yanks the neckline down and tucks her arms into it. "Was stuck there for a sec." She sweeps back sweater-frazzled wisps of hair from her face.

"I'm so sorry, my dear," Mrs. Medeiros says, "I wanted a moment with you to talk about that Karl man."

"Okay."

The sun is almost finished and the twilight glow blackens Mrs. Medeiros's pupils. "I met him," she says. "I went to the university to visit Helen and we saw him. He talked to me."

"What did he say?"

"Oh, all kinds of nothing. He has a little fluffy dog. He gives money to a charity Helen supports, something with animals." She flings her hands in the air to dismiss the idea of him. "But, he is really strange. He gives me a bad feeling. And I know when I have a gut feeling about someone, it means I should listen to it."

"In what way is he strange? I mean, yeah, he's pretty awkward."

"When he looks at you, he stares and twitches," Mrs. Medeiros says. "His eyes and lips move. Like he's thinking of something else."

"Yes, well, that is a side effect."

"Side effect? Of what?"

Fuck. What to say? Her head is a little woozy from being sweater-born again. "When I met him at the pharmacy, I noticed the name of his medication. I looked it up."

"What kind of medication?"

"Um, Zyprexa I believe."

"Zyprexa? What did you learn about it?" Mrs. Medeiros leans in closer. Her eyes are caverns. Might as well tell her. She'll just look it up for herself.

"There are a number of side effects," Wanda says. "It's a medication they give for mental disorders."

"I see." Mrs. Medeiros stands up straight. "So, this man has real problems then."

"I think so, yes." Her sleeve chafes against the eczema sores. She digs her nails into the spot.

"This is something to think about," Mrs. Medeiros says. "I'm glad I talked to you." She turns on her heel and crunches back over the gravel.

Wanda sighs. Holy shit, this woman. Now that it's almost summer, Wanda should prepare some ideas to keep Mrs. Medeiros occupied. A weekly outing or a hobby they can share. Something she can fixate on.

She makes her way back to the cooler by the picnic table. The ice has melted and a few cans of beer swim in the cold water. She opens one with a pop and fizz. The bonfire is going strong and makes shadows across the lawn.

She feels a light touch on the base of her spine. Leo. "How are you doing?" he says. He gives the spot on her back a little rub. Everyone is always touching her back these days. Like they're congratulating her on a great goal.

"I feel like that Jenga puzzle." She gestures to the tower of wooden blocks on the kids' table.

He tilts his head. "Taking a little bit off here and there? I think I know what you mean."

"And now, everyone wants me to go to a fucking carnival."

"Well, it might be a carnival, but I figure it's part of the reason he wants Trish's art," Leo says. "He needs to bring a bit of class to his event."

"Class indeed. He should serve canapés."

"Ooo, yes. And a champagne fountain." Leo sips his drink. "Whatever, though. Maybe it's something we all need."

"Who's we?"

"I mean the city at large. This place is a small town, really. Murders are big news. Shootings are huge. Shootings that get stopped are The Big Bang." Leo waggles his fingers over the hand holding his glass, like he's casting a spell. "People need to shake it off. To quote Taylor Swift."

"Why don't they just stay drunk as often as possible, like the rest of us?" She says it with a laugh. Leo stares at her. She drops her gaze to her can.

"Most festivals are kinda gross," he says. "They're excuses for people to carry on. Get Dionysian with it. That said, I don't think you should feel pressured to go."

"Yeah. Well, I don't." She clinks her can against his glass.

"Anyway. Brighter things." Leo takes a drink and swirls the ice in his glass. "I'm glad you and Ivan worked things out."

"Yeah." Ivan didn't say he talked to Leo. "I didn't know you knew about that."

"Honestly, he was being pissy, so I said, it's not that he was doing something wrong with Trish, it's because you didn't know about it," Leo says. "It's what's unspoken that worries people, not the obvious."

Wanda nods. Perhaps Ivan wasn't so understanding. For such a direct person, it seems he was quoting Leo. And *pissy*. He was *pissy* about it. The disappointment slides in like quicksand in her core. "So, you knew they have coffee together, all the time?"

"Oh yes. Trish has coffee with everybody, on the regular. She's got wings, that one. Always on the fly."

"Leo, I hope you don't think—I mean, I trust them both. We're a family, all of us." She sputters to get it out. Again, Ivan's words.

"Hey, don't apologize for feelings. Yeah, we're all tight, but it can make fear more intense. We all know bad things can happen with the best of people." His eyes hold hers for a moment and something flickers there, sadness, anger, regret, she can't tell. He looks out at the party. Ivan and Trish are silhouetted against the bonfire, standing away so Mrs. Medeiros can't see them smoke. Ivan leans into her and says something. Trish arches her back in laughter and, for a second, her blond hair is indistinguishable from the flames.

"Anyway. Family. What does that really mean, anyway?" Leo drains his glass. "Refill time," he says. He smiles at her and walks away.

17

TWO stacks of papers face each other on her desk. The twin towers of procrastination. Wanda locks her office door and readies a red pen. Last week at work and it's obligation laden. Sit down, get to it, finish up.

She separates out the final exams and assignments. Her computer chirps. There are two new emails.

To: JaynesWanda@nlil.ca
From: Holdenshat@mail.com
Subject: nothing really

Just thinking about you. Hope you had a good long week end.

Yick. She forwards it to Constable Lance. Does he even read them? It's like flicking a gum wrapper into a landfill.

The second email is from Trevor Dowden, Department Head.

Subject: A little chat

Hi Wanda. Please come see me when you get this.

Vague requests for meetings with your supervisor are generally not good. Her stomach does a curdling forward roll. Why be nervous now? The whole program is scrapped. *But she shouldn't burn bridges. She'll need references. And things might change.* Thoughts in Dad's voice: *Keep your options open. Networking is important.*

Trevor Dowden's office is shades of beige—tan carpet, taupe

walls, a long pine desk. Wooden picture frames display photos of his plump, smiling wife and their two teenage sons, spotty and damp with puberty. The room irritates her with its bland plan, as if bad news presented here can be softened by the inoffensive decor.

Dowden is beige himself, his aging hair the colour of porridge, his tie a long custard smear draped over his protruding paunch. How many people has he had to reprimand or layoff in this room? Years of it until his edges were blunted and he became a rounder, muted version of himself.

"Hullo, Wanda," Trevor Dowden says. "Please have a seat." He gestures to the cushioned camel-coloured chair on the opposite side of his desk. Wanda sits politely with her hands folded.

"How are things going?" he says. "It's been so busy lately, I've hardly had a chance to touch base with anyone."

"Things are good. I have lots of marking, but that's normal."

"Oh, I imagine it is," he says. He reaches towards a stack of file folders on his desk and slides the top one down. "So. One of your students. Evan—"

"McKinnley."

"Yes. He came to see me. What's going on there?"

"He passed in his paper late and I took off marks." She flattens her gaze to the wall behind him.

"Understandable. However, he said when he explained his situation, you told him it was okay."

"I told him I'd see what I could do." She crosses her legs and forces the small of her back into the chair. Sit up straight, sit like a person who's done nothing wrong.

"What kind of student is he?"

"He was hard-working at the start of the term, but around the middle he slacked off. His attendance went way down."

"Yes, he had a lot to say when he was here. However, his mother did call to back him up."

Wanda laughs. Dowden's face remains blank. "Of course she did," she says. "Isn't that what parents do now? Mom'll probably show up at his first real job interview to inform them what a good worker he is."

Dowden opens the file and pulls out Evan's paper. He lays it on the desk. "Both Evan and his mother say this paper was late because he wasn't able to get into his ex-girlfriend's house to access his work or belongings. His mother says he had to return home without most of his clothes. He had to wear his brother's things for a while."

Sure, that didn't stop him from buying new t-shirts. "In the student handbook," she says, "it states students require doctor's notes if they're sick, death certificates for bereavement. I understand Evan had a domestic issue, but he should have known better than to keep all his work in one place without backing it up. He could have saved it to the institute's network, or saved it on a USB. I tell all my students to do this." She should stop talking. Doth not protest too much.

"I agree students should be more careful. But I think he's learned his lesson. He was quite inconsolable while he was here." Dowden clears his throat. "And we've had female students with similar issues in the past. It would be unfair to not extend the same consideration."

Jesus Christ. Like Evan McKinnley is a battered wife. Hot frustration streams up her spine. She can't meet Dowden's eyes. A fierce-looking zit has manifested on his chin. Looks like it will come to a head soon. Is he a popper? Maybe he borrows his sons' Clearasil.

"What do you suggest I do?" she says.

"I think you should take another look at his paper and grade it accordingly. If you feel it should lose marks for lateness, do so. But if it's a passing grade, I think he deserves a break." Dowden closes Evan's paper back in the white file folder and slides it across the desk to her.

"K. Will do."

"Perhaps this experience supports a revision to the student handbook. We can stress the importance of backing up work. Maybe we could provide links to some online software for this purpose. A cloud application or something."

"Yes. Good idea," she says. Dowden's zit is the reddest thing in the room.

"How are things with other students?"

"Oh, fine. No major issues."

"That's great. Any summer plans?"

"Not really, Trevor. Hard to plan a vacation when you're getting laid off."

"Oh, I can imagine. Believe me, we've all been through it." Dowden sighs. "I'm sorry I can't give you any news for September right now. With the cutbacks and the layoffs and dealing with the permanent staff, it won't get sorted out for months. We're losing a lot of great contract workers. It's a shame."

"Well, that's all you can do," she says. She pats the folder. "Let me know if you hear of any changes." She stands and smiles warmly at his pimple.

"Oh, definitely."

Oh mos def. Wanda shuts the door behind her with a subtle click. Her right hand worms up her left sleeve and her fingernails bear down with vengeance on the mountain range of crusted gashes above her elbow.

Twenty minutes later, she's settled into a plodding rhythm of marking. She scours the multiple-choice sections first and matches them to the key. Her pen gives robotic ticks. The selected response areas are done when her office door rattles with Andrea's 'shave and a haircut' knock. Wanda's head swims a little as she stands to open the door, a little rush, like the first puff of a cigarette. Andrea is all set, track jacket zipped up to her chin. "Oh, look at you! Busy lil' marking bee."

"Shit, is it time to go? Sorry." Wanda grapples the piles of papers into a canvas bag. Normally, she'd come into work early or stay late to get this marking done, but Andrea has to get home to her dog and cat.

"Gotta get home by four to let Kiki out," Andrea says. "Inside or out, by 4:03, she's done her pee. Hee-hee-hee, don't mind me."

"No problem, I'll just take all this home," Wanda says. Final exams from the ABE English Language course, comparison essays, comprehension exercises, all ungraded so far. But she has five days to get it all in.

"Sure, just do what I do," Andrea says. "Chuck the tests down the stairs. The ones that make it to the bottom? *As.* Ha-ha-ha-Ha! I'm some bad." She clangs with laughter as Wanda locks her office door.

In the Rav4, Andrea blasts the Steve Miller Band so loud Wanda barely hears her phone ding. One new text message. At first glance, the contact picture looks like a spearmint candy, all white and green. On closer inspection, it's a selfie of Trish, her white-blond hair swept into her face. She's holding up a martini glass of something bright green. An appletini perhaps. Wanda swipes the screen to open the message.

> Hey Sweets! See you at
> The Duke tonight!

Trish made the date to discuss the show over pints. "You should go," Ivan said. "The two of you hardly ever hang out together." This is true. Wanda can't remember the last time it was just her and Trish without the XY chromosomes. And she never did anything with Wanda when Nikki and Sharon were around. But it's hard to believe Trish would be friends with her if they had met independent of Ivan and Leo. Trish's female friends are like her: fashionable, artistic, gregarious.

And the meeting is not about being girlfriends. Wanda has tentatively agreed to go to the Festival of Healing and do a little bow and wave on stage. The decision was settled on the return drive from the May 24th picnic. "Why not go?" Ivan said. "You've been friends for over four years. This is a significant exhibit for her." He kept his eyes on the road, but drove with one hand, the other airborne to stress his points. "If you had some big event happening, you know she'd go."

Wanda slumped in the passenger seat and stared out the window. She was tired all over, tired from a day of drinking outdoors, tired of Mrs. Medeiros's smothering mothering. "Fine," she said, "I'll go. Better to say yes and get it over with."

"That's my positive-minded girlfriend," said Ivan.

"You're awfully quiet," Andrea says. She turns down the volume. Her eyes dart from the road to the phone in Wanda's lap. "Bad message?"

You're awfully nosey, Wanda wants to say. "No. Yes, a bit. I'm annoyed at some people in my life at the moment."

"I hear ya," Andrea says. "I tells Boyd, he's lucky I run the kitchen at home and not the one in the women's penitentiary. Cause I could easily be in there for homicide the way he gets on." She chuckles. "Jet Airliner" comes on over the stereo and her fingers tap its beat on the steering wheel. "How long have you and your man been together now?"

"Almost five years."

"Ah, five years. That's a telling time."

"How so?"

"Well, five years is when a lot of people decide if they want five more years." Andrea's voice drops. "It was five years with my ex, the one before Boyd, when I knew I'd had enough. Really, we were coming up on our fifth anniversary and a friend of ours mentioned it. And I realized I didn't want to celebrate it. Hard to ignore a gut reaction like that. How are you two doing?"

"Good. Well. It's been hard lately," she says. She realizes Andrea is totally silent, waiting for her to continue. "Sometimes I feel like there's a wall of Plexiglas between us and I'm smacking my head off it trying to get him to understand me. Like, he just doesn't get it and then I end up agreeing to things because it's easier than making him see where I'm coming from." Now she's embarrassing herself. Like she sprayed spittle during a conversation.

"Answer me this," Andrea says. "If you came home and caught him with someone else, how would you feel?"

"What?"

"That's how I knew I wanted to break up with my ex," Andrea says. "Just imagine it for a moment. I drop you off, you walk in and catch him boning someone else. How do you feel?"

"I don't know. Numb. Betrayed."

"That's good. If you felt relieved or," Andrea removes both hands from the wheel and swipes them together in the wiping-dust-off-your-hands motion, "it means you're done. God, I used to fantasize about catching Rex with someone. It meant I could leave him. No one would blame me. I wouldn't have to feel guilty about him, about what he would do now, how he would look after himself."

"How did you do it in the end?"

"His mother. She caught me alone in the kitchen after Christmas supper and said, 'It's not your job to look after him, Andrea. If you're unhappy, do something about it.' I ended it right after New Year's."

"I don't know if I could think about breaking up with things so crazy lately. I don't really know how to feel about a lot of things." She forces a laugh to warm things back up. "He just makes me so angry. It takes nothing for me to get pissed at him."

"That's good then. Anger means you've made the decision to feel strongly about the issues at hand. I guess you have to ask yourself if it's really him you're mad at."

Wanda points to the stereo. "Hey, I haven't heard this song in a long time," she says. She leans forward and turns up the volume.

The Duke is busy with an upscale crowd: lawyers, politicians, the financially successful musicians. A cluster of well-dressed thirty-somethings stand around the bar, all power suits and slippery, over-processed hair. A few of them perk up as Wanda passes. Elbows nudge and jostle, phones make appearances.

Trish scored seats on the red-velour chairs in the back. She is decked out in a rockabilly-style dress, black with a print of little red cherries. Wanda has the nagging sensation she is going on a date. Perhaps she should have brought flowers or candy.

Trish stands to hug her. She presses her chest to Wanda's and the bodice on her cherry-print dress feels like it could make a dent in her. "Good to see you," Trish says. "Mmm, you smell nice." Wanda wonders what that scent could be. Trish's perfume is honey and citrus delicious.

Trish plops back down so air puffs out the hem of her dress. "I'm glad you're here," she says. "I'm getting so nervous about all this. This weekend! There's already, like, 1500 people following the event on Facebook."

"Yes. It's like the Regatta." Wanda takes off her jacket. "I'm going to get a pint, do you want anything?"

"Pike said he wants to get us drinks," Trish says. She nods towards the bar.

A lean, lanky figure approaches. Darryl Pike walks with a perk in the middle of each step, like he's hiking himself up to reach a high shelf item. He wears a black t-shirt cut in a low v-neck with a thick chain that dangles and bounces. His head is clean shaven and he has a small square of facial hair under his lip. What are they called? A soul patch. An asshole tickler, Ivan would say. As he leans down to kiss Trish on both cheeks, Wanda notices he has added to his neck tattoo: the symbol ∞ next to *infinity*. Things must be looking up for him.

"Wanda. It's a pleasure." Darryl Pike takes her hand and pecks her cheek at the same time. His cologne fills her face and eyes. Musky undertones which might be pleasant if there wasn't so much of it. "What would you ladies like to drink?"

"I'll have gin and tonic. Wanda?"

"Um, a pint of Harp is fine," Wanda says. She tries to catch Trish's eye, but she stays focused on Pike until he walks away.

"You didn't mention he was joining us," Wanda says.

"Ugh, I didn't? I'm so sorry. So, I tweeted about meeting you at The Duke and he responded. Said he was in the neighbourhood, would get us a beverage." Trish waggles her iPhone at Wanda. "He's quite the dude."

"Quite. Why is he here?"

"Shit, girl," Trish says, "he's your biggest groupie. He's been dying to meet you."

"You'd think taking a video of me would be enough."

Trish strokes Wanda's hand. "I understand how you must feel. Honestly, when I saw that video and his interview on the CBC, I thought, what an opportunistic ass. And just showing up like this? Bold!" Her fingers dance over Wanda's wrist. "But since I've been involved with the festival, I have to say, I think it's going to be really good. He does have vision for this kind of thing."

Wanda takes a deep breath. Trish's fingers make airy motions along the top of her hand. She glimpses Pike at the bar. He's waiting for her pint to be poured. A drink would be good. He owes her that, at least. She turns to Trish's expectant face. "So, this weekend. What's the plan?"

"There will be tents set up all over the park. I get one for the photo exhibit," Trish says. "Lots of local organizations will be there, non-profits, mostly. And music all day. I'm so happy Ivan and Ray will have a chance to play. Although not the main act. Pike's doing that."

"Of course."

"So, at the end of the night, Pike wants to get everyone up on stage, just as a big shout-out, you know? Maybe a song."

"Like *We Are The World*."

"Ha, ha. Maybe. But with just the real musicians playing," she says. "Oh, here he comes."

Pike rests the glasses in the middle of the table and sits down: "I just want to say how awesome it is to meet you, missus." He reaches out and covers Wanda's hand with his. Everyone is touchy-feely tonight. "And also, it's awesome you've agreed to be part of Healfest." The v-neck of his t-shirt droops. His Adam's apple is large and vulnerably exposed.

"Oh, thanks." Trish, the information sensation. The girl can't have a crap without tweeting what colour it is.

"That day, you know, it's one of those things. Like, we lived through it, right?" He squeezes her hand. Something pinches the skin on top of her knuckles. His three large silver rings act like teeth on her flesh. "The people I worked with at the store, the ones on that day…man, we're totally bonded now. We all lost Mike. I had just talked to him before he went on cash. And now, all of us, we got these memories. We felt that fear as one." He lets go of her hand and brings his fists together. "The strength of our connection now, you can feel it. It's wicked powerful."

Wanda nods. He lowers his eyes to swallow some emotion. His Adam's apple waggles a little grotesquely. Those neck tattoos look dangerously close to it. Imagine the tattoo artist's forearm brushing that huge-ass Adam's apple. Stop thinking of that.

"Do you remember me from earlier that day?" Wanda says. "Before the shooting started?"

Pike's face is blank. "What, like we met before?"

"Well, kind of. I was looking for the coconut milk and asked you where to find it."

"You did? Oh my God." Pike leans back with the impact. "So, I helped you find it? I helped find what you used as a weapon." He looks from Trish to Wanda with shining eyes. "It's like I said. Connected. Layers of connection and meaning. Did you see Deepak Chopra speak when he was here? I totally agree with his ideas on quantum entanglement. We are all part of a physical machine."

"Never saw Deepak, nope," Wanda says. Should she tell him he wasn't actually helpful and she found the coconut milk on her own? Sorry, Pike, you were more of a rusty gear in the physical machine.

"Wild," Trish says. "Totally wild." Her red lips pucker over the straw in her gin and tonic.

"So," Wanda says, "Trish said the festival will be pretty laid back."

"Oh yeah, really casual. Me and my crew are going to play a couple of sets. After the second set, I'm gonna do some thank-yous and call up people on stage. Volunteers, Trish here and people like Lydia Heffernan—do you know her?"

"No."

"She's the head of the Coalition Against Violence. Trish's portrait of her is stunning."

"She's amazing!" Trish says. "She does such good work."

"Oh man, she's a gift to the city. Also, I wanna give props to the cops on the scene that day, and you, Wanda, of course." Pike swirls his drink so the ice cubes jingle.

So, people who devote their lives to helping others and some chick who threw a can. Wanda tries not to grimace. "I come out last?"

"The best for last, my dear," Pike says. He grins at her. Something gold twinkles from inside his mouth, a cap or something.

"It's not really cool that I'm a finale—I mean—those people are deserving of recognition. I really don't feel comfortable being put on the same level."

"Just like you said, Trish," Pike says. He reaches across the table and squeezes Trish's shoulder. She smiles and nods. "See, this is why you're so awesome, Wanda. Trish said you were the most humble person ever and I can see it all over you. This is why you're so loved."

"That's nice of you to say. But it's way too grandiose for me to come out like that." Pike and Trish continue to beam at her. For fuck sakes. "I don't mind coming out on stage, but I'd prefer to avoid fanfare."

"Oh honey," Pike says, "the fanfare is there, even if you don't care."

"Ha! You are totally a rapper," Trish says. She play-slaps him on the arm. Wanda's phone flickers. Trish has texted her from across the table:

> He's such a case!
> Hilarious!

Wanda picks up her pint. "It's nice to meet you. But I stand by what I think. I don't want to be a big deal."

"Okay. We'll work something out," he says. He raises his glass. "Cheers to you, Wanda. This weekend is going to be ah-mazing." They all clink and drink. Wanda notices other customers—a couple at a nearby table, a guy seated at the bar—holding out their phones. They could be reading. They could be taking pictures.

The street is tranquil and it is close to midnight when she gets home. Ivan is at the computer. "How was it?" he says.

"Fine. Darryl Pike joined us." She kisses his cheek. He tucks one hand around her waist.

"What's he like?"

"He's pretty flaky. Tries to be smooth."

"Does it work?"

"It seems to." Her phone beeps. Holdenshat@mail.com:

I hope you do not think I send u things to bother you. Its so you will be aware of the monsters. The monsters, their mothers and the religion they misuse!

Wanda shows the message to Ivan. He strokes his chin mock-studiously. "Unhinged comes to mind."

"Lexicon on you. Funny stuff."

"Would you rather I panic?" Ivan says. "Forward it to the cop."

"Every time I click 'send' to Lance, I feel useless. Here's another piece of crazy for you to ignore."

"Let's get on his case."

"I don't understand why nothing is happening. Does there have to be an incident with this guy for action to be warranted?" She rubs her belly. "I think I'm getting an ulcer."

"You should see a doctor," Ivan says. "You're losing weight. And this," he points to the eczema on her arm, "Seriously. You obviously can't leave it alone. It's gonna get infected."

The sores above her elbow have spread up to the bottom of her triceps: angry, pink welts which throb with the lightest contact. "Man, you've really been itching at them," he says.

"You don't have to guilt me out about it."

"How is stating the truth guilting you out? Just go to the doctor." He stands up with a jerk. "Want anything from the kitchen?"

"No thanks, I'm okay." She takes his seat by the computer and opens her Facebook account. She's checked Karl's page so many times, it pops up as soon as she types K in the search engine.

Karl Prendergast: Having a nice quiet night in. Sometimes it just good to sit and dwell on ones thoughts.

Sometimes it's just good to proofread. She wonders if he's added her on Facebook with the hopes she'll read his updates, put things together. Maybe he's waiting to be seen.

Ivan shuffles out of the kitchen with a bowl of chips. His phone vibrates on the desk and he swipes it up as he passes by. Wanda gets a glimpse of Trish's green and white on his screen, the colours of spearmint candy.

18

THE blond girl in the poster wears a bright white grin. "*Sexually active? Regular pap tests save lives.*" Wanda's eyes dance over it while Dr. Jalaal goes over the paperwork.

"Ok, this cream is a corticostcroid, so only apply it to the affected area on your arm. Stop as soon as it heals." Dr. Jalaal tears the page from her prescription pad. "We won't know what's going on with your tummy until we investigate. I'll fill out requisitions for blood and urine tests. The stool sample you'll have to bring in. First movement in the morning is best."

Wanda's face goes hot. Ugh, a stool sample. Pap Test Poster Girl stands nonchalantly, hands in the front pockets of her jeans. "*Talk to your doctor about having your first cervical exam.*"

"Until we know what's wrong, you need to watch what you eat. Here's a list of foods that are considered mild—celery, garlic, onions, lots of fruit, special teas. Some possible over-the-counter antacids there too." Dr. Jalaal's voice is tender. She is splendidly gorgeous: long, sumptuous black hair, high elegant cheekbones, creamy clear brown skin. "You need to avoid coffee and spicy food. No alcohol either."

Wanda averts her eyes and nods. Pap Test Poster Girl smiles down on her. She does what she wants. So smug.

"Do you keep a journal?"

"Not really," Wanda says. "I used to, but it's been a long time."

"It might help," Dr. Jalaal says. "Take note of when you're getting the discomfort, what you ate that day, the time, the temperature, anything you can think of. In your situation, stress can be a factor." She gives Wanda a smile that goes all the way to her warm brown eyes. Wanda fights an urge to hug her. To rest her head on her shoulder. Ask to be taken care of. "Thank you," she says.

No sign of Ivan in the waiting room. The only sound is the burp of Wanda's shoes on the laminate floor. Damn farting shoes. A guy in a red ball cap scrolls through his phone. The girl sitting next to him stares at the notices on the wall beside her. Blood-donor clinic next week. A list of reasons why you should get the flu shot.

Wanda stands in the porch and looks out the glass doors. Three cars in the clinic parking lot. None of them are Ivan. No new messages or missed calls on her phone. A black car pulls up. Not their Honda Civic. He was supposed to get groceries before coming to get her. Texting will slow him down. She turns up the volume on her phone. She counts the fingerprint smudges on the glass door, twenty-three, mostly small, childlike hands. This is the third time he's been late this week. The sky outside piles on more layers of grey. She shivers in spite of herself. Someone should wipe down the glass door. By the time he arrives, she's been waiting for twenty-nine minutes. She says this when she gets in the car.

Ivan shrugs. "Everyone is late sometimes."

"Text if you're going to be late," she says. She unzips her purse and stuffs the papers into it. He hasn't asked how the appointment went. "Or call. It's considerate."

"I was busy."

"Everyone's busy."

"That's why they're late."

She folds her arms. Why can't he just say "sorry?" It's not saying uncle, it's not please. He turns up the radio volume. She turns it down.

"I want to hear the news."

"You know, I wouldn't feel angry if you gave a shit."

"Fine. I am sorry. But you should accept the fact that people are late at times."

"At times. It's a habit for you. Three times this week."

"It's been a busy week."

"I think busier people than you know to text or call when they're late."

"I think sometimes those people get too busy even for that."

For the rest of the drive, the only sound is the occasional tsk of the indicator. It's not until they're back in the house with their jackets off that she realizes there are no groceries.

"Did you go to the store?"

"Shit. Sorry. Totally slipped my mind."

"What have you been doing this whole time? I gave you a list."

"Work. Getting ready for the festival. You know, if I'm going to be the chauffeur and the errand boy, sometimes, I'm going to forget things." He shoves on his jean jacket and leaves. She waits for the door to shut to say "fuck."

A low rattle. Ivan has left his phone on the table by the door. The flash on the screen is white and green and familiar. Trish's bleached pixie cut and appletini. Wanda's jaw tightens. We all text each other. Not a big deal. Her and Leo, her and Trish, her and Ivan. We're all textroverts, it's okay.

But how often is okay? How many touches on the shoulder and lingering hugs are okay? She picks up his phone. Her hand hovers over the smooth black screen. Her pinky drops, the screen flashes open. If her pinky slides up, the phone will reveal the first few words of Trish's message. The phone will lock itself in a minute or so if it goes untouched. Her pinky nudges upward.

Oooooh! Sooo cute! ☺ ☺ ☺

She swallows. Her pinky taps the message icon. Trish's message is in response to a photo of a chipmunk, crouched next to what looks like Ivan's shoe. Okay. She likes chipmunks. No big deal. Wanda didn't get a chipmunk photo, but whatever. She scrolls down. Many of the messages are photos. Bathroom graffiti. Chinese fortune cookie fortunes. The written messages are jovial and read like icebreakers/conversation starters.

> Feet or farts? You have to endure the constant odor of one for two years straight. And not subtle feet stink. Sweaty hiking toes.

Like yer Nan's feet after makin' Sunday dinner?

> Like yer Nan's feet after White Russian night at Lottie's.

What kinda farts we talkin' bout here?

> Pungent. Beer & salami night.

At yer Nan's.

Really, your olfactory senses can get used to anything. That's why smelly people don't know they have B.O.

> In this case, the stink wavers just enough to always reek. A thousand layers of stenchatude.

I'd probably still go with feet. I'd pretend it was Doritos.

> Yer Nan's always eatin Doritos.

And on and on. Not sexual or overly flirtatious, but regular. Plentiful. An easy camaraderie. Wanda and Ivan have never had that. Even though Wanda is good at puns. Wanda's pretty fucking funny, actually. But Trish, he appreciates on so many levels, beautiful and pert and alert and such a joker. At least when she has a minute to think about it.

She scans other messages. 3:46pm on Thursday. She met Trish at The Duke that night.

Just texted W to remind her about 2nite.

Cool.

Should I tell her Pike is coming?

:S Not if you want her to show up.

Ok. ☹ feels dishonest.

Well, she's in a place that's hard to approach right now.

Understandable. How u doing?

Just watching my step.

K. Ugh, so many eggshells, huh?

You know it.

☹

Her stomach is a fist-full of dry sand. She should write that in her journal. *Major abdominal discomfort when reading insensitive comments from my common-law husband and my "friend."*

She lays the phone down. Her fresh fingerprints are obvious on the screen. Hands should be washed after being in places like medical clinics. Hands should be washed after dealing with greasy characters. She goes to the bathroom and lets the water run warm. In the mirror, her lips are dry and peeling. Her hair droops defeated over her ears. A face that can't be faced. *Hard to approach right now. You know it.* The steam rises from the tap. She washes her hands until the lather is thick and slippery. She rubs in into her nails, her cuticles, in between her fingers. Where did Pike's tacky rings pinch her? There. Furious bubbles on the tops of her hands. She looks up again at her face, cheeks flushing now, mouth downturned and dour. Did Trish really send a sad-face smiley when they discussed her "hesitation"?

She dries her hands and stomps down to the living room. Opens the phone again.

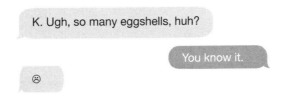

Sad fucking face. What's the emoticon for being a condescending bitch?

She flicks back through more messages. They scroll quickly, like a slot machine. A picture, lots of exclamation points.

What do you think?!!

Six photos. The first shows a white teddy bear, a red ribbon around its neck. The words *Thank You* are printed on the end. The teddy bear's face is in profile. The background is grey, overcast light, a parking lot. A figure stands in a long black coat. *Her* long black coat. It's her, at the vigil. The other pictures are close-ups of the offerings, flowers, notes, *Thank you to the hero. Whoever you are, thank you.* In three, the focus is on a gift tag with a slightly blurry Wanda, in three she is clear, her white face morose under the black hood. Trish photographed the gifts and offerings with the person they were intended for. Candid, standing unknown to everyone.

OMG THEY ARE AMAZEBALLS!!!

You think?

I have goosebumps. Jesus. I didn't even see you take these!

I'm trying to be subtle these days. Working on my inner Vivian Maier.

They would be fantastic with the exhibit. But you know you can't.

Oh yes, I know. I mean, it's hard, but yes, obvs.

Maybe after more time passes.

So Trish knew. Wanda asked Ivan not to tell anyone and he told her. Trish knew and made art with it.

The screen door squeals. She continues looking. Ivan enters with plastic grocery bags in both hands. "What are you doing?"

"Reading." She waves his phone at him. "So, you and Trish basically live in each other's pockets, huh?"

His mouth is clamped over gritted teeth. He lays down the bags. Slowly, he pries open the breast pocket of his jacket, looks in with one eyebrow raised. Pats pants pockets, front and back. "Nope. She's not there."

"Don't react like I'm overreacting."

"You're invading my privacy."

"You two are in constant contact."

"Really?" Ivan holds out his hand for the phone. "Let's see about that." Like he's going to say ta-ta, like asking a baby for its toy.

She throws the phone. It clatters across the floor. "Don't step on it. Might be like walking on eggshells."

Ivan picks it up and brushes his finger across it. "What is so upsetting?" He leans his back against the wall as he scrolls through the messages. "Let's see. Yesterday, we talked about farts. This morning, she sent me a joke her ten-year-old neighbour told her."

"You talk about me!"

"Yeah, of course we talk about you."

"She knew at the vigil! She fucking took pictures of me!"

"Okay, yes, but — "

"And you knew that Pike douchebag was going to meet us! You're both greedy assholes!" She lets out a sob and wraps her arms around her belly.

"Wanda. Leo and Trish knew as soon as it happened. I called them from the police station."

"Why did you do that?"

"It wasn't until the next day you said you wanted to keep it a secret." He runs a hand through his hair. "And as for the other night, you've been kind of…reactive with me lately. I thought if you heard about the festival from him *and* Trish, it might ease your concerns." He puts the phone into his jacket pocket and looks to her, his palms open at his sides. "And you didn't seem too bothered by it when you came home."

"Why is it so important I go?"

"Wanda, you've been closed off since the shooting." He takes a step towards her. "I don't know. I thought it might help you see how others see you."

"Bullshit. It's good for Trish's art. It's good for the new album and your *music*." She makes quotation motions with her fingers.

Ivan's face flushes. "What does that mean? You have an opinion on that now? You haven't been to watch us play in ages."

"You never invite me."

"You have to be invited now?"

"It's so obviously you and Leo and precious fucking Trish's *thing*." Her quotation fingers are on automatic now.

"Okay. Jesus. My *things* are not separate from yours. I've never excluded you."

"Yeah, the way I feel has nothing to do with your behaviour. You never fail to dissect the way others act. You should try looking at yourself."

"Fine. Look." He holds his hands out to her. "Let's calm down."

"I'm too disgusted to calm down. I'm going out."

"Okay, get some air, come back. We can talk." Ivan steps out of the way as she strides towards the door.

"By the way, my doctor thinks I might have an ulcer," she says. She grabs her coat and purse. "Don't forget to text Trish about it." She slams the door on the image of his hanging head.

Her footsteps make echoing slaps in the mist as she pounds down Empire Avenue. The fog blurs all lines and edges. Good. She wants to be an anonymous shape. She walks a straight line downtown, past the brewery and its yeasty stench, past the sheltered cluster of Georgetown houses. She jaywalks across Military Road and strides so briskly down Prescott Street, she feels her feet may catch on themselves and she could tumble, head over arse, straight down the hill. She forces herself to take slow, deliberate steps down the steep sidewalk, past colourful houses standing willfully against the grey air. The Fort Amherst foghorn sounds, each monotone blast the opening note on a pitch pipe, setting the tone, as if the ocean is about to break into song. Just to remind the city it is still there, just to announce it will continue no matter what horrible things people do, no matter if minds shatter, no matter what injustice occurs, no matter how many lovers turn out to be selfish shits, the ocean remains, it pushes the tide in and out, it keeps doing its job.

At Duckworth Street, she turns right and darts across the street. She scampers down the first steps of Solomon's Lane and enters The Ship. Happy hour is descending. She perches at the bar and orders a rum and coke. She thought she would want a whiskey or a glass of dry red wine, something that hurts a little, but the cool air and speedy walk require sugar and caffeine.

She lays her phone on the bar beside her. No messages. No missed calls. She may have to go to the bathroom and cry. She may have to go outside and bum a smoke. What the fuck is she going to do? She tries Sharon's number. Voice mail. Nikki's at work right now. She's so hard to get a hold of. Who to call? Mom would pitch into instant worry-mode and insist she come home. She imagines herself lying fetal on the twin bed in her old room, gazing up at pictures of Corey Haim and River Phoenix. Dead teen idols watching over her while Ivan plays a show to over a thousand people in a park and parties all night. With Trish. Who else can she call? Everyone has husbands and kids, everyone is occupied. There's Andrea. No. Can't do it.

"They let any old riff-raff into this bar."

Leo's face by her ear. "What are you doin', missus? Where's your mister?"

She opens her mouth to speak, but instead, she leans into his shoulder.

"Oh. Oh Jaynes," he says. "It's going to be okay." The collar of his flannel shirt wedges behind her nostril and she inhales the scent of his skin, fresh-baked bread with undertones of marijuana.

"You should let him know where you are." Leo places another pint before her. They have claimed the tall table in the darkest corner for the privacy and people-watching angle.

"I think he should ask me where I am."

"Man, you guys need to press reset or something," he says. "Sit down, clear your heads, and talk it out."

"I've made it pretty clear how I feel about things," she says.

"Ivan is my brother, but some people, you know, they're great every day, but suck in a crisis. And this is uncharted territory." He sips his beer. "For the whole city, really. The whole province."

"It's not even about recovery. It's the notoriety. It's a pleasant side effect to him. Like, 'hey, too bad you broke your leg, but at least you got some free morphine out of it.'"

"Ivan thinks of things in possibilities. After his dad died, they didn't have much. He said it felt like everyone around him had more options. So, even though this is a fucked-up situation, he recognizes what might be possible."

"I know how he feels. But he can't expect his point of view to be universal."

"I agree. And it is gross. Even the little bits that have fallen our way—like this Pike guy? What a dipshit. Trish has to deal with him for the festival. It's half hippy-peace-love-in, half business convention."

"Do you guys disagree about it?"

"No," Leo says. He sips his drink. "She's always been very entrepreneurial. You should see some of the crazies she's had to work with."

"You know Ivan and Trish are bosom friends, right? Always with the texty-text."

"She texts everyone. It's part of her temperament."

"Come on, Leo. It doesn't bother you?" She reaches forward and ruffles his hair, drags her hand down his shirt. "Oh, your hair's so nice. Oh, this shirt is so soft." She squeezes his knee. "Are these jeans 100% denim? Ah-mazing!"

"So? She's tactile." For an instant, his lips are stiff, a minus sign. Maybe she went too far. But he shrugs. "She's always been that way."

"It's never been an issue?"

"I wouldn't say that. In the first couple of years, yeah, I had some insecurity. I see how other men look at her. I see them getting hopeful. But she always comes home to me."

"I guess. Maybe it wouldn't bother me so much if I felt like I did anything for Ivan anymore."

"You don't think you do?"

"I feel like a fad about to lose its novelty."

"You're not a fad. You're trendy as hell, but a fad? No way."

"I am. I'm fadulous."

"Like Beanie Babies?"

"Like Pogs."

"Like a No Fear t-shirt?"

"Like Crystal Pepsi."

"You know what never loses its novelty?"

"What?"

"Tequila shots."

"So, what happened?" Wanda leans against the brick wall and lights her cigarette. "Back when you were feeling insecure."

"I got over it."

"But was there a thing? Did you fight?"

Leo fishes in his cigarette pack. "Yes, there was a thing. She had a roommate, this guy Jeremy. They were really close, roommates long before I knew her. She'd walk around the apartment wearing just a towel, he'd do the same. It bugged the shit out of me." He pulls out a joint and wets it. "One day, I stopped by her place and the door was unlocked. I walked in. She and Jeremy were lying on the couch together, watching a movie. They had a blanket over them."

"They were messing around?"

"No. Just cuddling."

"Huh," she says. "Was Trish the little spoon?"

"Yes, she was," Leo says. "So I walked in, saw them, turned around, walked out. She chased after me. We had a row. She said for her, cuddling is natural, not sexual. Even so, I said, it's physical intimacy."

"But you worked it out okay?"

"Yeah. She told me Jeremy was gay." He lights the joint and inhales.

"Well, that's good then. Sounds like you were both pretty young at the time? Younger? More to learn?"

"You can say childish," he says. He studies the joint for a moment before passing it to her. "Want to know something? I've never, ever brought this up to her."

"Yes. Tell me."

"I see that Jeremy guy with women all the time. Fucker is totally straight."

Wanda laughs hard from her gut, a laugh to blast through a foggy night.

Back in the bar, session players set up. Guitars, violins, a bodhran. Wanda checks her phone. Over four hours and no messages. Each time the door opens, her eyes dart to it.

"Just call him, sure."

"No." She gets up for another round. She sways slightly at the hip. "Same?" she says. She points to Leo's glass.

"One more. Then we get out of here. Enough sorrow drowning."

"But they're still breathing."

She clomps off to the bar. She looks back at Leo while the pints are being poured. He studies the players tuning up. Her phone vibrates in her pocket and she pulls it out.

To: JaynesWanda@nlil.ca
From: Holdenshat@mail.com

U should watch the company you keep.
Photo attached.

She presses the attachment link. At first she's not sure what she's looking at. Bright lights, a club of some kind. Two figures face each other. The woman wears a short black dress with a red pattern, her laughing face tilts up at the man. The man gazes down on her with pursed lips, his hand reaching out and over her butt. Maybe in mid-caress. Maybe about to go for it. It takes her a few moments to register it's Trish and Darryl Pike.

"You're looking pale," Leo says when she returns with the drinks. "I should get you home." She hands him her phone. He looks at the photo. His lip curls upward. "Where did you find this?"

"My crazy admirer sent it to me, just now."

"Where is it?"

"Don't know. That's the dress she wore on Thursday when we were at The Duke." She shrugs. "I guess they went dancing after?"

"When did you leave?"

"Around midnight."

Leo passes the phone back to her. He picks up his pint and takes a sip. "She didn't come home 'til three."

"I'm sure it's nothing."

"She never mentioned she went dancing with him."

"Maybe she didn't think she had to."

"No," Leo says. "She knows I think the guy is a tool." He picks up the phone and looks at the picture. "Look at him. Who dances like that with a girl when you know she has a boyfriend? That fucker shook my hand."

"He probably doesn't know any other way to dance."

"She does," he says. "She went to dance school. All 'round artiste, Trish."

"I shouldn't have shown it to you," she says. "I'm sorry. I should just block these emails. The cops have done nothing." Fuck sakes, Trish. For someone who takes candid photos, she should know better.

"No, I'm glad you showed me."

They drink in silence. The session players play one reel after another, frantic, churning music. Wanda's and Leo's feet tap involuntarily.

Leo empties his pint. "This music makes me feel like a leprechaun on speed." He plunks the glass on the table and stands. His knees buckle. Wanda leaps up to support him. She can feel the prickle of other patrons' eyes roaming over them.

"Look at 'em all," Leo says. "Havin' a fine gawk."

"Let's get you home."

"Good idea. There's wine there." He starts to do up his coat, third button into second hole. "Bout time you came by. Sure, you never comes over anymore."

They trudge up the steps by the LSPU Hall. Trish and Leo rent an upstairs apartment in a heritage home on Gower Street. The stairwell is dark with a faint smell of cat piss. Leo scrabbles the key in the deadbolt and the door swings open to their apartment. He flicks the light switch; the bulb flashes on and immediately fizzles out. "Piece o' crap."

The apartment is still sparsely furnished, as Wanda remembers it, their round kitchen table, futon couch, an ancient television set with rabbit ears that Trish has painted with rainbows, polka-dots, animal prints. More art on the walls. Most of it looks like Trish's work.

"Where's Trish?"

"At her cousin's," Leo says. He yanks on the laces of his right boot and shucks it off. He unties the left and tries to remove it without loosening anything. "Ow. I'm going to get a charley horse." He collapses into a chair by the kitchen table. Wanda clasps his foot between her knees and plucks the laces loose.

"The nice thing about relaxing at home is that you can use the bong. So economical," Leo says. He opens a small wooden box from the middle of the kitchen table and rustles out a small bag of weed, a few green crumbs spill out.

"When will Trish be back?"

"Tomorrow. She's babysitting overnight." Leo tilts his head towards the kitchen. "Be a dear and get us some wine? Bottle's on the counter. And two glasses. And the bong is under the sink."

"Do you want me to make you a sandwich too?"

"I would never degrade you like that. Bad enough you took me boot off."

The wine has a twist-off cap. Wanda cracks it and brings everything out to the table. Leo stuffs the bong bowl. "It's not so much she went dancing with him," he says. "Trish loves to dance. Dances all the time. But man, she made so much fun of that guy. She said he was puffed up. Like a macho little balloon."

"Good description."

"It all makes me wonder where the line is drawn." Leo makes a line on the table with the side of his hand. He looks up at her. "Have some wine, my dear. You know, we only have so much time on this earth. Life is too short to spend it with annoying people."

"That's exactly how I feel. I'm surrounded by annoying people all the time. It's inescapable." She thinks of Sharon and Nikki, what are they doing right now? Will they eventually find new friends who fit better in their lives? It's so hard to make friends when you're all adults. She pours a glass of wine. "When I have my own time, I want to be with people I actually like."

"Yes. Your top-tier friends. And I hate to be one of these *times are a-changin* jerks, but sometimes I get this feeling that lately, everything is a cheaper version of itself, including people." Leo waves towards the burned-out light. "I swear I changed that friggin' light bulb last week. Nothing is quality anymore."

"Maybe you got the wattage wrong."

"Maybe. But even with friendships, the people you surround yourself with. I don't want to hang out with knobs like Pike because of what they can give me." Leo sparks his lighter and touches the flame to the bowl. He inhales, neatly pops out the bowl and stem and passes the bong to Wanda. "Lots of smoke there for you."

"Thank you." The extra smoke floats from her mouth to the light fixture above. "Perhaps it's the millennial generation's influence or something. Saturated with image over substance."

"It's not any one group. My parents even. Now that they're retired, it's like suddenly they want this polished lifestyle." He pauses to fill both their glasses with wine, splashing some over the rim. "Last year, Mom redecorated our house in Holyrood. Painted, bought new rugs, fancy lamps, all that stuff. Anyway, she found this wall hanging, this quote thingy in wooden letters. Has a little shelf on either end, for fuckin' knickknacks. It's a Chinese proverb." He presses his fingertips to his chest: "*A family in harmony will prosper in everything.* So, one Sunday, she invites everyone over to check out the house. And I'm looking around and I realize something's missing. The spot on the wall where she hung this saying is where Nan's rug used to be. It was this hooked rug she made for Mom and Dad's wedding. I said, 'Mom, where's Nan's rug?' And she said she sent it to Aunt Maureen in Oshawa, to hang up in her cottage. 'I've been looking at it for thirty years, someone else can enjoy it now.' So now, there's friggin' font art explaining the importance of family harmony while an actual symbol of it, the fucking work and effort of familial love, is in a cottage. To be seen on long weekends and holidays. Because it fits in with the rustic décor."

He slumps in his chair and sips his wine. His eyes shine in the dim light. She realizes he is close to tears.

"Let's get you to bed," she says.

She stands in front of him and holds out her hand. He takes it and brings it to his lips. "You're a good person, Wanda."

"Thank you, sweetie."

He hauls himself up. She leads him towards the bedroom. He follows her, his head dangles over his heart. The door sways open with a sigh. The walls are barren except for a few small photos in frames. The room is stuffy, but comfortable with the faded odour of sandalwood candles and warmth.

Wanda unbuttons Leo's flannel shirt and lays it over the dresser. Once he is under the blankets, he takes off his own pants.

"Goodnight. I'm going to get a cab."

"Stay for a while?" Leo says. Tears drip down his face. "Just lie here with me for a bit. Please?"

She considers him. He is melting with sadness. She'll make sure he's okay. He'll pass out soon. She lies next to him, facing away. He curls one hand around her waist. "You're a good friend to me." He presses his face into the back of her neck. She can feel spots of dampness forming from his breath in her hair.

She closes her eyes. Sleep is like blowing out a candle.

The clock glares 7:48am. Leo's arm is warm and sticky against the flesh of her belly. Her top shifted up in her sleep. Or his arm snaked its way in there. She sits up. No great hangover pain, but technically, she still feels drunk. Her mouth is wet. She has drooled a tiny pool onto Trish's pillow.

Leo's face is slack and peaceful. She pokes his shoulder. "When is Trish back?"

He sniffs loudly and turns to the clock. "Soon."

"Gettin' a cab."

"Okay. They're pretty fast around here." He pulls up the covers and is out again.

Should she ask if he will tell Trish or Ivan she slept over? He is already lightly snoring. She'll ask him later. Fuck it. Nothing happened.

The cab arrives quickly and as soon as she settles into the back, the roughness starts. The air freshener says French vanilla, but it smells like bubblegum. It tries its best, but she can still identify the ancient stench of damp cigarettes.

As the cab pulls away, she catches a flash, a tiny glimpse of Trish's familiar platinum head, appearing around the corner. She slumps down in the seat. She closes her eyes and tries to ignore the droning cadence of the taxi dispatcher; every beep and burr of the radio makes her belly twist.

The house is cool and musty when she comes in. No sign of Ivan. A note on the fridge.

W,

In case you're wondering why I didn't call, Leo texted and told me you were with him. I guess he couldn't convince you to get in contact with me.

I need to clear my head. I'm at Sylvie's for a couple of days. Call me if you need anything.

I.

The letters are pressed hard into the paper. Is he really upset or was it just a shitty pen? No apologies or affection. What does "clear my head" mean?

She gets a Gatorade and gulps a third of it. What will she do if he leaves her? All alone. She imagines calling her parents to tell them, the nervous twang of Mom's voice, the placating, the "Oh love, that's too bad." Dad's silent, shrugging disappointment. Who would get the house? Would she get a roommate? Are these really her main concerns?

She goes upstairs and lies down. Bit woozy. Still kinda drunk. Her eyes fall on the canvas bag of unmarked assignments from work next to the bed. Ugh. Her bag of nag. And why? The program won't exist soon. Her students will be the last ABE graduates. No more students. No more work. No more boyfriend. Her stomach's contents shudder and wheeze.

Her phone goes off. Trish. Ignore. She silences the phone. Then turns it off. Just no. She squeezes her eyes closed until sleep takes her.

It's afternoon when she wakes up. Small cracks and water stains in the ceiling stare at her. She thinks of the things she does not want to do and lists them on her fingertips. She takes the stairs to the attic with the canvas bag. It slaps her hip with each step. She counts the steps from the top to the landing. Thirteen. Pretty ideal, actually.

The first stack of papers doesn't distribute well and only a couple make it to the bottom. By the third toss, she's developed a good arch and the momentum and distribution is quite even. When they're all gone, she surveys her handiwork. Not bad.

She scoops up the three on the top stair, closest to her, and lays them in a pile. For the next three stairs, she stacks the papers by corresponding grade: D-, D, D+. When she gets to the bottom and inspects the A section, she laughs out loud. "Evan McKinnley, you made it all the way." She grabs his paper and puts it on top of the A+ pile. "Have a great summer."

19

CONSTABLE Lance moves a chair so Wanda can sit next to him and they can both see the computer monitor. When he jerks the mouse, his screensaver vanishes, but she gets a quick glimpse of a family picture: him in uniform next to a petite blond woman with a wide-eyed baby in her arms.

Constable Lance bites his bottom lip as he types in the web address, his eyelashes cast shadows on his cheeks. She is reminded of a Cabbage Patch doll she had in grade four. What was the name on the adoption certificate? Alyssa. He frowns at the screen and a tired breath drains from him: coffee and beef stock. All grown up on the inside.

"Here it is," he says. The wallpaper on the MySpace page is wine coloured with titles in a light yellow. Designed to look like the cover of the book, but slightly off: the font is Comic Sans. "The MySpace Page of Holden Caulfield." There's a bio and links to music videos they figured Holden Caulfield would like—The Smiths, Simple Plan, The National. Various pictures of emo-looking guys with sad faces and hair in their eyes.

"It's a high-school English project," Constable Lance says. "The kids had to create online profiles for characters from their novel studies. I spoke to the teacher who had this class. Each group got an email account and shared passwords so they could contribute easily. Holden's hat was chosen as a user name because they were focusing on symbolism in the book. They also had characters like Phoebe Caulfield and Ackley." He picks up a clipboard beside the computer. "The MySpace page is over ten years old. It took a while to get the list of student names that made this particular project." He pulls out a sheet of paper from the clipboard and hands it to her. "Do any of their names look familiar to you?"

She scours the list:

Sam Katsman

Daniel Burke

Melody Chen

Jody McKinnley

Mia Nguyen

She studies each name, says it out loud. Nothing. No recognition. "So, how old were these students at the time?"

"It was level three, so seventeen, eighteen."

"So, now they'd be twenty-seven, twenty-eight?" she says. "No one rings a bell."

"What about your own former students?"

"There's been so many." And names change, people get married. Is Jody a boy or girl? Does she know any Mias? She's taught a few Melodys and Mels. She knows way too many Daniels.

"I can cross reference," she says, "but I'm usually pretty good with recognizing names. So, if these six people knew the email password, they could have given it to someone else?"

"It's possible. However, I noticed a couple of things." He clicks on the "photos" section of the MySpace page. There are several stock images posted: a picture of a red hunting hat; the Museum of Natural History in New York; a photo of a little girl looking melancholy. The caption reads, "This is Holden sister Phoebe. He thinks she is a little angle."

"Since it was a group project, they all had to contribute. Quite a few entries read the way your admirer writes. I think it's one of the original students."

"Really? That's a relief." And it's not Karl. His empty bottle of Zyprexa pops into her head. Ugh. Stupid Wanda. The scabs on her arm tingle. Resist, resist.

"I'll keep looking into it. The emails continue to come from public computer labs at the university. The messages are not directly threatening, so the most we could do is keep track of them. But I will personally look into each student."

Guilt pecks her insides. How many times has she cursed Lance in the past few weeks and he was actually doing his job? "Thank you," she says.

"Continue to forward any emails you get. And call if you're concerned about anything," he says. She resists the urge to muss his hair.

On the way home from the cop shop, the wind bites at her exposed hands. She shoves them in her pockets and her phone presses against the inside of her wrist. She checks it. She still hasn't listened to Trish's voice mail. There are two new missed calls: one from Mrs. Medeiros, one from Mom. Both have left voice mails. The idea of hearing them speak brings thick ripples of exhaustion through her. The timbre of Mom's worry. The artificial frothiness of Trish's voice, like whipped topping.

Four text messages.

Ivan: How are you? Doing ok? Don't forget to put out the recycling.

Leo: Let me know if you need anything.

Sharon: Missed your call, what's up? Get on a plane, come to me.

Nikki: I miss you Meme Dream. Talking to Sharon. This summer, the 3 of us, together again. Make it happen.

She gets in the house and faintly realizes she remembers little about the walk there. She's on autopilot. She swings open the refrigerator and drinks orange juice straight from the container. A small rectangle of notepaper lies in the centre of the dining-room table. Yesterday, she made a list of things to do and they've all been done: price security cameras, marinate chicken, put in final grades, organize desk. Each entry is sliced with a red line through it. Her pen is a guillotine, executing tasks.

New tasks for today:

Stop scratching fucking eczema.
See if Leo can bring some weed.
Sleep.

The festival is tomorrow. If she can lay low and avoid everyone, it will pass quickly. Bah-humbug to it all. She texts Leo about pot, slathers cortisone cream on her scabs. She opens a bottle of wine and settles on the couch. The rule is to only watch comedies. Intense drama or violence or romance cannot be handled right now. And nothing in a school or post-secondary setting. Leo replies and says he can come over in the morning. Hooray. She can smoke the rest of the weed and get more tomorrow.

At 1:53am she wakes on the couch. Two empty red wine bottles and an empty baggie on the coffee table. She totters to bed and collapses stomach down. Her eyes squeeze shut. C'mon sleep. Reappear. *Don't forget to put out the recycling.* A sound outside, a sharp bang. Her heart jumps. It's a car door. Pascale's probably. Or someone outside. *Let me know if you need anything.*

She staggers to the bureau and fishes in the top drawer. It was here the last time she checked, amongst her socks and underwear. Her fingers touch the plastic canister and she pulls out the pill bottle. One last pill, the last Valium from Mrs. Medeiros. She swallows it without water and slumps back to bed. The dulling comes, velvet and numb. Thoughts alight on her mind and make no impact. Pictures appear: Ivan's slumping shoulders, Mom's jaw moving as she chews the insides of her cheek, Frances Rumstead seated on her sad, drab couch. Florescent lights and moist killer eyes. Her mind becomes a thick slurry where ideas form and float and evaporate without residue. This is good. This was a good idea. Her eyelids leaden and seal like an ancient sarcophagus.

20

SHE wakes to the doorbell. Everything external is dry cotton while her inners are infused with a stinging, brackish solution. Slight movements kill. Phone is beside her head. It flashes a text message. She slithers out one hand to check it. Leo.

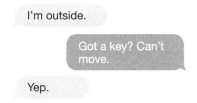

I'm outside.

Got a key? Can't move.

Yep.

She hears the front door swing open. His feet patter upstairs. He sighs at the sight of her. "Jesus Christ, Jaynes."

She waggles fingers at him. Even that hurts.

"So, the doctor says no booze, huh?" Leo says.

"Oops."

"Guess you're not going to the festival, then?"

"Can't. Sick, see?"

"I brought something to fix you up," he says. He holds a large plastic cup with a bubble lid and a straw. Real big, venti size. The liquid inside glows bright pink and radioactive.

"What is it?"

"All the good stuff. Beets, carrots, celery, pomegranate. I was looking up ulcer-friendly foods last night. This has a bunch of them." He holds it out. "Drink."

She worms her body across the bed and dangles her head off the edge. Leo holds the cup while she sips from the straw like a caged pet at a water feeder.

"Is it good?"

"It's hydration," she says. "What time is it?"

"About 1:30."

"Wow. I was out like a light." A light-blue pill.

"I'm worried about you."

"Yeah, well, you got off your face completely the other night. Worry about yourself."

"I don't deny things aren't great. But I'm scared you're going to bottom out." Leo stirs the mixture with the straw. "Did you talk to Trish?"

"Nope."

"She knows you stayed over the other night."

"Oh well." She takes the cup from him. "Thanks for this. I think it's working."

"She's upset with both of us."

"Why? We didn't do anything."

"Yeah, but can you please talk to her?"

"Oh, for fuck's sake. Does she ever look at herself? Did you tell her about the photo of her and Pike?"

"Yes. We discussed it."

"What's her excuse?"

"I'm not getting into this," Leo says. "Anyway, talk to her, please? She says you haven't returned her phone calls."

"I wish everybody would just leave me alone." She sits up and rubs her face. "Just get off my ass."

"You seem pretty alone already."

"Whatever." She straightens her t-shirt. A red wine stain stretches down the front. Class-say. "Have you talked to Ivan?"

"A little. He isn't saying much." He checks the time on his phone. "I gotta head over to the festival to help him and Ray set up, but I can't stay there. I think he'd like it if you came down."

"Did you bring me some green?"

He stares at her. She blinks to show she's waiting. He rummages in his jacket pocket. He tosses a small baggie on the bed. "Try to take it easy. Drink that juice."

"Okay, Dad."

He leans forward and kisses her forehead. "You are loved, remember that."

She closes her eyes. "Bye."

Leo's footsteps descend to the front door. She listens for his key in the lock and closes her eyes. Breathe in, breathe out. Any sudden movement can ignite pain. Don't think about bodily functions that require getting out of bed.

At 4:13pm, her phone goes off. Go away. But it's Constable Lance. Take the call.

"I have some information on your pen pal." Lance sounds like he's shuffling papers. "One of the students who worked on that project has a definite connection to you."

"Really?" She sits up. Her head roars in complaint.

"I spoke with the original teacher. One of the students used a different name in high school. Melody Chen. She used the name Melody because her classmates had a hard time pronouncing her Chinese name and she got teased. Her name is Liang-Yi Chen. Who we know, of course."

The woman in the grocery aisle next to her, the sob and thud to her right. Her pleading voice. Sitting in the parking lot at the vigil, her face in her hands. Here is Wanda, going slowly mad about what she doesn't remember doing. And Liang-Yi probably remembers very well. Wanda sinks her teeth into her knuckle to halt whatever cry or grunt or wail might exit.

"Ms. Jaynes? Are you okay?"

She removes her hand from her mouth. "Yes." She swipes at her eyes. "Sorry. It's just coming back or something."

"I understand. How would you like to proceed?"

"I don't know. I'd rather she'd get help than charge her. I mean, could she be dangerous?"

"We also have reason to believe she may be giving the shooter's mother a hard time."

"Frances Rumstead?"

"Yes. We don't know about the phone calls, but someone who fits her description threw a can through her window."

"Jesus Christ.'

"If you see or hear anything from Ms. Chen, call the station."

"Yes, of course."

"And if you have any questions, you know where to find me."

"Thank you. I realize you didn't have to go to all this trouble."

"It's no trouble." Lance's voice is gentle professionalism. "No trouble at all."

She hangs up and coils into a ball. More sleep please. But it doesn't come. Sleep is all she's done and now Leo has filled her up with vitamins she'll have to burn off. Just get up and eat something solid, get on with it. There's leftover pizza. There might be soup. In the freezer, there's lasagna that Mrs. Medeiros gave them at the birthday party. Her voice bubbles into Wanda's mind: "*When he looks at you, he stares and twitches. His eyes and lips move. Like he's thinking of something else. He gives me a bad feeling.*" Wanda shoots up in bed. The ache sloshes in her brain. Mrs. Medeiros needs to leave Karl Prendergast alone.

She calls. Mrs. Medeiros's phone rings. The voice mail would be sweet relief. She could explain it all in a message, not have to answer concerns as to why her son is at Sylvie's and not here. But Mrs. Medeiros answers on the third ring: "Oh, Wanda, thank God. I have to talk to you."

"Me too. Listen, I was just talking to the cops. We were wrong about Karl."

"No, no, it's so much worse," Mrs. Medeiros says. Her voice is high and eerie. "It's so awful. He is a monster. He needs to be stopped."

"Why? What happened?"

"I was in his house." She pauses, pants. "He has things, set up. Equipment."

"You went to his house?"

"Yes! Remember I told you he is involved with the same charity as my friend, Helen? Well, I rang his doorbell, told him I was going door to door, looking for donations." She pauses. Wanda hears a clicking sound like a bottle cap popping. A signal indicator.

"Are you driving?"

"Yes! I've been following him for two days." A car horn blares. "I have to, you see. I have to make sure he doesn't do anything bad."

"Bad like what?"

"I saw it, in his house." More car horns: a series of angry honks.

"You should pull over." Wanda pictures Mrs. Medeiros balancing the phone between her chin and shoulder, turning the steering wheel hard, the flashing lights of a police car through the rear window. "You shouldn't drive and talk. It's dangerous. You'll get a fine."

"I have to follow him. I have to make sure. Don't worry, I've been looking at his Facebook too. After he goes home, he's going to the festival. I can follow him on foot there."

"Please, I think you should pull over."

"He's almost home."

"I'm scared you're not thinking clearly," Wanda says. Hot nervous sweat envelopes her. "We should talk about this."

"Ah, he's parking now." Mrs. Medeiros sighs. "I'm going to follow him over to the festival." She hangs up.

Wanda closes her eyes. Fucking hell. What to do. She starts to text Ivan, but stops. Texting your boyfriend to tell him his mother is off the rails. Good idea. Christ. She presses call. Straight to voice mail. The time is 4:41. He's at the festival by now. She opens the Facebook event, checks the lineup for musical acts. 4:30. Ray and the Autumn People. They started playing ten minutes ago. When she shows up, they'll be finished. Everyone can tell her what a nice fucking girlfriend she is.

Wanda scrambles around the room. Yesterday's jeans are in a pile and her navy-blue hoodie hangs on the doorknob. She throws it all on. Her stomach moans in hunger. She grabs the cup of veggie juice and flies down the stairs. What else does she need? Sunglasses. Secrecy would be nice. She puts them on and charges out the door.

The festival grounds occupy half the park, starting at the playground and stretching to the end. Signs and decorations skirt the sides of the walkway. Wanda strides up the dirt path under the maple trees. Tibetan prayer flags are strung from tree to tree, homey-looking Bristol-board placards are propped up on plywood posts:

To the Festival of Healing! ☺ Painted rainbows and doves juxtapose with corporate signs and logos: *Proud Sponsors of the Festival of Healing.* A haze of activity hums in the distance. A few scattered clouds on an otherwise idyllic sky. Where the Jesus is Mrs. Medeiros?

As she nears the playground, the noises intensify and separate: music, voices, the grinding of generators. Booths and tables line a wide walkway through the park: games of chance, crafts, organizations with stacks of pamphlets and badges, cotton candy, popcorn, samosas, cupcakes, and coffee. No Mrs. Medeiros.

Burly men with tight black t-shirts and folded arms hover by the entrance to the beer tent. On its right, people have set up deck chairs and blankets on the grass facing the tall, black monolith of the stage. "Test, test. One-two, one-two." The next act prepares to perform. Which means Ivan's around. Maybe she can find his mother and leave unnoticed. She stops by a craft table and scans the area. Where would Karl be? If she can find Karl, she can find Mrs. Medeiros.

A roundish woman in a royal-blue t-shirt walks towards her. There is something familiar in her gait that makes Wanda push her sunglasses up and tug her hood around her face. The woman's eyes catch on Wanda. It's Pascale Aggressive. Wanda gives her a quick nod. Pascale's face pales. She makes an abrupt right turn and crosses to the booths lining the other side of the walkway. A gaggle of others wearing the same t-shirt cluster around one of the booths. A glossy royal-blue banner hangs over it with yellow letters: Keeping in Touch: Workers for Modern Christianity. A picture of a smiling Joseph Workman in the lower right corner. Pascale is a member. Well then. Guess it was easy for them to get her address. Maybe Pascale would like being added to every flyer distribution list in town. What a cow.

Pascale scurries to the Workers' booth and whispers something to a woman with long red pigtails. The red-haired woman turns and stares at Wanda. She is familiar. Geraldine Harvey, the woman who was shot at and played dead.

Geraldine tugs the sleeve of the person next to her: a stick-thin figure in a black toque. Wanda averts her eyes from them; she examines the items on the closest craft table. Glass-bead necklaces, earrings. She pretends to be enthralled in a stained-glass sun catcher shaped like an owl.

"Excuse me?" Three furtive taps on her shoulder. Geraldine's brassy braids are coated with a froth of orange frizz. They dangle along the sides of her large breasts, like the floor path lighting on airplanes. This way, please. The woman beside her is chiselled and frail, the black toque tight across her skull. Her eyes shine with intensity. Both wear royal-blue t-shirts with "ASK ME WHY I BELIEVE IN MIRACLES" in bold gold letters across the chest.

"You are her, yes?" says Geraldine. "Wanda Jaynes?"

Wanda nods. Geraldine smiles with her lips shut, but her eyes stay direct. "My name is Geraldine and this is Ruth. We are both members of Workers for Modern Christianity." She points to a button above her giant right boob that states the group's title. "But I believe you've heard of our founder, Joseph Nigel Workman?"

"Yes, he sounds vaguely familiar." Why is she trying to be funny? Her glib reply does not amuse. Ruth's eyes roll up to the sky. Geraldine's chin juts out and she smooths her pigtails in one long, quick stroke with both hands.

"Yes, I'm sure he does," Geraldine says. "I don't know if you might have seen me on the news. I was in the store as well, that day."

"Yes, I saw. How are you doing?"

"Well, you know, such a tragedy. But we were lucky God was on our side," Geraldine says. "I'd like to invite you over to our tent to talk. You can meet some of the other members."

"Um, that's very nice of you," Wanda takes off her sunglasses. Maybe she'll seem sincere if they can see her eyes. "Unfortunately, I have to meet someone here. Thanks, though." She steps to the right. Ruth matches it to stand in front of her. She glares up into Wanda's face. Ruth has a fierce, reptilian look. It takes Wanda a moment to realize she has no eyebrows or eyelashes. Cancer survivor.

"I'm sorry, Gerry, but I really need to hear her say it," Ruth says. Her left eye twitches.

"Easy, Ruth," Geraldine says. Her cheek quivers with pleasure.

"No, I'd like to hear this woman say she stopped the shooter herself," Ruth says. "I'd like to hear her deny God's power."

Geraldine speaks into Wanda's ear, her breasts press into her arm. "You'll have to excuse, Ruth, Miss Jaynes. Ruth is a miracle.

Like you and I." Geraldine places her hand on Ruth's shoulder. "Without the power of prayer, she would not be here."

"Stage three cancer." Ruth puffs out her bony chest. "It was everywhere. And I was Satan's cohort back then. I drank. I smoked. I tarnished this gift from God, this body. And Satan was winning. I was a goner." She holds out her skinny arms to the sides, displaying the miracle that is her. "But I believed. And I prayed, every day. And thanks to people like Geraldine, I had an army of believers praying for me. And now, remission." Ruth's arms rise up over her shoulders. She smiles up to the sky. Then the arms descend to fold in front of her. Her eyes drill into Wanda's. "So, I find it very hard to take people who can stick their noses in the air and ignore God's blessings."

"We all saw the video," Geraldine says. "God acted through you. If you won't take it from me, take it from this woman. She knows miracles."

Wanda swallows. She is unbelievably thirsty. "I'm glad you're okay now, Ruth." She occupies herself stirring the straw in the pink vegetable juice.

"Thank you, Miss Jaynes."

"But, no offense," Wanda takes a quick sip. "You had chemo, right?" Maybe she's still drunk. Or high.

Ruth's eyes narrow. "I prayed every day."

"Yes, but you know, you also had radiation therapy, right? I mean, you do also take that into consideration, yes? The work of doctors and nurses?" Wanda takes another sip and can't stop. So thirsty.

"Wow," Geraldine says. "You're something else."

"Conceit," Ruth hisses. A thin droplet of spittle lands on Wanda's cheek.

"Leave her alone." The voice booms. Two people appear next to her. The speaker is a tall man with cropped green hair. His earlobes reach his jaw and gape open; the round plugs in each are so wide, she could watch the concert through them. The person beside him comes up to his elbow, red bucket hat, tiny fierce eyes. Dallas Cleal.

"Oh look," Geraldine scowls. "It's Dallas and the philosophy society."

"Maybe you should take a class," Earlobes says.

"Then she'd have to read a book," Dallas says. "Geraldine only reads propaganda. And distributes it. Thanks for keeping me on your mailing list. Kept the woodstove going all winter."

"What do you want, Dallas?'

"I want you to stop badgering this woman," Dallas says. Earlobes glowers beside her.

"Badgering?" Geraldine says. "You're the one with the goon." She grabs Ruth's hand. "Pretty low to gang up on a cancer survivor."

"You call yourself Christian, but you're an insult to Christians," Earlobes says. "You come to a peaceful festival and harass people?" Dallas nods, hands on hips. Wanda glances around. More people in blue t-shirts are approaching. Others stop and stare.

Ruth laughs. "Oh, Gerry, isn't it refreshing to see how little things change? Dallas always brings her most smug first-year philosophy student to explain how things work."

A hand clamps down on Wanda's shoulder. "There you are." She looks into Darryl Pike's beaming face.

"Everyone enjoying themselves so far?" Pike looks slick. He wears dark jeans and a silver-grey t-shirt made of some kind of gauzy material that clings to his pectoral muscles. His black sports jacket looks tailored and expensive. He removes strips of tickets from the inside pocket. "Here are some complimentary tickets for the beer tent and local treats. Enjoy them, give them to your friends, on me." He tears them in quick, neat rips and hands them out. Ruth and Geraldine glare at Wanda before skulking off. Dallas hands her tickets to Earlobes. She nods to Wanda and walks away.

"Well, you're a sight for sore eyes, missus," Pike produces another strip of drink tickets and slides them into the pocket of her hoodie. "C'mon, let's get you outta this chaos. You gotta backstage pass, after all."

He places her hand on the crook of his elbow and steers her past the line of vendors and tents. People mill by them, dragging children, balancing Styrofoam containers of fried food. Pike greets them with nods and winks: "Hey there. Whaddya at? How ya gettin' on?" He never waits for a response. People's faces register the two of them and glow with recognition. Great. Wanda didn't shower today—did she yesterday?—and she is decked out in her grubbiest, non-descript clothes. She imagines she exudes booze in a sour, pungent aura. She tries to shrink further into her hoodie.

"So many people have asked about you today," Pike says. "Did you just get here?"

"Yes. Actually, I need to find a friend of mine."

"Good luck! Massive crowd on the go. The vibe is truly amazing, Wanda." He rubs her hand on his arm, pressing it into the silky fabric of his jacket.

"Thanks for getting me away from those Workman people back there, but it's kind of important I find my friend."

"Who is it you need to find?"

"Ivan's mom, actually."

"Oh, well he might know himself. He's in the backstage area— the Green Room, I call it. Lotsa green goin' on there all day." Pike grins. He smells like Axe body spray and Listerine. He eyes Wanda's hoodie. "Did you bring a change of clothes? For later, on stage?"

"Um, no. I need to talk to you about that."

"No worries, my dear. We have lots of clothes in the Green Room. We'll find something sharp."

She withers a little more. How to get out of here. She'll check out the Green Room to be polite, make a quick exit.

The Green Room is actually a large tent with red and white stripes. Pike opens the flap with a generous sweep of his arm. "Ladies first." Inside, Wanda recognizes several local musicians sprawled across worn couches against the tent walls. They ooze a practiced nonchalance. Two bearded guys with dark-framed glasses rummage in a cooler. There are tables full of liquor. Racks of clothes along the far wall with a curtained-off dressing room.

"What's your poison, my dear?" Pike gestures to the bar area. "Wine or beer? A rum and coke? Vodka with something fruity?"

"A rum and coke sounds good." The pink juice is down to the dregs.

Pike takes the cup. "A girl after my own heart," he says. He waves at a svelte black girl with cornrows twisted into a high pile on her head. She wears a beige suede dress that looks designer and amazing. "Rachel, get Wanda and I a couple of rum and cokes, please." Rachel gives them a perfect smile, exposing rows of even white teeth. When she turns, Wanda sees the dress is backless, exposing the long sweep of her flawless brown skin. Pike's eyes dance down her spine as she walks away. "Rachel is great. She'll help you pick out something for onstage as well." He points to the rack of clothes. "Lots of stuff here for you to go through."

"About that. I don't really think I'm up to going on stage," Wanda says. "It's almost 5:30 now and I'm feeling really gross."

Pike's face hardens with concern. "Oh no. People have been asking about you all day. There are people who came just to see you."

"See, that's it too. I find all this extremely stressful."

"Stressful? Oh, honey, my stress has gone through the roof! Smoking a pack a day and nervous diarrhea all week for me." He tosses his head back and laughs. A gold-capped tooth on the top front row of his mouth sparkles. His head levels with hers. "Seriously though, whatever you need. There's a soundproof trailer a street away if you want a nap. We can get you food, drinks, a massage, anything you need." Rachel appears with two fizzing plastic cups. Pike takes one and coils an arm around Rachel's shoulders. "You're among friends here, my dear. We'll take care of you. Won't we, Rache?"

"Anything for the Wandawoman," Rachel says.

"See? No stress here." He smiles. His hand disappears from Rachel's shoulder and from the flicker in her dark eyes, Wanda suspects it made an appearance somewhere on her naked back. She thinks of his hand poised over Trish's behind in that photo. What a dicksmack.

"That's all very kind, thank you. But I really—" The flap in the tent parts. Ivan enters. Her heart jerks in her chest. His eyes meet hers and he deflates a little, like some vital energy was just siphoned out of him.

He raises one hand to her. She matches it. He nods his head towards the exit and mouths the word "outside?"

She nods. "Pike, I need to talk to Ivan, back soon." She tips her cup at Rachel in thanks.

Outside, they scan the area for a place to talk. A band of about a dozen musicians in colourful tie-dye clothes have taken the stage, pounding out hyperactive ska. People dance writhing-hippy-style on the grass before them. Sloppy bellows of laughter echo from the beer tent. They pass lines of vendors: the Potters Association, handmade hemp products, Inuit crafts and sculpture. A few people pat Ivan's back as they walk by: "Good job, man." "Deadly set." Ivan thanks them. These are the only times he smiles or speaks. Wanda tightens her hood over her head. She scans the area. No sign of Mrs. Medeiros.

Ivan points to a blue tent, set off from the main stage. "Trish's exhibit," he says. A silver banner bearing the words "Local Heroes in Their Element" drapes over the opening. Wanda looks sideways at Ivan. His face is sullen and unreadable. He's so angry with her.

They continue walking to the edge of the park where it's just grass and trees. A few people sit on blankets under trees, sipping from thermoses and unmarked bottles. Three cop cars line the street at the park's end.

"Here is good," Ivan says. He leans against a tree. The music thumps in the distance. A dog yaps. Marijuana smoke wafts by.

"You look tired," he says.

"I am." Her fingernails on the hand holding her cup have ragged, dirty ridges. Tiny bubbles rise from the black drink. "I've never felt so tired in my life."

"What are you going to do about it?"

"What are *you* going to do about it?" she says.

His eyes cast down from hers. "I'm trying, Wanda. I'm trying to help you."

"Really? Because I wonder if you even want to understand how I feel."

"I guess I thought we were at a place where we're close enough you would tell me how you feel," he says. "That if there was a problem, you would tell me."

"I feel like I have been telling you."

"I feel like you're just reacting."

"Well, yeah, I'm reacting to you. To your…lack of acting or…acting in ways that aren't cool." Nothing she says is right. It's like scratching a slab of granite.

"But, I don't know, Wanda," he says. "If you don't tell me, I don't know what I'm doing wrong. Or what you need." He moves in front of her and touches her cheek inside the hood. "I missed you these past few days."

"I missed you too."

"I'm sorry everything has been so fucked up," he says.

"Me too. I feel like everything I do is wrong. I'm becoming a lunatic."

"Ridiculous. I mean, you're not ridiculous. Don't think like that." Ivan sighs. "Here, you wanna see a lunatic? Look at that dog. That dog is bananas."

He nods to a bopping, yapping Pomeranian, a fluff ball of orange fur. Lumbering beside it is Karl Prendergast, lips moving subtly, eyes swimming in his thick lenses. Wanda's face retreats turtle-like into her hood.

Once he moves beyond them, she pulls her hood back and looks around. A head of wild black curls juts out from behind a tree about twenty feet away.

"Just…give me a second," Wanda says. She strides away. When she glances back, Ivan is checking his phone.

Mrs. Medeiros steps out from the tree. Her hair rises off her head in a frazzled snarl. A pale-pink windbreaker is tied around her hips; one of the cuffs is stained yellow-brown, like coffee or tea. She wears a saggy grey t-shirt, large, dark circles of sweat shadow the armpits. She waves Wanda over.

"There he goes," she says. "We need to watch him."

"Are you okay?" Wanda says. "You look...when was the last time you ate? Let's get you some food."

"Wanda, honey, you should go. Follow him to his house. Go and watch there." Mrs. Medeiros's eyes widen. She wipes at her mouth with the back of her hand. "Get Ivan, he can come with me. Ivan can stop him."

"We don't need to stop him, remember?" Wanda tries to keep her voice steady. "I talked to the cops. Karl didn't send me those emails."

"But it's worse, so, so much worse. It's in his house."

"What did you see?"

Mrs. Medeiros starts to shake her head. "He went to make tea. I asked to use the powder room. And I saw all the equipment, set up in the room. The computer, the telescope, the high-powered camera. All trained out the window. All watching the school next door."

"Are you sure?"

"I looked through the camera. It's aimed at the playground. The telescope looks into the windows of the school, the little girls' room." Her breath sucks in sharply. "When I think about what he's doing, what he's taking pictures of, I could kill him." She stops suddenly. "Where is he?" Mrs. Medeiros whirls around. "Where?" She brings her shaking hands to her face. "I lost him. I lost him. He can do anything now. He'll do bad things." She bends forwards and lays her hands on her knees, panting.

"Are you okay? C'mon, Ivan's here. We can take you home." Wanda looks back at Ivan and waves. He is still face and eyes into his phone.

Mrs. Medeiros jolts upright and points to the end of the park. "Police. Police! There! They can help me." She kisses Wanda hard on the cheek, her lips tight and sticky. "There they are. It's like they knew I needed them." She sprints towards the patrol cars, dodging between and around trees.

"No, stop!" Wanda calls. She runs. Ripping pain erupts in her stomach. She staggers. Ivan looks up. He follows her gaze to his mother standing before a police officer. Mrs. Medeiros makes animated gestures.

"Ma?" Ivan starts towards them. The officer nods at her and motions to the car. "What's going on?" Ivan says. They are too far away to hear him. The police officer walks to the back door of the cruiser and opens it. Mrs. Medeiros gets in. The door shuts and he moves to the front. He speaks into the radio as he pulls out. They catch a glimpse of Mrs. Medeiros's profile in the back seat, straight-backed and head high.

Ivan turns to Wanda. "Why did my mother get into that cop car?"

"I don't know. I mean, I don't know what she said to him. She's freaking out about that Karl guy."

"What Karl guy?"

"Karl Prendergast. The Facebook guy, remember? She's convinced he's the one sending me emails."

"Is he?"

"No. I found out today and told her. But she believes he's

into…other stuff."

"Like what?"

"Like…kid stuff. Pedo stuff."

"What? How does she know that?"

"From what she's observed." Wanda licks her lips. How to phrase this.

"She saw him with kids?"

"No. She was in his house," Wanda says. Ivan stares at her. "I don't know," she says. "She was pretty incoherent when I spoke to her."

He stares at her. "I called her earlier today," she says. "As for her and Karl, she's been…fixated on him for a while. I told her I suspected him and it turns out her friend knew him from work."

Ivan's eye twitches. "What do you mean, *fixated*?"

"She's been trying to find out stuff about him. Asking questions."

"Jesus, Wanda. Since when?"

"I don't know." Her insides are cold. "Since…well, before the long weekend. And she followed him around today."

"When you say *followed*, what do you mean?"

"I don't know what she's been doing. But I called her this morning and she was following him in her car."

Ivan holds his head. "Why didn't you call me?"

"I…I came here to find her. I wanted to find her first."

His hands smear down his face. "So, for at least three weeks, my mother has been discussing *some guy* with you and, what, spying on him? Stalking him? This didn't strike you as alarming behaviour?"

"She didn't want you to worry."

"She's my fucking mother," Ivan says. "She's been a wreck on and off for years. You know this. You know it's why she has buckets of pills. I've told you about the nerves and the wild imagination stuff. And if you thought you knew who was creeping you, why wouldn't you tell me? Don't you think the person who shares your *home* and your *bed* should *know* that?"

"Please stop yelling at me."

"Well, Jesus Christ, Wanda." He streaks his hands through his hair. "Who else knows?"

"About your mom? No one. Leo knows about what I thought about Karl."

"So he's your confidant now?"

"Don't start with who talks to who."

"That's not fair. I'm the one you should be talking to. Friendship is one thing, confiding is another. Confiding is fucking intimate."

"Maybe I wouldn't feel a need to confide in someone else if you showed me more understanding."

"Oh, Christ. This is just circles now." He takes out his phone. "I don't know what to do. Okay. I have to go. I have to go find my mother."

"I can come."

"No. Just…give me a reprieve, please." He turns and walks away, taking wide steps.

Her stomach twists in complaint as her legs scrabble to keep up with him. "Wait!" A couple sitting on a blanket turn and stare at her. Her muscles are tender and slow and she cannot keep up as his back disappears into the crowd. When she gets to the stage, she catches the sight of his frame slipping into the candy-cane stripes of the Green Room.

In the Green Room. Pike will be there. Smooth beautiful Rachel and all the cool people. And she's filthy with grime and shame. It's all so embarrassing. Better to wait for him to come out. She can go with him. They can talk things out, far away from all this shit.

In the pocket of her hoodie, her fingers touch the cardboard strip of Pike's drink tickets. The beer tent is surrounded by a temporary fence of posts and plastic netting. From the edge of the fence, she'd have a view of people entering and exiting the Green Room. She could get a drink, sip it casually, not standout, wait for him to exit. She has her phone if she wants to act like she's waiting for someone. She dons her sunglasses and heads inside.

The beer tent has long, industrial wooden tables set up close to the bar area, their sticky surfaces peppered with plastic cups and beer cans. She hands in three tickets—might as well get three at once, save a trip, avoid looking conspicuous in line. She finds a spot near the fence, lays two cans at her feet. The red and white tent is pristine against the black stage and the myriad of plastic tarps and tents. A sea of people filter in from all sides. City bylaws dictate the festival has to end by eleven. Everyone will come to fill up on junk food, beer, and free music before moving to bars or house parties. It will be a nice night. First good party of the summer. Wanda pours beer down her throat, each mouthful is an improvement. Clusters of drinkers are scattered throughout the space between the bar and the fence. They chatter and laugh. They take photos of each other: keepsakes, evidence. No one looks like they're hiding or stalking.

She lays the empty can down and takes up another. Should check her phone, to not be so obvious, gawking about.

A notification from her work email. Soon not to be her work email. Grades will be posted on Monday. She'll get some notifications then. Mos def. For a moment, she considers the numbness she feels towards her job. Like it was an insignificant errand she had to run, putting gas in the car, dropping off the recycling. She touches the icon for her work inbox.

To: JaynesWanda@nlil.ca
From: Holdenshat@mail.com

They try 2 make a funeral into a festival. A fun funeral.

Liang-Yi. The message glows in her hand. Shrill laughter blares from a nearby cluster of women. The speakers squeak angrily from the stage. Wanda presses reply.

To: Holdenshat@mail.com
From: JaynesWanda@nlil.ca

You need to stop doing this. I know who you are. Please leave me alone.

Wanda

Send. Your message is sent. She regards the glowing screen, flicks it off and pockets it. The entrance flap of the Green Room hangs still. No sign of Ivan. The song ends, the crowd whoops their approval.

Her pocket vibrates and chirps about an email received.

To: JaynesWanda@nlil.ca
From: Holdenshat@mail.com

Why? How does it hurt you? You have family, friend, you live in a big house with a handsome man. I have only monsters. Media monsters, monster mothers making monster babies, religious monsters, racist monsters. All i have done is try to talk to u about this.

She swallows. Her throat is dry and depleted. She glances around. A guy in a Toronto Maple Leafs jersey lays a chip bag in an overflowing garbage can and staggers off. The chip bag slides to the ground. She taps the reply button.

To: Holdenshat@mail.com
From: JaynesWanda@nlil.ca

I think you should talk to someone who can really help you. Your messages scare me. And I soon won't be available at this email address. Please get some help.

Send.
Response.

To: JaynesWanda@nlil.ca
From: Holdenshat@mail.com

No one can help. They can't change what i see when i close my eyes. They can't make me stop seeing white men with guns. I saw him decide to take me first. And u saw it too.

U are the only one who really saw. If others saw, it wouldn't just be about u the hero. It would be about what kind of killer he was. And this makes me so scared.

And I know you are also scared. Everyone loves u and u still hide.

She's right. Edward Rumstead did make a choice. Motivation is unknown, but it was there.

To: Holdenshat@mail.com
From: JaynesWanda@nlil.ca

I'm sorry you are going through this. Yes, I did see that.

To: JaynesWanda@nlil.ca
From: Holdenshat@mail.com

Then u must understand my heart. He was a stupid man who knew nothing. But he knew I should go first. He was taught someone like me should die first.

She drinks deeply. Oh god. She can say nothing to this poor goddamn girl. She presses respond.

To: Holdenshat@mail.com
From: JaynesWanda@nlil.ca

> Ok. You should know that I have been sending all your emails to the police since they started. I'm going to send these too and I think you should try to help yourself.

Send.

She presses forward and sends the whole chain to Constable Lance. Then she presses block. "Block Holdenshat@mail.com?" Yes. Done. No more. Wanda stabs at the off button. The screen darkens and she stuffs it into her pocket. She looks up and yelps. Trish stands before her, arms folded, all in black: a sleeveless top and a straight maxi skirt. Art-dealer chic with her pale face and red lipstick.

Trish appraises her up and down, unsmiling. Wanda realizes she's bracing herself for one of Trish's threadbare hugs. There is no move to embrace her.

"A lot of people are wondering where you are," Trish says.

"I'm waiting for Ivan."

"Here? He left to go to the police station. Ages ago," Trish says. Her round eyes narrow. "You were there when they took off with his mother. Surely, you don't think he would stick around drinking and leave her stranded?"

Wanda stares at the beer in her hand dumbly. Of course she knew he would go to the police station. It's what a sensible person would do.

"Sorry. Sorry, I guess I wasn't thinking."

"Oh, don't apologize to me," Trish says. "Oh, wait, yes. You should definitely apologize to me." Her chin juts out. She's going to haul off and give Wanda a dirty look.

"Apologize for what?"

"Maybe for the long brown hair you left on my pillow. I know Leo told you."

Trish knows that Wanda knows that Trish knows. "Well, if it upset you, that's your choice," Wanda says. She sips her beer and shifts her posture to affect nonchalance. Her heels roll back too far and she wavers on her feet.

"Choice? To be upset?" Trish says. Her open red mouth like a blossom. "So, you would choose not to be upset if I crossed that line with you and Ivan?"

"Trish, you and Ivan have never given me any choice," Wanda

says. She sips from the can. A dribble of beer runs down her chin. Her hand jerks it away.

"Ivan and I have been friends for years. Before you and he even met."

"Which gives you the right to do whatever you want. Text him night and day, hang off him, talk about me behind my back. Take fucking candid photos of me after the worst day of my life." Her voice rises. She steers it back in. "You can't suddenly set up boundaries."

Trish's red mouth closes. A berry in a bowl of milk. "I have no intention of publishing those photos. And if we talk about you, it's out of concern."

"Your high art-ly concerns," Wanda says. She makes a flourish with her hand, beer sloshes over her wrist. "So concerned about me. And your photography. And your Twitter account. What's sincere and what isn't, Trish?" She wants it to come out stinging, but her voice cracks.

Trish sighs and smoothes her skirt at her hips. The material shifts, exposing a side slit and the shock of white legs underneath. "You're all over the place, Wanda. You say you want to help Pike. He's been looking for you all day. You say Ivan has hurt you. Then you get involved in…whatever is going on with his mother."

"Of course, you know all about that," Wanda says. "Texty-text. He won't even answer my calls."

"He's upset, Wanda. You might want to think, if he's this upset now, how will he feel when he knows you slept in my bed, with Leo?" She steps forward slightly. Her foot appears in a red patent-leather flat.

Wanda stares down at the shoe: a mocking red arrow. Her shoulders are waterlogged with guilt. She pictures Ivan at the police station. Talking to a bored-looking cop at a desk behind a plastic barrier, a perfect circle cut to voice your complaints through. Last year, he might have brushed off her and Leo getting drunk and passing out together. Last month, even. Now, it might be just the excuse he wants. Like Andrea's hands and the swipe-swipe motion. All done. A dirty job completed.

"I guess I thought he already knew."

"Nope. Leo hasn't had a chance to talk to him. He only talks about that kind of stuff in person."

"So, you don't blame Leo for this?"

"Leo drinks too much," Trish says. She pauses, a slight recoil at her own abruptness. "Things have been a little rough with us lately." She tightens her arms around herself and shrugs. "We all go through rough patches."

Wanda nods. Ivan packing his things. Or her, packing her own things. Or her things in boxes on the path. Pascale Aggressive watching her carry boxes.

"Look," Trish says. She moves in front of Wanda, ducking to look into her downturned face. "Come back to the tent. We'll get you cleaned up."

"I don't think so."

"What else are you going to do?"

"Go home."

"What will you do there?"

"Not be here."

"I don't think you should be alone right now." Trish looks around. "You've been drinking. Half of St. John's has been drinking. Lots of nosey eyes around. Have you eaten?"

Wanda's stomach growls in betrayal. She shakes her head.

"Come on, there's food in Pike's tent."

"The Green Room?"

"Yeah. It's private." She tilts her head towards the bar area of the beer tent. "It's turning into a shit show here." Loud whoops peel from the crowd as if to prove her point.

"I just want to go home. This whole getting on stage, photo-op bullshit is too much for me right now."

"I know." Trish's voice is soft and low. "I've been with the exhibit all day. It's madness. I've sold at least fifty prints of your photo, my dear." She smiles into Wanda's face. "Everyone asks about you. And most of the proceeds are going to the Coalition Against Violence. You did a lot of good today."

Another guffaw falls out of Wanda's mouth. She clamps her hand over it. Her eyes well up. "All I do is make poison." Her throat chokes on the words. "I can't do anything else anymore."

"Impossible." Trish puts her arm around Wanda's shaking shoulders. "There are thirty poster-sized photos of you in the Green

Room people want you to sign. That's not poison. That's goodness."

"Yay posters. Dead trees." Wanda swallows hard to control the sobs. In the corner of her eye, she sees faces turn towards her. "I wish it had never happened. I wish I'd just gone straight home from the gym that day."

"More people would have died if you hadn't been there."

Wanda's eyes heat up with tears. "But, now, it hurts so much to think about. It physically hurts." She senses movement; two women, double-fisted with drinks are taking tentative steps towards them.

"Come on. We need to get food into you." Trish gently grips her shoulder. Wanda lets herself be guided out of the gate. Their footsteps fall together in unison towards the circus-style tent.

Trish sits Wanda down inside the Green Room and brings her a Styrofoam bowl full of chili and a clean, white plastic spoon. Rachel brings her a beer from the cooler.

"You poor thing. So wound up." Trish jiggles Wanda's knee. The chili on the spoon is lava-hot and scorches the top of her mouth. She takes a gulp of beer to extinguish it.

"Tomorrow, I'll talk to Ivan," Trish says. "I'll tell him to stop being a turd and be more attentive to you."

"Really?"

"Yes! He should be more focused on you." Trish tugs Wanda's hood down and strokes her hair. "You're finished work for the summer. You two should take some time, go away for a while or something. You can go out to my folks' cabin in Bonavista." She pushes back a strand of hair from Wanda's face. Wanda fights the urge to yank the hood forward. Her hair feels like oily string pressed into her skull and neck.

"We'll just hang out here, eat some food, listen to music." Trish checks her phone. "Two acts until Pike wants everyone on stage."

"Trish, I really don't want to."

"The guys up next are really good. Leo has one of their albums at home."

"I think I should try to slip out or something."

Trish's eyes latch onto Wanda's. "Oh honey. I know you want to. But you know, there are people who came here tonight just to see you." Her eyes gloss over with emotion. "I've talked to families today. Ella Collier's family. D'arcy Fadden's family." She runs a finger underneath her eye, damming in her mascara. "When I think about how much worse it could have been." She swallows deeply. "It's important you're here tonight, Wanda."

"I look and feel like a value pack of crap."

Trish laughs. "Oh, honey, that's why Rachel is here. She helps everyone." Trish waves at Rachel, who waves back from the other side of the tent and approaches in tidy, elegant steps.

"Rachel, do you have anything Wanda can wear?"

Rachel appraises Wanda, seated on the couch. Wanda averts her eyes, blows on the chili to cool it. "Oh yes. Come." She strolls to the far corner of the tent, not checking to see if Wanda is behind her. Wanda lays the bowl of chili on the coffee table and shuffles after her.

Three stuffed racks of clothes are lined up against the tent wall. Rachel slides the hangers along. "There should be several things in your size." She pulls out a long grey tunic and holds it up to Wanda's face. "Hmm. We need something to make you pop." She pulls out a bright purple blazer.

"I don't think that's really me," Wanda says.

Rachel's eyebrows raise a little. Perhaps at the idea that Wanda has established an idea of what her "style" is. "This, maybe." She selects an off-white blouse, long, hitched at the waist. "Yes. It wouldn't look bad with those jeans, either. Kind of funky/dreamy. Try it on?" Wanda unzips the navy hoodie. Underneath, she's still wearing the t-shirt with the long red wine stain. She glances at Rachel, who looks away, straight-faced.

In the dressing area, Wanda yanks the t-shirt over her head, wincing as she hears the static fizzle of the fabric against her hair. The t-shirt is ripe. She should throw it out; she blushes at the thought of other occupants of the room wrinkling their noses at it. The off-white blouse smells like lilacs and soothes her skin. When it's buttoned up, it hangs smartly at her hips.

"Yes. You look like a classy number now," Rachel says when she sees Wanda. "Let's find you something to dress up that lovely long neck of yours." She produces a wooden box and opens it to an assortment of necklaces. "This one, I think." She hangs a thin golden chain around Wanda's neck; a solitary pearl nestles just above the opening of the blouse. Rachel gives one brisk, approving nod. "Now. Your pretty face. Sit." She slides out a sleek black makeup bag and takes out a package of disposable facial wipes. Wanda closes her eyes as Rachel runs the cool wet square over her forehead and cheeks. She almost moans as Rachel wipes her neck and behind her ears. "Feels good," Rachel whispers. Wanda remains still while Rachel applies foundation, powder, and eye shadow in little swipes. "Your hair. I'm just going to brush it back." She smoothes Wanda's hair back with a soft brush. Wanda catches a whiff of something floral and fresh from Rachel's wrists close to her face. "Okay. What do you think?"

Wanda opens her eyes. Her hair, flat and stringy from being tucked under the hood all day, now cascades from her face in soft, shiny waves. Rachel has covered up the dark circles and red blotches on her face and played up her eyes, shades of peach and grey.

"Thank you."

"You're easy to work with," Rachel says. "Great hair, good bone structure."

"You're very good." She flushes with shame. "I've been having a rough couple of days."

Rachel scoffs. "Please. I've been doing this for ten years. I've covered all kinds of bruises, scars, cocaine faces. You're a piece of cake."

Wanda turns her face, inspecting all its angles in the mirror. "I might be able to do this now. Maybe."

Rachel tilts her head at Wanda. "You smashed in the head of a gunman. You can smile and wave to some drunk people."

On stage, Pike bounces behind turntables. The floor throbs with the overpowering bass. There are other musicians—a keyboardist, an electric guitar, a backup rapper—but the volume is so high, it's all muddled soup to her ears. Perhaps if she wasn't backstage, if she was in front of the speakers, she might be able to distinguish his lyrics from the blare. Once in a while, she can make out a "yeah" and a "fuck" and "haters." But the crowd before him are on low boil. They gyrate and sway. 10:27pm. Pike will stop in a moment and call everyone out on stage, one by one. Then he'll do one last closing number. Then she can go home and lie down and shut her eyes.

She stands backstage at the end of a line. Trish, Lydia Simms, the head of the Coalition Against Violence, and a tall man in a police uniform all wait in front of her. It's like they're about to accept their high-school diplomas.

She peeks out at the audience. Beyond the dancers, people stand in clusters, smoking, talking. Security guards circulate, talking into headsets.

The song ends. Pike bows deeply. The crowd whistles and thunders with applause. Pike makes a sidelong glance backstage, a little wave. Everyone in front of her gives a little wave back, like a synchronized dance move. Wanda waves last. Pike points at her and cocks his thumb. Shooting a finger gun at her. What a tool.

"Ladies and gentlemen, thank you for making this day, this festival, the fuckin' best!" Pike says. Again, he bows deeply to the audience. Whistles and whoops. "Before we wrap it up, there are some special people I want to bring out. Hardworking people who make things happen. People who save lives."

Pike goes through the list. Volunteers, staff, security. The organizations and vendors who *make this city what it is*. The park staff. Then he turns his attention to the people in front of her. "Patricia Samson, who created these beautiful photographs on display today, truly inspirational." Trish crosses the stage. Wanda gets a glimpse of her white leg jutting out of the slit in her skirt. Whistles from the audience. "Lydia Simms, who has worked tirelessly with the Coalition Against Violence in the province for over twenty years." Lydia crosses the stage, her silver hair glistening under the lights. She moves to shake Pike's hand; he kisses her cheek.

"Officer J.J. Woods, who was there, on that day, and is here with us tonight, representing the Royal Newfoundland Constabulary and police officers throughout the province." J.J. Woods walks a straight line to Pike's outstretched hand. Claps and cheers.

"And now. We've all seen the video. We've all been captivated by her. A woman who will be known, throughout history, as a hero, Wanda Jaynes!"

Wanda steps out from the curtain. The whoops and cheers boom around her. The lights bear down. Beyond them are a thousand shadows, hands up, clapping, waving. A child is being hoisted up towards the stage; a little boy with dark hair, hands full of flowers. She moves forwards and stoops to take them. The little boy smiles at her, something pink and sticky in the corner of his mouth. Other people press forward, armloads of flowers, teddy bears. Security stream out, scooping the bouquets from extended arms. "Wanda! Wanda! Love you!" She smiles hesitantly into the darkness. Placards, Bristol-board signs, her name in hearts, her name in huge letters. Her hand flutters to her mouth involuntarily. She didn't know it would be like this. Her eyes fill up.

She stands and waves. People jump up and down, waving and clapping. A sign reads *Wanda = Hero*. A sign reads *Wandawoman!* A sign reads *Thank You Wanda*. A sign reads *Ignorant Bitch*.

A hand appears in front of the Ignorant Bitch sign and it is blurred by the black backs of security guards. Wanda can see a line of royal blue as the members of Workers for Modern Christianity face the stage. They hold signs over their heads: *Conceited Atheist. Miracles Are Real. Atheism is like a fish denying the existence of water. Believe!*

Security and audience members scrabble around. Wanda recognizes the green-haired man, the Earlobes guy, snatching down a sign. The sign holder jumps to get it from his hands, but he holds it up high, like Monkey in the Middle. He throws the sign and grabs another one. Ruth shakes a wiry fist: "We have every right! We have the right!" She pushes the back of a woman in a red hat, Dallas Cleal, who whirls around with her arm raised and delivers a solid crack to Ruth's face. Wanda gasps as Ruth's slight frame crumbles. People gape at the growing squabble. Cries of "What the fuck?" and "Call the cops!" People point cellphones at the chaos. More security guards move in. Blue t-shirts being dragged away, Dallas too, with her hands held behind her back.

"Okay, cool it! Cool it everyone!" Pike's voice booms through the speakers. "C'mon, b'ys. I know it was fun in the beer tent, but let's all relax." Laughs and mutterings from the audience. "I know, I know. It sucks when some people can't put their feelings aside." He raises his hand out over the crowd. Scattered applause in response. "Even at times like this, when people get together for healing and happiness and togetherness, we can lose ourselves. We shouldn't forget that."

The applause warms and grows. "Let's hear it once more for these amazing heroes." Pike gestures to the line behind him. The crowd whoops once again.

"And before we do our last song, ladies and gentlemen, I want to bring one more person out," Pike says. "And actually, it refers to what I was saying before. It's hard to put our feelings aside. It's hard when things have been difficult to forgive. And to heal, you need to forgive."

Pike waves to someone off stage. A small figure shuffles forward. She raises a hand to block out the stage lights and takes timid steps towards Pike's beckoning hand. Confused applause peppers through the crowd. The woman is familiar. Dark hair and an aged, sad face. Wanda recognizes the purple blazer from Rachel's wardrobe. It dangles on the woman's frame; she looks small inside.

"Everyone, this woman has had a hard time lately and I think, since the message of this festival is healing, that we should let this woman, Frances Rumstead, heal as well."

The crowd sucks its collective teeth in response. A few claps.

"C'mon everyone, let's welcome Frances to the stage." Pike makes big clapping motions. A few more claps, dark murmurs. Frances's head hangs low. A male voice, slurry and deep: "Bad move man." Hushing sounds. "Well, it is."

Frances Rumstead trembles. What did Pike say to convince her to do this? Wanda stares at him. He stands defiant, arm clamped around Frances like she just struck a home run. Tasteless attention-seeking bastard. If she ran, bolted forward, she could shove him. He would tumble head first off the stage.

The movement is a flicker in the corner of her vision. Two hands and a face, like a mounted heart, appear at the corner of the stage. Wanda watches Liang-Yi Chen hoist herself up and stand on the stage. Her eyes hold Wanda's. For a moment, there is understanding. Wanda feels herself nodding. Yes, yes she knows.

Liang-Yi unzips her jacket. Underneath, she wears a t-shirt with a close-up of herself, her blurry image on its knees, begging to be spared on the floor of a grocery store. It looks faded. She's been wearing it for a while.

Liang-Yi's face shines with tears and sweat, her mouth moving, saying something in another language, something angry and urgent. She moves forward and grabs a microphone stand. "Monsters," she says. She lifts the stand and holds it sideways. She starts swinging.

"Whoa!" from the audience. Security at the bottom of the stage, ducking as she whips the stand back and forth. Liang-Yi takes long, sidesteps towards Pike and Frances. Wanda's feet are encased in petrified earth. Every muscle seizes up. The creamy blouse is slathered on her back with fear.

Liang-Yi Chen stares at Frances Rumstead. Wanda cannot hear what she says, but sees the word mouthed over and over. Monster. Or Mother. Mother Monster. Closer with each wide step. Frances is frozen. Pike back-pedals. He falls on his rump at the edge of the curtain.

"No," Frances says. "Please. Please leave me alone."

"Now you know what it's like," Liang-Yi says. "What it's like to know it's you. What it's like to be a target."

"No," Wanda says. "Just stop it."

Her legs are electric. They move in wide slicing steps, once, twice, three times, gliding her into position directly in front of Frances Rumstead.

The bottom of the microphone stand piles into Wanda's gut. Her mouth drops open to expel the wind in her lungs. Her stomach reverberates in shock and pain.

"Lord Jesus, help us," Frances says.

Wanda's body buckles. She crumples to the stage floor. Her eyes close.

21

THE people in the hallways have places to get to or things to wait for. Wanda's eyes canter over them as she is guided past signs and posted reminders: Radiology, Mammography, Scent Free Workplace, MRI, No Cellphones Please. The nurse steering her stretcher wears lavender scrubs with a butterfly print.

"We'll check your x-ray and get some fluids into you," the nurse says.

"No rush," Wanda says. "This is the most relaxing ride I've had in weeks."

There is a line-up at X-Ray: people in wheelchairs, a pink-eyed child with a puffy arm. Wanda thought there would be more pain, but she's been lying still for so long her body seems to have forgotten. Or she's in shock. Or a rib has broken and dust-like shards of bone are seeping into her bloodstream. Maybe this is what an embolism feels like.

Her phone rattles at her side. Trish shoved both her hoodie and phone into her arms as the paramedics lifted her into the ambulance: "Omigod, omigod! It's all going to be okay!" Wanda didn't think an ambulance was necessary, but by the time she managed to lift her head off the stage floor, it had arrived, paramedics, a stretcher. Security, cops, and strangers witnessed her horizontal departure: "God love ya, Wanda. Good job, girl." Pike stood by the stage, smoking a cigarette with a shaking hand. She flipped him off.

"Fourteen people arrested at that festival," someone says. One nurse to another.

"That's madness."

"I knew it was going to end badly."

"Yes. Too soon for a big idea like that."

The nurse's voice drops: "Sure, it was the Chinese girl from the video who attacked her on stage."

"Oh my God." A high inhale from one, Butterfly Scrubs Nurse. "Oh, that hurts me. The poor lamb."

"I know, it kills me when I see her in the video. When she's begging. I can't even deal with it."

"I can't imagine what she's been going through. But fourteen arrested. That's ridiculous."

"What's this place coming to?"

"Soon they'll have armed guards at everything."

"Makes you wonder what they'll have to do for the Regatta this year."

Clucking tongues and sighs. They converse in a steady rhythm of busyness with the awareness of being overheard. No privacy for those in the trenches. Wanda's phone hums. Incoming call. She should turn it off with the amount of dings and pings and tags she's getting. But Sharon's contact avatar smiles at her on the screen. She answers:

"Sharon."

"Jesus, finally. I was starting to think you'd gone AWOL."

"No. Witness protection maybe."

"So someone's hit you now? What's going on?"

"It wasn't at me purposefully." Wanda shifts her weight. There it is, the pain, yanking through her torso. "I got in the way."

"Fucking hell." Sharon's breath sucks in. "First you're almost getting shot, then concert violence. This is bullshit." Wanda catches faint music in the background, the chirp of a bird. "Come visit me now," Sharon says. "I mean it. I'm in Cape May. Housesitting for a coworker until July. There's four bedrooms, a view, close the beach. It's sick. Nikki's coming this week. Join us. I'll buy you a ticket."

"It sounds great." Unless she has busted ribs. Or an embolism. "I might not be the best company though."

"Lies."

"Sharon." If she sobs, it will hurt her chest more. Nurses will approach and fuss. "I'm not doing so good."

"How can you be? I'm not even in Canada and I can tell it's nuts."

"My job is gone. I don't know what's going on with Ivan. I'm fucking up. A lot."

"All the more reason for you to come. Everyone's too rich around here to read or pay attention to the news. You'll be anonymous." Shifting sounds in the background, a breeze, clicking glasses.

"I'll think about it."

"Let Nikki know either way. She's worried. She sent me a text with some video of you at this show."

"Really? Oh fuck."

"No phones allowed." Butterfly Scrubs Nurse frowns down at her. "You need to turn that off."

"Sharon, I have to go."

"Call me tomorrow. I love you."

Butterfly Scrubs waggles a finger. "Put it away. At least until we figure out if you're all in one piece."

There are no broken bones. "You'll have bruising," the doctor says. "It will get quite colourful over the next few days. You'll be tender, so take it easy. Don't lift anything more than five pounds." Wanda gets a wheelchair for the excursion out. Ivan guides it to the car and helps her into the passenger seat. She waits until he's buckled his own seatbelt to ask if he's okay.

"Me? I'm exhausted."

"How's your mom? What happened with the cops?"

He starts the engine. His hair droops along his face and his eyes are bloodshot. "Mom's a mess. The cop told me she freaked out in the car. She kept telling him she knew about a pedophile, a guy who was targeting kids. She wanted him to go to Karl's house and watch him. The cop brought her to the station—I guess he wanted her to be supervised there or something. Then he went himself to check on him."

"What did he find?"

"Well, there wasn't much he could do without a search warrant." He puts the car in reverse. The parking lot is nearly vacant. Early morning light bounces off parking meters. "The cop talked to Karl, said someone had seen something unusual in an upstairs room. Karl invited him in. When the cop asked about the camera and telescope pointed out the window at the playground, Karl said he likes to watch people walk their dogs there."

"With a telescope? That guy is weird."

"Maybe. Or he likes dogs." He twitches with impatience or exhaustion. "The cop goes back and tells Mom. She gets *belligerent*. His word. She says he should have looked at the computer. That he should get a warrant and search the house. He tries to explain how all her notions have no proof and she breaks down. Crying, cursing him."

"So, where is she now?"

"They brought her to Waterford Psychiatric. Overnight observation. They think she's having a breakdown."

"Oh no." Mrs. Medeiros in a small, white room in a hospital. Like the one she was just in, but with rigid walls and locks.

"And, unfortunately, it's not the first time with her. I guess I was hoping that part of her life had passed," he says. "So. I'll check on her tomorrow. Hopefully, they'll let her go home."

Wanda nods. "I'll come. We can both talk to her."

He nods. Pause. "Sure."

They drive in silence. She turns her phone on. Notification City. Tagged in at least three Healfest videos so far. "Oh God."

"You don't want to look at that stuff now."

"No. I need to know." She taps the play button. The video shows the stage, Pike, Frances, and the others. When Liang-Yi appears at the edge and starts swinging the microphone stand, the crowd near the front scatters, like when she was a kid and shook salt and pepper into a bowl of water and added a drop of dishwashing soap. Liang-Yi is silhouetted against the stage lights, narrow shoulders, purposeful steps. Wanda moves towards Frances's cowering shape: two side-steps like the opening and closing of scissors. And bang. She falls. People scream. And then, Wanda's body convulses. The spray of vomit out of her face is a flood of neon orange.

"Oh. Oh fuck." Wanda covers her eyes and curls up. She immediately winces in pain from her buckling stomach.

"Be careful," Ivan says. "You're a giant bruise."

She swipes to read the comments beneath the video:

Maury1212: BAZOOKA BARFFFF!!!!

ELzoidzoo: OMFG. Like the exorcist.

RicePatty7000: Hawt. :p

Sheldononhigh: I don't understand why everyone is reacting to her puking. She just saved that woman's life.

ELzoidzoo: @Sheldononhigh saved a life? It's a microphone stand.

Sheldononhigh: @ELzoidzoo She was being threatened with it!

taylormaidTT: I think she's brave, but this still makes me sick.

JimmyJoJardon: What did she eat? A Costco case of spaghettios?

Samalot0325: ^^ LOL @ JimmyJoJardon

"I will never live this down." She looks at the bottom right corner of the video. 2,632 views. Not even home yet. "How many other videos exist, do you think?"

"Well, there's another from the side stage. Some roadie with a phone."

"So, other angles?"

"I guess so." He turns onto Bonaventure Avenue. "Let's just get home and go to bed. The cops need to know if you want to press charges against Liang-Yi. They said call them tomorrow. And we have to deal with Mom. Your folks wanted to come in, but I told them you need a couple days rest."

"Thank you for that."

"No problem." He slows for a stop sign. "I'd like it if everyone packed off and left us alone for a month."

"Sounds perfect."

"And through all this, you know what's so annoying?" He shakes his head as he flips the turning indicator. "Ray bugging me all night. He left the festival and went to some party or something. High as fuck and texting me for hours with ideas for the name of the album.

Phone's going off and I keep thinking, *Is it Mom? Is it Wanda? Is it the police?* No, it's Ray: 'What do you think of Random Impulse, for the album? Or Heroic Hits? What about Hero Inaction for a title?' For fuck sakes."

"Hero what?"

"Like inaction, as a play on the word. Inaction like no action."

"Oh." She examines her front. The long white blouse is puffed out from the gauze bandages covering her stomach, navel to sternum. She runs her hands lightly over her front. Why would Ray suggest names like those? Because of her. Because Ray wants a name with current validity, less than one degree of separation from him. A tweak of anger flutters through her, but is too tired to grow.

"Those are awful names," she says.

"Fuck yeah."

"Might as well call it Zero Downloads."

"Might as well call it Record Store Discount Pile."

In the house, she washes as best as she can with the bandages still around her. Ivan is fast asleep when she enters the bedroom. She regards his closed eyes, his soft breathing. When everything calms down, how much will he resent her? And tomorrow, more new decisions, more dealing. Will she press charges against Liang-Yi? Will Genevieve Davey want to interview her again? Will people make barfing sounds when she walks down the street? She plugs in her phone. Unchecked voice mail, new text messages. Twitter notifications: twelve contacts have retweeted Pike:

> @Pikeitalot: All great changes are proceeded by chaos!
> #deepakchopra #forgivenessforchange

What a fuckhead. She turns off her phone. She sleeps as soon as her eyes close, with no extra assistance.

In the early afternoon, they wake and pack. They will fetch Mrs. Medeiros, they will stay with her until she's "better." Ivan drags out his duffle bag: "I hate not knowing how long this will take."

Wanda stares out the window. No one outside, no media or gawkers. Pascale Aggressive exits her house. When she glances up,

Wanda slowly raises one hand, then gives her the finger. If Pascale notices, she doesn't let on.

She gingerly checks her phone. A message from Constable Lance; he will be by in two hours for her statement. Liang-Yi must be in custody. A filmed assault. A mental-instability defense, if she's lucky.

"Sylvie's going to leave Fiona with Alex," Ivan says. "She can help with Mom too. Which is good. We need time to get on top of things."

"What things?"

He yanks t-shirts from the closet. "Right now, I have about seventy thousand messages to deal with, how about you? We could use a break."

Her phone buzzes in response. It never ends. Yes. They could use a break. She holds up her phone. A text message from Nikki. Her sweet, smiling face. Colourful emojis in the text.

"I want to go to New Jersey," Wanda says.

He tosses a pair of black socks in the duffle. "Well. Who doesn't."

"To see Sharon and Nikki. Sharon's got a place in Cape May 'til July."

He takes pairs of boxers from the drawer. "Sounds nice."

"She offered to buy me a ticket."

"For when?"

"As soon as possible."

"Is this what you want?"

"Yes. I want to. I want to be around people who...I need to not feel like I'm on a platter." She winces. That was too much.

"If it's what you need." He pushes items around in the bag. "I'd like to get back into the studio, finish the last touches on the album. It would be nice to dive into that. Get it done."

"Okay. And if I'm gone, it's easier to deal with, I don't know, anyone who wants anything from me...you can just tell them I'm out of the province."

"And when you return, you can just threaten to vomit on anyone who gets in your way." He grins. Finally. "Too soon?" She gives him the finger too.

Ivan goes to the Waterford alone. She contacts Sharon, who buys the ticket for the following evening. Wanda will sort out the house,

Ivan will return when Sylvie's ready. They'll talk tonight. Before leaving, Ivan offers to invite Leo and Trish, so she can say goodbye to them as well. He retracts the offer as her face falls.

Constable Lance takes notes for a final statement. When did the emails from Liang-Yi start, how did she perceive them. How did she respond yesterday, can she confirm no other contact happened on her part. Then on to what Wanda saw on stage. What happened when she was hit. When she describes the impact and the puking, she has to stop. Her name and *vomit* on the same notepad, written by Constable Lance and his handsome mouth.

"How am I supposed to live this down?" she says. "I will forever be known as the Healfest Barfer."

"More like Healfest Hero, I think."

"Please. There was no real danger."

"She could have seriously injured Frances Rumstead," he says. "People have died that way."

"When? At Aerosmith concerts?" She pictures Steve Tyler dancing with a microphone stand. Constable Lance blinks. He doesn't get her reference. "It's all so ridiculous," she says. "And I know I'm being childish, but it's unfair. Freaky things happen all the time and escape notice. Now, everything is filmed and attached to you."

"Stuff gets filmed, but only special things make history."

"I don't want to be history."

"But you are," he says. "The grocery store might have been a fluke. Or a miracle. Or luck. But you've just added another event. It's something now, like a matching set. If people were convinced before, they'll be twice as convinced now. I know I am."

"And so, more scrutiny. It all feels like water torture."

"I see it this way: None of these people online know you. All they know are these two videos which show amazing things you've done. It's enough to label you as something special. And that's how fame works. You can be a one-hit wonder and people will remember you forever. "

"I wish I could understand it."

"Well, how do you feel when you watch Pike's video?"

"I never have."

He stares at her blankly.

"I can't," she says.

"I see." He nods. "I understand, but if you ever do watch it, perhaps you'll end up in the cheering section with the rest of us." He closes his notebook. The details are there, but she's decided not to press charges. Frances Rumstead is the one who is Liang-Yi's victim as far as she's concerned. Constable Lance says goodbye. He goes home to his wife and infant child.

That evening, Wanda slips on Ivan's jean jacket to take the garbage out. It was warm when he left and he didn't bother covering up. She carefully places each arm in its sleeve. The frayed collar brushes against her cheek. It feels stiffer than she remembers; tight across the back, it emits cigarette smoke and cut grass. She fastens the buttons over her t-shirt, over the thick white bandages on her front.

Last summer, she wore this jacket at a cabin party. She ducked out for a moment because she'd forgotten something in the car. When she walked back to the cabin, she could hear Ivan inside, laughing, his guitar strumming, and she shivered, a deep, rigorous, delicious shiver. Even though he was inside and she was outside, if anyone saw her at that moment, they'd know Ivan and Wanda were together. She took the steps leading into the cabin two at a time.

How does it feel now? She stares at the lawn. The jacket feels like a jacket.

She reaches into the pocket. A small note. *Groceries and to-do*:

Cheese

Olives

Milk

Eggs

Ask Ray about Clarenville dates

Oil change

Show Wanda she is loved, everyday

She holds the note in her palm. Presses it to her lips.

Back in the house, she turns on her phone. She responds to Sharon's and Nikki's text messages, matches their enthusiasm. On Facebook she is tagged in another video from the show and she taps it absently. Same thing, chaos and upset.

She can see Pike's infamous video is there, underneath the new one. Her and Liang-Yi, frozen in time. And how many times has Liang-Yi watched it? She said she remembers everything, this moment when they both believed it was the end and they both began to unravel. They'll have to face each other at some point, in court or at a hearing. Wanda should at least try to understand her better.

The phone is light and easy to toss away, to the table, to the chair if it bothers her. Her finger hovers over the thumbnail. Tap.

She sees herself and Liang-Yi standing frozen and separated by the aisle shelves. As Rumstead turns, Liang-Yi falls to her knees in a begging stance, asking to be spared in her own words.

When Wanda throws the can, the motion is a flash, like she is raising her hand to catch something, rather than throw. Or hitting a button that makes him stop. A button only she can see.

Edward Rumstead falls. Liang-Yi stays kneeling on the floor. Her hands stay clasped, but her shoulders sink. She is safe. She is saved. It is the moment she had printed on a t-shirt, the moment she wanted Wanda to understand.

Wanda raises her head and wipes her eyes. Tomorrow, she will board a plane. She'll see her two long-term friends for the first time in over a year. There might still be a strong connection there. Or something won't match like it used to. And when she returns to St. John's, her life may not have changed. Or she'll see what has petered away. Whatever is left, it will be scary, but new. Deep in the fragile numbness of her core, it is there, a feather turning, the slightest spark of anticipation.

The tiny screen in her hand waits for her. She presses replay.

ACKNOWLEDGEMENTS

Big thanks to the early readers of this book for their feedback and guidance: Paul Butler, Glenn Deir, Linda Abbott, and Mark Callanan. Thank you to James, Rebecca, Rhonda, and the entire Breakwater Books team.

Deep thanks for dear friends who offer advice and encouragement: Jacinta Cameron, Jenina MacGillivray, Justin Merdsoy, Lisa Moore, Tamara Reynish, Liz Solo, Deirdre Snook, Liza Ann Tucker, and Tracey Waddleton. Thanks to my writing groups, the Naked Parade Writing Collective and Soft Pants: A Comfortable Writing Group.

Thanks to my loving family: Mom, Liz, Patrick, Jason, Michelle, Mary Anne, John, Harvey, Gail, Sharada, and Travis.

All the love and gratitude to my partner, Jon Weir, for his unwavering support, assistance, devotion, and for being the best human I know.

AUTHOR PHOTO: SHEILAGH O'LEARY

BRIDGET CANNING's work has won the Cox and Palmer SPARKS Creative Writing Award, the BC Federation of Writers Literary Writes competition, Newfoundland and Labrador Arts and Letters awards, and has been shortlisted for the Cuffer Prize. *The Greatest Hits of Wanda Jaynes* is her first novel. She lives in St. John's.